I0723214

RUNNING AWAY TO BOSTON

ANNE LOUISE BANNON

HH
Healcroft House, Publishers
Altadena, California

ISBN 978-1-948616-31-7

Library of Congress Control Number: 2023906582

Healcroft House, Publishers, Altadena, California, United States of America

Contents

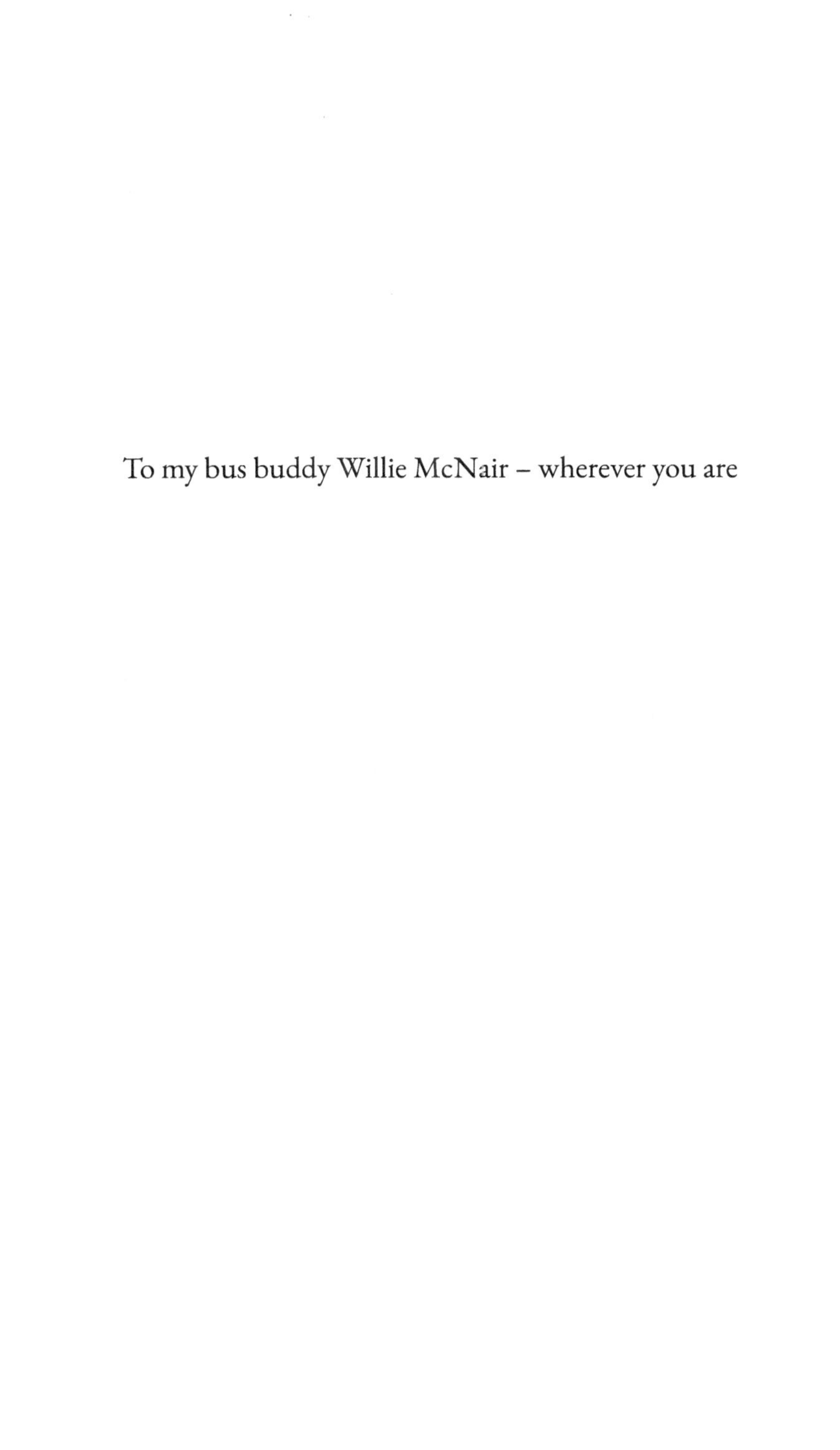

To my bus buddy Willie McNair – wherever you are

Acknowledgements

No matter how lonely the act of writing can be, it is also absolutely true that creating and producing a novel does not happen in a vaccuum.

My first thanks go to Willie McNair, my bus buddy. I have never met anybody who had more cause to be bitter and angry and who was also anything but. Instead he was filled with a joy that was utterly infectious. Willie and I spent so many rides just laughing our backsides off with each other. He also came up with the bus shooting that happens in this novel, and which laid the foundation for a fair amount of the action.

My second thanks go to Michael Starch, Scoops Adamczyk, and Mike O'Brien. Compared to most of my writing and other friends, I'm considered pretty geeky. And it is true that I don't panic when asked to set up a Google Form or a spreadsheet. Yes, I know my way around the back end of WordPress and can even get to a website's deep backend and set up email addresses. But these three guys blow my skills out of the water. We're talking guys who can write computer code from the ground up. The fun part was when I asked them to check my text for any technical goofs, they not only agreed to do it with enthusiasm, they all found different issues, including several goofs that had nothing to do with the tech stuff. Anything that got missed was probably me accidentally editing in errors while correcting the ones they found.

Then there was my friend and colleague G.P. Gottlieb, whose comments really helped smooth things out. And I cannot function without my good friend and editor Carol Louise Wilde, who not only keeps me honest, she keeps me clear.

Finally, as always, I have to thank my long-suffering husband, Michael Holland, who listens even when he's heard the story far too many times already. And my daughter, Corrie Klarner, who loves to listen and always has great suggestions to make. My writing will always be the better thanks to you two, but also my life is so much better just because you are there.

PROLOGUE

T he silence struck her first. After the roar, the deafening, bone shaking, ear-splitting roar, there was silence. Not quiet, with twittering birds and the soft whisper of cars on the highway in the background. Dead silence.

She couldn't hear it, but felt the thudding of her heart in her chest. She took a deep breath, suddenly aware that she'd been holding it, then bent over and choked from all the dust floating everywhere.

She was alive.

A shaft of sunlight shone through where the living room ceiling had been. She looked up. The shaft came from a tiny break in the ugly dark green clouds that still hovered. There should be rain any second.

Something wood fell, maybe a two by four. She jumped. It seemed as though the only wall left standing was the one she'd huddled against, the one between the living room and the kitchen.

She was alive.

An anguished wail split the silence. It came from down the street. Another wail joined in, this one from the other direction. She slowly got up, stretching each limb. Her cheek stung. She wiped it and felt the blood, then saw it on her hand. There wasn't much. It was probably just scratches. She felt her cheek again. It was intact.

She looked around. There wasn't much left of the house, her husband's house. She turned the corner from the living room. The kitchen walls still stood, or at least three of them did. The cupboards had been blown open. Half the dishes sat in place on the shelves. The other half lay in pieces, splattered in a trail out of the opening where the one wall had been.

She turned to the front of the house as the faint cry of sirens began, underscoring the wails of her neighbors. Her first instinct was to go to the school. That was all that mattered, really. She prayed the tornado had spared the school and her baby. That's when she knew it was time for them to escape.

She made her way through the debris to the refrigerator. There was a slim box between it and the counter. Her husband had never noticed it. As long as he got what he wanted, he seldom noticed what she did. Her precious laptop and modem were in the box, plus cash, and the two fake I.D.s she'd already gotten from the online bulletin board. She wasn't quite ready, but the tornado had made that moot. She'd transfer the rest of the money later, after she and her daughter had gotten away.

She gathered the contents of the box and slid the empty box back between the counter and the refrigerator. A briefcase had somehow landed on the kitchen floor. She didn't know whose it was, but she took it, dumped the contents on the floor, and put the laptop, modem, power and modem cords, money, and I.D.s inside. The sirens were getting closer, and the wailing was not stopping. Her wallet and the rest of her belongings she left behind.

She swallowed, then slid outside to the backyard, and looked back at the street as if to say goodbye.

There was only one person who mattered now. She made her way across the yard to the path through the woods to the school. The trees closest to her house had been stripped of their leaves, but the trees and bushes closest to the school yard remained intact. The school was relatively new and consisted of two long rows of rooms. The windows had all shattered in the winds. Grim-faced women and a few men were slowly pulling out small bodies from the building and tenderly laying them on the grass.

She crept along the bushes that surrounded the school, wondering how she was going to find her daughter. And was brought up short by a flash of lavender and glitter. Her baby's shoes. The two had laughed all the weekend before as they had painted the new pair of tennis shoes. Her daughter had insisted on wearing them to school that day.

The shoes were her daughter's. She could see the bits of DOS commands on them. But how was there a white sheet over the top of the body laid out on the grass? An ugly red stain seeped through the covering where her daughter's head would be.

Her heart stopped, and her stomach wrenched. Her baby? Her darling daughter? The only other person who loved computers as much as she did? The giggling, sweet, incredibly intelligent, and witty little eight-year-old?

She started toward the too-still form, but then other adults, one bearing another white-sheeted body, appeared from the building. She shrank back into the bushes and puked. She wanted to run to her daughter's body, to cuddle it again, maybe bring her back to life. But she couldn't. The others would see her and know that she was alive.

It hadn't been her original plan, but the tornado provided her escape hatch. Her husband would not come after them if he thought she and her daughter had perished. She gagged. Her daughter was dead.

Her throat closed again. How could her daughter be dead? Just when they had their path to freedom. She blinked and wondered if it made sense anymore to run. But staying would not stop the beating, the rage. She'd tried leaving him before and he'd promised to kill both her and their daughter after the last time she'd tried. She did not doubt he would make good on that promise. Only her daughter was dead.

The anger filled her. If only he'd let her go, her baby might still be alive. She and her daughter could have been someplace else when the tornado hit. Someplace safe. Staying would not bring her baby back. Staying would only give her husband the satisfaction of keeping her. If her daughter was dead, then there was even less to keep her there. Suddenly numb, she tore herself away and turned into the woods.

She felt like she had been walking for hours, though it had only been half an hour or so according to her watch, when she saw the small sedan in the tree. The driver's side door hung open, and the car was upside down. Yet there was no body nearby. Only a purse and its contents scattered on the ground in a small circle underneath. She wondered what had happened to the driver, then spotted the red leather wallet. Her conscience pricked as she picked the wallet up and opened it. The name on the driver's license seemed familiar.

She winced and wondered if it would really matter in the long run. Which is why she put the wallet in her briefcase and continued on the path until she reached the highway. She followed the highway, oddly empty of traffic, passing McDonalds, grocery stores, and shopping center after shopping center until she felt confident that she was far enough away. The clouds had somehow moved on without unleashing their rain and the sky was clearing even as the sun sank lower.

She found a Walmart and bought underpants, t-shirts, a couple pairs of jeans, and a small suitcase.

"Are you all right?" The clerk asked kindly.

"Yes," she said softly, not looking up. She wasn't all right, but what else was there to say?

"You look like you got caught in that tornado today," the clerk said. "It's all everyone can talk about. Three towns just flattened. I was scared out of my wits."

"I know," she said, hoping the clerk wouldn't say anything about her scratched cheek. "I was, too."

Fortunately, the clerk seemed too wrapped up in his own narrow escape to question someone else's. She paid with a credit card from the red wallet. The clerk asked for a driver's license, then barely glanced at it.

She left the store. She was close to the center of the small city, one just large enough to have a Greyhound station. Dark closed in as she got there. The next bus - and it was still running despite the weather - was headed to Chicago. She bought the ticket with the credit card from the red wallet, then dumped the card and wallet in a trash can just before she boarded the bus. It was full night by then and the bus pulled onto the highway and into the darkness.

She had never been able to sleep in a moving car before, but she slept on the bus, a weird, restless sleep filled with the roar of the wind and children covered with bloody white sheets. The bus pulled up in Chicago as the sun began to rise and fight its way through the clouds. She debated finding a hotel room but decided to save her money. The bus station had a pamphlet detailing all the stops on the Elevated trains. She picked the one for O'Hare airport.

She spent the morning wandering past all the ticketing desks, looking for something, although she did not know what that would be. Then she saw the flight she wanted. To Boston. She'd never been to Boston, knew very little about the city, but had always wanted to go there for reasons she could not explain to herself, let alone anyone else. Her daughter might know to look for her there, but her daughter was... Dead. Her gut clenched at the thought. The plane to Boston was just what she needed.

It was afternoon when the plane landed at Logan airport. Still numb, she waited at the baggage claim for her one suitcase, and looked at the ads for hotels plastered all over a nearby kiosk. It didn't matter which one she picked, so she chose the one that seemed to have the most modern amenities and a free shuttle from the airport.

The room was more comfortable than anything she had ever seen. It was a little intimidating, but well worth it. Once settled and showered, she knew her next step immediately. She got out her laptop and modem, then unplugged the cord from the room's phone. She plugged in the modem, waited while it squeaked and wailed, then directed her laptop to her husband's bank.

It took only a few minutes - she had hacked this account many, many times before. It was the account her husband had set up because, based on the terms of her grandfather's will, he could not directly spend the funds. But he could (he thought) keep her from spending the money. She knew she was giving herself away, but she emptied the account of the money her grandfather had left her and transferred the funds to her offshore account, the one her husband had no idea she had.

Then, finally, she caved in to her grief.

Chapter One

I was in one lousy mood, and it wasn't just the sea of traffic ahead of me on the 134 freeway out of Pasadena. The traffic didn't help, and I would have taken the bus, but, damn him, Brent had sounded worried when he'd called me a half hour before.

I spotted a gap between the cars to my right and pushed my new black Ford MachE into it, ignoring the beeps from the accident prevention system, then pulled onto the offramp.

Now, I am not so paranoid that I will not use Google Maps or their other services. I have friends who won't. Me? Let's just say that you'd have to know it was my account or have some crazy mad skills to connect it to me. No, the reason I wasn't checking with the gods of Google was that I was worried enough about Brent to drive and pissed off enough not to give a rat's ass if I was on the fastest route or not. It's called being conflicted.

I hit the accelerator the second I turned onto Figueroa, then promptly hit the brake to avoid skidding through a red light. A minute later, I was on Colorado Boulevard, heading west.

I was on the way to my favorite coffee joint in Silver Lake, a community in northern Los Angeles that was rapidly gentrifying, which meant the shop would not be my favorite for much longer. Special Agent Brent Mikkelsen, F.B.I., had said he needed me, damn him, and so I had dropped everything and driven off to do his bidding yet again. At least I'd be on what I considered my home turf.

Any hold on me that Brent had was completely in my own head. I knew that. That didn't help. He called, I showed. It was infuriating, really.

My friend Dina Mendoza, barista and amateur psychologist, insisted that it was my parental issues at work - resentment of authority figures, yet powerless to disobey. I had snorted. I'd disobeyed my father plenty of times, although I had to concede that I kept my disobedience to behind his back. Given my father's tendency to come unglued whenever confronted with something he couldn't control, it was safer that way.

My name is Jannie Miller, and I find people. That's why Brent called me. I'm really good at finding people. What annoyed me was that the only time Brent called me was when he needed something from me. The rest of the time, he expected me to call him. One of many reasons why unresolved feelings really suck.

When I finally got to Silver Lake and found a parking spot on the street, the heat of early August wrapped around me. Brent stood outside the shop, looking peeved. Too fucking bad.

"Finally," he said as I walked up.

I held my hands up. "Traffic."

I pushed past him into the shop. It had a comfortable, frowzy feel, with mismatched chairs at small tables and electrical outlets everywhere. Abstracts in black, white, and gray lined the walls. While hardly subtle, I had to admit the paintings were better than the bright orange and blue atrocities that had been there the week before.

"Do you always have to do the passive aggressive thing?" Brent asked as we waited in line for George, the bald barista, to take our orders.

"You know I really hate it when you psychoanalyze me," I replied.

Brent rolled his eyes, but by then George had turned to us and Brent ordered a regular coffee for himself and a latte for me.

"I also really hate it when you decide you know what I want better than I do," I continued as George bent to the espresso machine.

"Was I wrong?" Brent asked, being more obtuse than usual, which meant he was not looking forward to our meeting, either.

He looked more like an actor than a G-Man, or perhaps an actor who would always get the starring role as a G-Man. He was tall, with brown closely clipped hair, round brown eyes, and the kind of build one spent hours at the gym for.

"That's not the point," I said. "You're supposed to check in with me. It's always possible I might change my mind. Maybe I wanted a matcha today."

Brent rolled his eyes again. "You hate matcha."

"I might try it again and like it."

Not that I would, but that was not the point, and Brent knew it, even if he wasn't acknowledging it. I led him to my favorite table and took the seat with its back to the wall, partly because it was my favorite and partly because I knew Brent hated having his back to a room. That particular quirk I got. I didn't like having my back to the room, either.

Brent sidled the chair around so he was at least sideways while I pulled my laptop from its case.

"So, what's the job?" I asked.

"That kid that was gunned down in the taco truck in Santa Monica last week," Brent said.

"That's not Federal jurisdiction."

"There's a cybercrime involved." Brent was part of the cybercrimes task force. That meant he was not above using that as an entrée to get involved in something that piqued his interest.

"Uh-huh." I glared at my screen as the laptop took its time booting up.

"Come on, you read about this."

I looked at him. "So, we're going to play that game?"

Brent rolled his eyes. "At twenty-two forty-six last Tuesday, the Taco Fuerte truck was serving a crowd outside a pop-up club on Santa Monica Boulevard. Manny Rios was behind the counter when he was shot and killed. Five people saw Tanya Coleman drop what turned out to be the murder weapon before running away. More interestingly, surveillance video shows her picking up something flat and black with her order, and Rios gave it to her. Even more interesting, she was not in the club or with anyone else, as far as we know."

"Okay, she iced her boyfriend."

"I doubt she iced anybody," Brent said. "Rios was an ethical hacker."

"Rios?" I saw that the laptop had booted, pulled up my browser and typed as fast as I could. "Holy shit. You mean Old Man River?"

Brent sat back with a self-satisfied smirk. "I do believe so."

The son-of-a-bitch. He knew damned well that I'd know Rios better by his hacking handle than his actual name. And he called me passive-aggressive?

George called Brent's name. Brent waved and George, with a long-suffering sigh, left the coffee bar and brought the coffee and latte to the table.

Brent sipped his coffee. "Rios got outed as part of a group going after the Wheeling Corporation a few days before he was killed."

"I saw that," I said.

Brent and I both hated the Wheeling Corp, a think tank known for its political biases even as they cranked out some impressive research. I did not share their perspective, though I gave them points for backing up their talking points.

What got under my skin – and that of most of the folks in the ethical hacking crowd – was we all knew that when someone needed some computer code that might or might not be entirely ethical, that someone went to Wheeling to get it. As in the think tank sold viruses, and how they got those viruses written was positively mean. Wheeling, of course, never copped to it, nor did everyone believe the rumors. And there certainly wasn't any proof you could use in court. The closest Wheeling came to admitting any-thing was saying that they emulated viruses to help secu-rity experts defeat them. Yeah, right.

Most of the rest of the world bought Wheeling Corp. as a model corporate citizen. Why not? The think tank funded all kinds of libraries, schools, and even childcare centers. And they did back up their research with what looked like solid data.

All the nice things Wheeling did were purely for cover, and unbelievably aggravating, since no one could prove that they were rotten to the core. Which is why the ethical hacking crowd over the years had taken it upon themselves to bring the think tank down. I'd helped here and there, but I couldn't do much since I was already on Wheeling's radar screen. I wasn't sure how, which made them even creepier. But Wheeling had enormous resources and used them relentlessly, only one of the many reasons that made it so incredibly hard to take them out.

There had been some chatter recently that a group had an actual plan to take down the rat bastards. Hardly the first time I'd heard that. The problem was, some idiot posted, "Old Man River is going after Wheeling. Way to go, Manny!" on a Reddit thread. It would have taken me maybe half an hour to figure out who Manny was, not that I would have, so you know the Wheeling people already had. Things had gone seriously whack-a-doodle when Old Man River's murder hit Reddit, which is when I checked out. I do not need whack-a-doodle.

"I need you to find Tanya Coleman," Brent said. He handed me a thumb drive, one of the boring ones you buy at Target. "She's in the wind with no trace of her."

I have to admit, that startled me. Government entities are insanely suspicious of thumb drives, and well they should be. It's appalling how often viruses get transmitted with the darned things. Still, they have their uses, and sharing a file without a record of it is one of them.

I also shook my head. A sudden disappearance with no trace usually means I'm looking for someone who has died.

"You know I'm not good at finding stiffs," I said, putting the thumb drive on the table.

"Surprise, surprise, I'm not looking for one," Brent said. He sipped his coffee again and nudged the drive toward me. "Check it out."

Sighing, even with my misgivings, I stuck the drive into my laptop's port. I knew I could trust Brent not to fuck with my system. He almost had the skills, but the really salient point was that he is not the sort to pull shit like that. The fact that he was resorting to a frickin' thumb drive to share information with me spoke volumes. Something was up and he either didn't want to tell me what it was, or he couldn't. And the odds were even which it was.

There was also the fact that my laptop runs Linux rather than Windows, which doesn't mean much to most people, but it does mean that the vast majority of viruses out there will not affect my laptop. Viruses are almost always written to work on computers that run Windows, which the vast majority of computers run. That being said, it doesn't pay to be too trusting. I looked at which files were on the drive. There were two video files and a text file, so I went ahead and opened the text file because that was the easiest.

"Woh. Coleman's a secretary at Wheeling."

"Yep."

"In human resources." I bit my lip in thought. "And you said Old Man River handed her something. Could she be part of the group trying to bring down Wheeling?"

"Hard to say." Brent scratched his nose, then gazed thoughtfully at the door to the outside. "We don't know what Manny gave her. Could have been a CD case for all we know."

"A CD case?" I tried not to roll my eyes. Compact discs are practically antiques.

Brent sighed. "The only reason we knew about Rios was because he got outed. That whole crew is pretty secretive."

"They have to be to have a prayer of succeeding. Still, he gets killed, and she works there?" I frowned. "I suppose it could be a coincidence. HR can be pretty innocuous."

"Or it's sometimes the heartbeat of the place," Brent said. "The only problem is that she's disappeared. So, either she's part of the group or she saw something that scared her, or she set Rios up."

"Okay. Why do you think she's still alive?"

"You may not have noticed this, but there hasn't been any chatter from Rios' friends about going after Coleman. Absolutely nothing. Dead silence."

I shifted. "Now that I think about it, you're right. There was plenty of conspiracy talk and, boy, were they mad about Beefsteak outing Old Man River. That's why I checked out so quickly."

"There hasn't been a thing about going after Coleman."

"So maybe one of Old Man River's friends killed Coleman and was smart enough not to post about it."

"Somebody almost always posts something." Brent said, with some justification. He put his coffee down and glanced around the room. "Coleman's boss has been sniffing around her family and her friends, asking if they've heard from her. Her mother said it felt really frightening, and one friend thinks she may have been bugged."

I frowned. "You'd think Wheeling would distance themselves from her, especially if she's an employee and Old Man River was known to be targeting the company. But that still doesn't mean that she's alive."

"Except for the one thing that has been floating around the conversation," Brent said.

"What?"

"Coleman is getting some high-level support," he said. "We don't know who or how, but someone seems to be hiding her."

"Some federal agency?"

"Not us, and NSA isn't saying."

"Which means shit."

Brent picked up his coffee again. "The conspiracy fans have decided that this is a federal plot to screw over the hackers going after Wheeling. You know how everybody thinks Wheeling is so squeaky clean. That the NSA or somebody set up the hit and are now hiding Coleman to cover their asses."

"Hm." I scrolled around Brent's file just to keep my fingers busy. "That is not outside the realm of plausible, you know."

"My liaison over there has two ways of 'not saying,'" Brent said. "There's the obvious not saying, meaning that they're hiding something. Then there's the way that usually means they genuinely don't know. All of which, as you pointed out, means shit, except that I can't really tell what my liaison is actually trying to say." He toyed with his coffee cup. "Which is why I've got a gut feeling that Coleman is still alive and hiding somewhere." He looked at me. "And I need you to find her for me."

I tried not to sigh and failed. "I need a retainer and it's not going to be cheap. If she's as deep underground as you've suggested, it's going to take some time and resources to find her."

Brent squirmed. "I don't know why, but McCaffrey has authorized it."

I didn't question the squirming. "Then tell that dickhead to send the contract to my lawyer, and I'm not doing squat until we're signed and court-proof."

"Sure," said Brent with enough grace to be embarrassed.

See, the thing is, thanks to a couple of spectacularly remunerative cases, I don't have to work for a living. I mean, I'm not buying-tickets-on-private-rocket-ships-into-space wealthy. I could run out of money if I go crazy enough, and that is surprisingly easy to do. On the flip side, I'm not a miser, either, and have enough cash to pay the bills, travel when I want, and buy the very latest new technology, never mind that I'm paying more for some piece of shit that probably won't work right.

Brent's boss, Phil McCaffrey, knew this and thought I should take his cases out of the kindness of my heart and work them for free. He even tried to screw me out of my fees every now and then, which is why I wouldn't work for him unless I had really good, solid proof he owed me.

"Okay, then." I started putting my laptop away and noticed Brent looking at me.

"So," he said, hesitantly. "You got any plans for tonight?"

Which, for him, was unusually close to actually asking me out. I debated having mercy on him. It wasn't his fault that he was allergic to asking for anything, unless he had to for work. But at the same time, I was so tired of doing all the work in the relationship and letting him manipulate me. And my shrink is very clear about me sticking to my boundaries.

I sighed. "Brent, you know what the rules are and why they are."

I waited. Nada. So, I got up and left the coffee shop, hopefully fast enough that he didn't see the tears in my eyes. He, more than anyone, understood why things had to be the way they were. If you haven't experienced the kind of hurt we have, you can't really know what it's like. But Brent couldn't get past his shit, and I was determined to get past mine, which really makes it tough on a relationship.

I got in my car and headed out, not sure where I was headed.

It was possible that I was being too hard on Brent. If I was going to be honest with myself (sadly, not a gimme), the whole reason I came running when he called was not because I couldn't wait to see him. It was because I knew I was genuinely needed. Brent was no slouch in the brains department, and he knew his business. No matter how frustrated I got trying to have a relationship with him, I did not intimidate him, and he was humble enough to admit his limits.

That's when it occurred to me that the case had him far more bugged than I'd originally thought. He had been unusually obtuse, and the more I thought about it, the more I began to suspect he hadn't told me everything that was going on. He probably couldn't, either, since Brent didn't ordinarily play that game. A lot of others, maybe, but he didn't withhold information on a case. So, Brent was worried and possibly even a bit afraid. That made even more sense. He did not deal well with his fear, which was understandable, given his profession.

I grumbled to myself, trying to shake off the emotions. But then my phone pinged with an incoming text and, when I pressed the button, my car's audio read it to me.

"Settled in at the Sheraton," said the toneless female voice with an English accent. "All set for the notary at four. When and where for dinner?"

I glanced at the read-out on my dash. The text was from Abe Pearlstein, the lawyer handling my Grandma Schmidt's probate. I had gotten tagged as the executor of the will, which wasn't all that big a deal, since I was also the primary beneficiary. Abe, bless him, had come out from Missouri, where we'd both grown up, to have me sign a bunch of papers. We were meeting at a local notary's office to get it done, then Abe had offered me dinner.

I liked Abe a lot, don't get me wrong. But dealing with Grandma Schmidt's death had been bad enough, between the grief and all the miserable memories that had come along for the ride. Dealing with the probate had only drawn the misery out, and while one could make the argument that getting the final papers signed would bring closure, I still had to get through reliving the worst parts of my childhood.

I dictated the return text that I was ready to go and took the long way back to Pasadena and the notary. Both Abe and I turned up a little early. The signing was relatively painless. Then Abe and I hit the streets.

The Pearlstein family has been taking care of my mother's family's business since my great-grandfather, Abner Smutz, made his first will. That's pronounced "smootz," by the way. My Smutz cousins get pretty pissy when you pronounce it wrong.

Abe and I were the same age and had been buddies in high school together. Then Abe horrified his family by heading to Columbia for his undergrad degree, and by Columbia, I mean the university in New York City, not the University of Missouri. Even more horrifying, he had chosen to go to the University of California, Berkeley, for his law degree. Mrs. Pearlstein (who was also a partner in the family firm) was supposedly grateful that at least Abe took up the family trade. Abe's dad was still getting over it.

Abe and I drove to a legacy seafood restaurant in Pasadena that still got written up as a great place to go, never mind that the hotter, trendier places are way further west on Colorado Boulevard. Abe really loved seafood, and while you can get great fish in Central Missouri, it's freshwater fish. Abe waxed ecstatic over the menu, and it took forever to get our order in. But once the waiter had brought our cocktails (a Manhattan for me, a martini for Abe) and our cold seafood sampler, we settled in.

"How are you doing?" Abe asked, after slurping down an oyster. He put the shell down and looked at me. "You know, I get it. Signing the papers seems like it would be pretty cut and dried, but I've never done one of these sessions without the heirs getting bent out of shape."

"I'm okay." I squeezed my eyes shut, then blew out my breath. "You're right. There's been a lot of the old crap cropping up."

"Like what?" he asked kindly.

I frowned and dipped a bit of cold crab in some cocktail sauce. "Not sure, really. I guess I'm mostly glad that we didn't get too much trouble from my dad."

Abe laughed and rolled his eyes. "He tried. Made the case that your grandma was not of sound mind."

"She wasn't," I said with a shudder. "When I visited her last summer, she kept trying to tell me my mother was still alive."

When I was eight, a tornado flattened three of the towns in our area. The worst day of my life. It had not started well, with Tiffany Klinger sitting on me and stealing my new shoes. I blinked at the memory. I had decorated them the weekend before with Mom. After Tiffany stole them, I had run to the cloakroom and hidden, which, as it turned out, saved my life. Mom hadn't been so lucky. When the tornado had ripped through the house, it had taken her with it.

"Your grandma was more with it than you thought," Abe said.

"I suppose," I said. "Other than the thing with my mom, she seemed pretty astute."

"Sharp as the proverbial tack," Abe said. He took a bite of octopus. "In fact, she may have had a point about your mother."

"The house was destroyed, Abe," I groaned. "There was no way Mom could have survived."

"There were several walls still standing," he replied, matter-of-factly scooping out a mussel.

"Nice try." I pushed my appetizer plate away. "I know. They never found her body. That doesn't mean a thing. Trust me, hers wasn't the only body they never found." I swallowed and blinked my eyes.

Abe reached over the table and touched my arm. "Look, I'm sorry if this upsets you. But I thought you should know. There's some weird shit connected to Abner Smutz's accounts. He had a bunch of them, each for a different member of your family."

I shrugged. Great-grandpa Smutz's legacy had been legendary in my family. He'd been some sort of city engineer or something very strait-laced. But he'd scrimped and saved and invested wisely and had left a freaking fortune for his two kids and their children. There had even been an account for me, as I had been born a year or so before he died.

"There's weird shit all over my family's finances," I said. "You're an officer of the court, so I can't say anything about my dad's accounting, but let's just say, off the record, that it's more than a little on the creative side."

Abe laughed. "I believe it. There have been all kinds of rumors for years."

"Another reason why I'm here and not in Lee Creek," I said.

Lee Creek is the town where I'm from. Abe grew up nearby in Klaxton Center, which is the county seat for Amberwick County, and was one of the three towns decimated by the tornado that took my mom.

The waiter came by and removed the appetizer plates and shells and placed salads in front of us.

"Look, Abe," I said. "I've looked at Grandma Schmidt's accounts and a few other things, but not much. I could go deeper, and you know that. I'm not because I don't really want to know. If I haven't gone deeper with my dad's finances, I seriously do not want to know. Okay. Maybe I have and I'm using what I find to keep Dad at a distance."

Abe looked puzzled. "Okay, your dad isn't an angel..."

"Not even," I groaned. I looked away, then caught his eyes. "This has almost nothing to do with the money. My problem is that I have no proof, and that I was a kid at the time." I stopped long enough to take a lungful of air in and blow it out. "Here's the thing. Dad is a traditional wife beater. He used to hit Mom pretty regularly. In fact, we were going to escape. We had a signal she was going to send me. When I got it, that meant that I was going to take everything in my school desk that mattered to me because we were leaving." I squeezed my eyes shut against the tears. "We were so close to getting out of there. Then the tornado hit, and Mom was gone."

"That sucks."

"Not nearly as badly as hearing Dad kill my first stepmother." I tried to eat some salad and failed. I put my fork down. "The yelling and the screams, I'd heard all that before. It was the dead silence after the fight. That scared the snot out of me. Dad told me that Janelle had run off. But then they found her body in the woods outside town. I looked up the police record a few years ago. Dad said they had been fighting, but that she'd run away." I shook my head. "I knew that was bullshit. Dad had been telling me since the tornado that my mom never loved me and that was a flat out lie. Mom loved me like no one else." The tears started running down my cheeks whether or not I wanted them to. "My other stepmother, Eileen, we have no idea where she is, and trust me, Dad is hell bent on tracking her down."

"Could that be why your mom is trying to stay hidden?"

"I would imagine so, if she's alive," I said.

"I think she is." Abe continued munching on his salad. "My guess is that she has good reason to fear your father. I've done a few of these abused wives cases. Those husbands are pretty scary."

"Okay. Dad qualifies." I took another deep breath. "That being said, he never usually hit me. If there was abuse, it was in his constant criticism and trying to control me all the time."

"And I can see that it worked really well on you." Abe's eyes gleamed with mischief.

It was just the right touch.

I shrugged. "Maybe not completely, but enough that I am seriously fucked up and constantly fighting it."

Abe chewed thoughtfully for a moment. "The problem, Jannie, is that your grandma's money should have run out years ago, and it didn't. I know how much she had when I started with her. I would figure it was about to end, but then there would be a deposit. She wouldn't say from where. My dad said that in this case, we shouldn't worry about the money coming in. We both kind of figured the money came from your dad, which meant it was in everyone's best interest not to look too closely. It was no surprise that your grandmother didn't want to talk about it."

"Why not?" I asked.

"She hated your father."

I made a face. "She didn't like him a whole heck of a lot, but I figured that happened after Mom died."

"I don't think so," Abe said, then sat back as the waiter collected our salad plates.

"It had to be. Mom always said Grandma had strong-armed her into marrying Dad."

"He must have had something on her," Abe said. "We'll probably never know what."

The waiter returned with ice-cold glasses of sauvignon blanc and shrimp scampi for me and poached sole for Abe.

I glared at Abe over my plate. "Go peddle your conspiracy theory someplace else, Abe."

"Jannie, I have to tell you this," Abe said. "When you go through your accounts, you're going to find a whole bunch of money that you can't account for. Your grandmother believed that it came from your mom. She wouldn't let me tell you this while she was alive, but now I have to. Just based on the comments I got from her, I think she didn't want you to go looking for your mother. She was afraid of what your father would do."

"Then why would she tell me last summer that Mom was alive?"

Abe shrugged helplessly. "Best I can figure is that she was feeling guilty. Or close enough to dead that whatever hold your father had on her didn't matter anymore."

"That almost makes sense," I sighed.

"Especially since she did sort of ask me to tell you something." Abe paused. "It was about a week before she died. She said that I wasn't supposed to tell you, but I got this weird feeling that she really wanted me to."

"Huh?" I speared a shrimp on my fork, then used my knife to scrape the tail off.

"Apparently, a couple months after the tornado, when they finally decided that your mom was dead, your grandmother got a phone call from a woman asking about Jannie's funeral."

"Okay. Maybe you were right about Grandma being delusional. Obviously, there wasn't a funeral for me."

"Which is why your grandmother hung up right away." Abe grabbed a really huge bite of sole and sighed. "This is fabulous."

"I know."

"Anyway, your grandmother told me that when she thought about it later, the voice had sounded an awful lot like your mother's. The reason Grandma hung up was that she thought it must have been some trick of her imagination, because her daughter was dead. But then she got another call when you were around fourteen. The woman wanted your grandmother to tell you that she and you would be running away to Boston that next week."

My stomach twisted and my throat tightened. Running away to Boston was our code that it was time to leave.

CHAPTER TWO

O kay. I was shook. Really, really shook. I'm not sure if I finished dinner, but I was glad that Abe took care of the bill and didn't complain about it. That's because shortly after he told me about Grandma Schmidt telling him about The Code, I ran like hell.

It did not help that there were two beefy guys in the parking lot, sitting on top of a big-ass American muscle car close to where I was parked. I did not recognize the guys specifically, but it did occur to me that I'd been seeing the black car with red stripes behind me every so often ever since I'd left the meeting with Brent.

"Oh, fuck!" I groaned to myself and popped the leather cover on the pepper spray can I keep on my key chain.

The two guys, both wearing jeans, black t-shirts, and closely cropped hair that stood up about half an inch on the tops of their heads, had the grace to pretend that they hadn't been following me, but it was obvious.

You see, my father would hire beefy idiots to follow me every so often. Ostensibly, it was his way of keeping me in control, even though it had never worked. That, sadly, didn't stop him from trying.

I guess the goons thought they were being really subtle. One was slightly larger and had a broken nose. He grinned at me and waggled his eyebrows at me in a lame attempt at being sexually predatory. Maybe it wasn't so lame, but I knew these guys couldn't hurt me. Dad always gave his goons strict orders not to even touch me. The one who did got a nice face-full of pepper spray before I tazed him. I never found out what Dad did to him.

Mr. Eyebrows laughed menacingly. So, I did the one thing he and his pal would not expect. I walked right over and got in their faces.

"Listen, assholes," I said. I folded my arms over my chest so that my left arm hid that my right forefinger was on my spray can. "I am so not in the mood for this bullshit. Which means you little peckers have a choice. Either stop following me or I call my dad and let him know his goons got made again. Now really. Do you want my dad pissed at you?"

"We don't know your dad," said Mr. Eyebrows with a grin. "And we're pretty big guys."

"With tiny little feet and hands, which is why you're compensating with that big, black thing you're driving. Red stripes? Seriously? Like I'm not going to spot that?"

The second guy looked like he was about to come after me, but his friend stopped him.

"Okay. We're busted," said Mr. Eyebrows, genially. "But you know it's only because your dad cares about you."

"So I've heard." I glared at the two men. "Get the fuck away from me. Stay the fuck away from me, or I'll find you two shits and set any number of government agencies on your asses. And that's after I've disabled all of your credit and debit cards, hacked your email, and outed your tiny little dicks on Facebook. Guess what? I can really do it, too. Ask my dad."

The second guy made a move toward me, but Mr. Eyebrows held him back again. Still, his eyes narrowed.

"That's not a nice way to talk to guys who are only trying to help you," he growled.

"Help me how?" I asked.

"We're here to keep you out of trouble."

"Uh-huh. Nice try. Now, scoot or you will regret it." I put on my best menacing smile. "I mean it. Do you really want all your Facebook friends laughing their asses off at you?"

The two guys looked at each other. The second one was looking like he still wanted a piece of me, but Mr. Eyebrows shoved him toward the passenger seat of the car. I memorized the plate and saw a rental company sticker on the side window. That was a little odd. Dad mostly hired local goons, but he'd sometimes send someone from home.

I went to my car, got in, and booted my laptop. As the laptop booted, I pulled out. The idiots were still on my tail. It didn't take that long to get home, and by then, the laptop was ready to go. I pulled into the garage, slid my car into my space, then signed into the car rental site. On those occasions Dad would send somebody, he'd have them get the car from the same company so Dad could get the points, and, yeah, I'd hacked it before. I pulled up the car's records and found the email the guys had used when they rented the car. It wasn't Dad's. A few clicks more and I confirmed it. The yutzes had violated the first rule of covert activity - never use your personal information unless you have to.

Grinning, I sent a rather nasty little email from my garage. I went up to my condo and went in without turning on any lights. I stumbled up the stairs to the living room. My front window looked down on the street, and I watched the black car as it slid into a parking space. A few minutes later, it peeled out. I guess they'd gotten the email.

"Damn, I'm good," I muttered, fumbling for the tone fob on my key ring.

I was alpha testing the gadget for a friend of mine, who had developed a new security system that used a combination of subsonic tones and biometrics rather than Bluetooth radio signals. Not only did you need a special microphone to record the tone, the fob also read my fingerprint, so I had to have my actual finger on it before the tone would register anything.

The idea was that it was more secure to use the fob than using just my voice to control my smart home. After all, if Hollywood has taught us anything, it's that biometrics aren't as secure as you might think. The catch, of course, is that the person trying to hack them must know the target well enough to get the mask, the recording, the fingerprints, the whatever, and know how to game the specific system. In short, if someone seriously wanted to turn my lights on and off, they'd have to do a lot of work to do so, which meant I was already pretty safe. The fob was supposedly another layer of security.

Actually, the fob was a royal pain in the ass. It mostly worked. I wasn't sure if the problem was in the fingerprint reader or the tone part of the controller. Or maybe it was my tendency to press the buttons on the fob too quickly. Slowing down usually helped, but not always.

I clicked the sequence to pull my blackout curtains and turn on the lights. Nothing happened. I tried another sequence. Bupkes.

"Curtains pulled, lights on," I announced.

The curtains slid closed and the lights finally came on. I sighed. Another failure to write up for Aileen.

It wasn't that late, and like a lot of geeks, I tend to be a night person. I went up two more flights of stairs to my study and sat down in front of the small file cabinet next to my main desktop. I'd built the computer from scratch, so it was pretty darned powerful. The desktop, however, was the last thing on my mind at that moment.

I opened the file drawer and pulled out the file filled with printouts. Oh, sure, I could have kept everything on a thumb drive, but those are easy to lose. Plus, believe it or not, paper lasts better. At least so far, it does. And hackers can't get to my paper files. The downsides are the space paper takes and that it's hard to update copies. I had a copy of the file in my safe deposit box. I hadn't updated that copy in a few months, but there really weren't any new data, either.

You see, I had lied to Abe. I told everyone that I believed my mother was dead, but the truth was, I knew she wasn't. And I strongly suspected I knew why she was hiding. It was exactly what Abe had said. My dad was still looking for her and would probably kill her if he found her.

That didn't stop me from trying to find her. Okay, it doesn't take a shrink to figure out that the reason that I was so good at finding people was that I'd been trying to find her for years. Yeah - the only person I hadn't been able to find, and just enough tantalizing clues. I had to figure the mysterious scholarship I'd gotten to MIT came from her. And there were other little, subtle signals, too.

Abe's revelations about my Grandma echoed in my brain. So it turns out that when I was fourteen, Mom wanted me to run away with her. I would have in a heartbeat. I loved Grandma, but she could be a real piece of work. She absolutely refused to talk to me about my mom, beyond telling me that Mom had been real wild and that I did not want to end up like her. It was almost like Grandma was trying to protect me from my mother and could never give me a good reason why.

I thumbed through the print outs yet again.

It's actually easier to find people than you might think. Yes, you have to have an idea of where to look, but once you've got that, most people give themselves away through their habits, those unconscious bits of behavior that we all engage in and are unique to each of us. My mom somehow had understood this because her main habit was to change things up periodically. Every now and then, I'd run across a bit of code that seemed to be her style, but chasing it down seldom did me any good. If the code was hers, then she'd written it with someone else whose name was on the project, and that someone else only knew a name that led nowhere. My mother was as close to being a ghost as one could get and still be alive.

Wiping my eyes, I put the printouts back in their folder. I had other work to get done, namely Tanya Coleman. Okay, I didn't really, since I didn't have my signed agreement yet, but I figured the odds were good that I'd have it soon and it was better than trying to figure out my mom.

I plugged Brent's thumb drive into my desktop computer and again did a thorough scan of everything that was on the drive. It was as clean as the day it came off the factory floor, with the dossier on Tanya Coleman and the two video files. The dossier only contained the facts of Coleman's life: her school records, where she'd lived, the resume she'd used to get hired at Wheeling, credit cards, Social Security and driver's license numbers, her mobile phone number, and her address, which happened to be her parents' address, as well.

Actually, that last bit was a bit off. Not entirely unusual. I knew plenty of young adults who had to live with their parents, but most of them either didn't have paying jobs or jobs that didn't pay a whole heck of a lot. Coleman had a full-time gig with a major corporation. Even as support staff, you had to figure she could have afforded her own place, or at least something with a roommate. So, either Wheeling was pretty chintzy with wages, or Tanya had some other reason to stick with her parents.

Her school records didn't show much on the surface, just a list of where she went and her Grade Point Averages. She'd been a so-so student, not terrible, but not all that impressive. I wondered how she'd scored a job at Wheeling, which generally went after the cream of the crop. I looked at her resume. It really hit all the right notes. It was almost as if a young kid, about to graduate with a less than stellar performance at a two-year college, had somehow found a way to endear herself to a think tank.

Then I looked at Tanya's photo. Her hair was done in a traditional 1960s flip and her nose was almost as narrow as mine, but it would have been hard to miss that Tanya Coleman was African American. I winced. She'd probably been hired because the upper echelons at Wheeling Corporation did not want to look as racist as they were.

Okay, maybe some of my personal biases were at work, but I'd seen it before and had some other friends who could verify that they'd been hired at some place or another for the exact same reason.

And yet, Old Man River had been seen giving Coleman a flat black box that could have been... What? A router? A hard drive? Some other device? And if he had given her something, why had he been killed and not her? Maybe because she wasn't part of the hacking group?

There were a couple of video files on the thumb drive. I was not surprised to see the grainy black and white of surveillance footage when I opened the first one. The camera must have been on the side of the building, because it overlooked the doorway to the club, but included a perfect shot of the serving window of the Taco Fuerte truck.

It was a busy night, and I almost missed Coleman picking up her order from Rios. I ran it back a couple times to be sure, but then I saw something flat and dark under her burrito as she grabbed it. I watched several previous orders go out, and none of them included something flat and dark. Less than a minute after Coleman picked up her burrito, a man wearing a wide-brimmed hat and medical mask approached the truck, pulled a gun, and I stopped the video.

I took a deep breath and opened the second video file. The camera angle seemed to be coming from the street level, like a car window, or someone standing nearby. The camera was focused on a knot of people near the front fender of the taco truck. I guessed they were selling something they shouldn't have been, and that was why the cops were taking the video. Other people stood around eating or ambled about. Just beyond the exchange, Coleman walked into the shot, heading away from the truck. A second later, people scrambled all over the place. Coleman turned back toward the truck and stood, gaping. The man in the hat and medical mask ran past her and shoved something into her gut. It fell to the ground and sure looked like a gun. The man kept running down Santa Monica Boulevard. Whoever had been shooting the video had had the good sense to keep recording the man fleeing the scene, but Coleman entered the shot, running like crazy toward the camera and past it. The camera stayed on the fleeing man until he took a left and disappeared. Then the video cut out.

I opened the file's metadata, basically information about when, where, and what had created the file. It was a Los Angeles Police Department video. They have a couple of unique fields and some weird shorthand that they use on their evidence videos. A couple years before, Brent had given me a few and asked if I could figure out which ones were L.A.P.D. and which ones weren't. It must have been another of Brent's little games, but I'd found it fun and picked up the metadata thing right away. Brent had been impressed because he hadn't been able to spot it.

And there I was, thinking about stuff that I did not want to be thinking about again. I shook my head for a second and took a deep breath. At least, I had some hint as to why Brent thought Coleman might be alive. I wondered if she was in police custody for a moment, then realized Brent would not be asking me to find her if she was. The Feds and local law enforcement tend to play nice with each other here in L.A., which apparently is kind of weird.

So where had Coleman gone? I rolled my head on my neck, then booted up my extra secure Virtual Private Network. VPNs are services that make it look like you're surfing from someone else's computer, and it's a great way to keep people who are spying on your network from seeing what you're actually looking up on the Internet. As in, I was about to engage in the sort of snooping that pulls in the kind of evidence that you can't use in court. I wasn't looking for a bad guy, at least, I was pretty sure I wasn't. Having seen that video really made me wonder, though.

Past is prologue someone once said (yes, I could look up who, but I don't want to right now). If people give themselves away by their habits, then it pays to remember that the vast majority of our habits are formed in our early lives. Which is why I hacked my way into the Los Angeles Unified School District system to look up Coleman's school records. There were the actual grade reports, which included notes from her teachers. Most noted that she was really bright and well-behaved for the most part, but lamented her lack of interest in playing with her classmates or doing her homework. Several noted that she still somehow managed to pass her tests with As. If she'd been a boy, I suspect the notes would have worried about her anti-social tendencies. As a girl, she was just quirky.

I had to admit, it was all more than a little familiar. My own elementary school record had looked pretty much the same. So had the records of many of the geeky kids that I'd known. I was about to curse the squashing of another mind under the boot of conformity when something else caught my eye. In sixth grade, Coleman had gotten into trouble for configuring the classroom computer to play Beyoncé's Single Ladies every time it booted up. Apparently, her teacher had taken it as an insult, as she was single and had recently broken up with her boyfriend. I could see Tanya thinking of it as a salute to her teacher's strength.

Which is when I sat up. Tanya was a geek like me. I scrolled through her high school records: more of the same, without the pranks, and plenty of math and science classes, which she passed just barely because she kept passing her tests without doing her homework. Her high school teachers had labeled her socially immature. I saw an introvert who was more at home with a keyboard than with other people.

From high school, she enrolled at Santa Monica Community College as a computer science major. She changed to a business major after her first semester. I wondered at that, especially when I saw that her first computer class had been with an old friend of mine, Dr. Leon Cortez. She'd gotten a D in that class, which didn't make sense. Any kid who could have set up the Single Ladies thing had to have some skills. Leon usually celebrated that and was really into making sure that girls were included in his classes. Coleman had graduated two years later and gotten her job at Wheeling.

There was something really fishy about that. Given Coleman's behavior as a kid, it certainly seemed like she could have been part of the hacking group. But it also seemed like she'd given up computers. Could she have set Old Man River up for Wheeling somehow? And yet, he'd given her something, not the other way around, unless they were trading drugs or porn or something. Did she have a connection with Manny Rios? I dug a little deeper and found it. It wasn't a direct connection, but it was almost as fishy. Manny Rios had also taken a computer class with Leon the semester before Coleman had. Only Rios had dropped the class within days of starting it. Rios had never graduated, either, and went on to work in the Taco Fuerte truck with his cousins.

I emailed Leon. The email bounced back. I looked again. The address was correct, but according to the server, it didn't exist. What? I emailed Leon's school address. I got an auto-responder email that Leon was on sabbatical for the fall semester and would not be checking his email. Well, that explained the dead email address. Leon apparently did not want to be bothered. It happened. Most of us changed personal emails every so often just to cut down on the spam and all the bots tracking us.

Except that I couldn't quite buy it. Something was off, maybe even wrong, but for the life of me, I couldn't figure out what.

CHAPTER THREE

I crawled out of bed at nine the next morning, feeling groggy and annoyed. I'd gone to bed shortly before one, but had not slept well, my mind reeling with all the reasons why Leon Cortez would want to drop his personal email address, and how that connected him to Tanya Coleman being missing and Old Man River getting killed. The last time I'd seen Leon in real life, a few weeks before, he hadn't said a word about any sabbatical. If anything, he'd been a touch edgy and evasive.

My watch chirped an alert, and, sure enough, Brent had emailed. I pulled it up on my phone. Brent had told Coleman's family about me, and they were eager to talk.

"Also, any progress yet?" the email read.

I glared at my phone, then thumbed the reply. "Not doing squat. You know why."

I probably should have held my breath another ten seconds longer before hitting send, but I didn't. No surprise, Brent did not respond.

I staggered in and out of the shower, made up my morning ration of caffeine, and popped a bagel in the toaster. I debated continuing to blow Brent off and wait until I had my contract before doing anything more on Coleman, but the thing with Leon had me bugged. I called Coleman's mother, Yvonne. She invited me right over.

"I'm going to be here all day," she said with a sigh. "My boss told me to take some vacation time until they find Tanya."

"That's very nice of you," I said, ignoring the skepticism in her tone. It had clearly been directed at her boss. "I can be there by two."

I checked my laptop bag for everything I needed, refilled my water bottle, and changed out the snack bars in there for fresher ones. I locked up the condo with my smart locks and set them to open with my fob. Then I walked to the Gold Line station, about half a mile away.

I use public transportation as much as possible. Besides having to walk more, the other advantage of going by the light rail and bus system was that I got a lot of work done. Oh, and it's harder to track someone when they're constantly moving. Maybe that was unnecessarily paranoid, but as I often explained to my friend and favorite barista, Dina, when you know how easy it is to hack some of this stuff, you take steps.

For example, as I settled into my seat on the Gold Line train, I saw an ad for Mrs. Goode's MarketPlace. "We deliver!" proclaimed the red, white, and blue banner over the owner and his mother. The company was a shopping site with pretensions of wresting Amazon's iron grip from that space. The owner, Jackson Goode, was making a big deal that their site was the safest on the Internet, with no tracking and no one hacking their data.

I did not believe that there was no tracking. Of course, they were tracking user data. Tracking is one of those things that makes shopping sites so useful to the rest of us. As for no one hacking their data, it was only a matter of time before some smart ass did just to say they had. Possibly already had done so. You just don't put temptation like that out in the world because there's always a way in. So, you harden your space as best you can and don't give anyone a reason to come after you. Or you try not to give them a reason.

I snorted and booted my laptop. I looked at the ad once more. Goode had that rangy, down-home look, with short, dark hair, and an arm around a sweet-looking old lady. I wondered if that was really his mother.

It didn't really matter. I had work I wanted to do, particularly looking at the rest of Tanya's family. Her mother, Yvonne, was employed at a nursing home as the front office clerk, with mostly good comments on her employee evaluations. She'd taken advantage of the company's volunteer hours policy to spend time at her kids' schools, although she hadn't done so in a while. Tanya's father, Wilson, worked as a floor supervisor at a parts plant down in the South Bay. He'd been written up a couple times for "talking back" to his supervisor, but otherwise was considered a good, conscientious worker. They owned their home, which they'd inherited from Yvonne's mother some years before. They paid their bills on time (which was more than I could say, thanks to my complete inability to pay attention to that sort of thing). Tanya had two younger brothers, and based on their school records, they were a little squirrelly, but mostly well-behaved, and both showed an aptitude with computers. One would be a senior in high school in another month's time, the other would start high school. Basically, a nice, stable family. I wondered how much of that would hold up when I talked to Yvonne.

While digging all this up, I had switched trains twice and eventually caught a bus to the Palms neighborhood where the Colemans lived. It was a small plot of single-family homes that had probably been built in the 1930s or '40s, nestled just below Interstate 10, interspersed with apartment buildings. A huge billboard facing the westbound traffic hovered over the neighborhood, put there by the Wheeling Corporation.

"Our job is thinking about you," read bright white letters on a royal blue background that also featured the Wheeling logo.

I shuddered. Those damned billboards were everywhere, and they seriously creeped me out. I guess I just wasn't buying the benevolent thing they were supposed to represent.

I'd arrived in Palms a lot sooner than two o'clock, but that had been my plan. I walked around a bit to get a feel for the area, then went and ate lunch at a nearby cafe. At two, I knocked on the door of a small stuccoed hacienda-style house fronted by a neatly kept lawn with just enough brown to show they weren't flouting watering rules. Yvonne, a busty woman with light brown skin, answered right away, then took me out to the backyard, where she put on a radio and turned up the volume.

"We don't know if somebody's listening," she said softly. "Somebody was watching us all last week. I wouldn't be talking to you if Anthony hadn't looked up that F.B.I. person and found that he was all right."

"Looked up?" I asked.

"Yeah. Anthony, he's my older boy. He made sure Agent Mikkelson really was with the F.B.I. and that he looked like the person who came to talk to us." Yvonne leaned forward. "Ever since those people from Tanya's job came nosing around, we decided we'd better not take any chances."

"What made you decide that?" I asked, frowning.

Yvonne looked over her shoulder and shifted. "Tanya hated that place. They were racist. Real bad."

"I've heard that," I said.

"One of her bosses kept calling her his cute little jungle bunny."

"Holy crap!" I yelped. "I can't believe it."

Yvonne shifted and almost shut down.

"No, no. I mean, I believe that it happened," I said quickly. "I'm just shocked that anyone would be so overt about it these days."

Yvonne rolled her eyes. "Tanya said he made like he didn't know it was offensive, like it was so old, she'd've never heard it before."

"Good lord! Why didn't she quit? Hell, I would have been out of there and calling a lawyer within five minutes."

"I told Tanya the same thing." Yvonne sat back and blinked back some tears. "I told her to get out of there. Nothing good would come of it. She just said she had a job to do there. I told her nobody that dense was ever going to get woke, and she said that wasn't the point." Yvonne took a deep breath as she fidgeted with her hands. "She also told me never to trust anybody from that place, but she would never say why."

"Could she have told her friends?"

Yvonne shrugged. "She didn't have a lot of friends. A couple girlfriends is all, and I asked them if Tanya had told them anything about her job or whatever. They said they hadn't heard anything weird, just that she hated her job."

"How about any online friends?"

Yvonne chuckled. "She used to have lots of those kinds of friends. She loved being on her computer. We were so proud when she signed up at the college as a computer science major." Yvonne looked down and sighed again. "Then, after her first semester, she suddenly decided she wanted to be a business major. She said she knew more than the teachers did about writing code. She also stopped spending so much time chatting online. Said those folks were just holding her back. I was glad about that. She was spending way too much time with them and not doing her homework." Yvonne shook her head. "After she switched majors, she got real secretive about her laptop. Kept it with her all the time. The boys would try to play with it sometimes, but she made it real hard for them to get on it. They couldn't get around her sign in or something. Especially the past few months, we got the feeling she was up to something, but we couldn't get her to say anything."

"She probably was," I said, then regretted it.

Yvonne looked at me in surprise. "Do you know what?"

"I don't know," I said, hedging a lot. "I just know the pattern of behavior. Can I look at her room?"

"Oh, yes."

Yvonne showed me to the tiny bedroom in the middle of the house. It was furnished almost more like a study than a bedroom, but the futon did double duty as a bed and a sofa. A large screen TV had been set up across from the futon. The closet was stuffed full of clothes, mostly office wear and workout clothes. There were only a couple going-out dresses and nothing sparkly. Tanya had a desk, but it was empty except for a couple of old thumb drives. I asked Yvonne if I could have them and she said yes. If Tanya was hiding an ongoing interest in computers and hacking, she'd done a fantastic job of it. But next to the futon, there was an ethernet cord. I traced it to the family's wireless router in the hall.

"She used to love playing computer games in there," Yvonne said softly, once we were back outside again. "Even after she changed majors. She had one of those desktop computers hooked up to her TV." Yvonne blinked again. "Then, it was right before Christmas, I think, she suddenly gave her desktop and her keyboard to Jamal, my younger boy, and told him that if anybody asked, to say they'd always been his."

"Hm." I looked at her. "This won't be easy, but tell me about the night she disappeared. Was she upset? Scared?"

"No. She seemed excited, like she couldn't wait to go out." Yvonne sniffed. "She told me right before she left, 'Mama, won't be long now. You'll see. It will all be good.' I tried to ask her what she was talking about, but she just left."

"Did she have her laptop with her?"

"Oh, yes. Then there was the shooting, and she didn't come back. I thought she was just upset about Manny."

"Manny? You mean you knew him?"

"Of course. They met at Santa Monica College. He was one of her best friends." Yvonne sighed. "Well, not the past year." She blinked again, and this time the tears fell down her cheeks. "Jannie, the police told me that she's a person of interest in the shooting. That means she's a suspect, right?"

"It can, yes."

Yvonne shook her head. "My Tanya wouldn't have hurt Manny. She loved him like a brother. Maybe even a boyfriend. I don't know why they stopped seeing each other so much, but she wouldn't have shot him."

"Well, we know she didn't do that," I said.

"Please find my baby," Yvonne said, grabbing my hands. "She's a good girl. She wouldn't hurt anybody, let alone Manny. But she must be in some terrible trouble to be away like this."

"I'll do my best, Yvonne," I said.

I left soon after, my brain going thirty different directions at once. The problem was, nothing entirely made sense. If Tanya was trying to hide that she was part of the group trying to bring down Wheeling, why would she hide her computer habit when she was at home? You'd think that would be the one safe place for her. Except for Wheeling's legendary resources. The shit they dug up on folks rivaled what I could find.

And if Wheeling had used her to hurt Manny, I could well see that she'd run away when she'd seen what happened. Maybe she'd been afraid her bosses were setting her up for something, and then realized it was to take the fall for Manny's shooting. That would explain some of the secrecy at home, but not the need to hide her computer stuff.

I was inclined to believe that Tanya was part of the hacking group. Her past skills, her connection to Manny, and the job thing, that made it all too likely. And I could understand the online secrecy. If they were going to bring down the nerds at Wheeling Corp., then they were going to have to really keep it under their hats. It wasn't like the folks at Wheeling were unaware that they were a target. In some ways, it was kind of like the Mrs. Goode's Marketplace thing - Wheeling almost begged for it with their arrogant attitude that their "emulated viruses" were only to help create better web security.

It was pure bullshit, and I knew that for a fact, even if I couldn't prove it in court. I'd had at least two young friends who'd been encouraged to write malware. One friend had been tricked into it when he'd been told that he was working on a fake virus that would help security experts find real ones. The other had been told she was helping solve a coding problem for something that would make computers more secure.

Both had come to me to find the people who had tricked them because they had been trapped and would be arrested if I couldn't prove they'd been tricked. There was money involved, and the trail led me to Wheeling Corp. through a couple shell corporations. The problem was I'd found that trail through means that are not admissible in court. Brent had been furious, but we'd gotten enough to get the Feds off the kids' backs. Brent also made a point of teaching me the rules of evidence and we'd both been gunning for Wheeling ever since.

Unfortunately, none of this got me any closer to actually finding Tanya Coleman. While on the train home, I used my hotspot and searched all of her debit and credit cards for the previous year, checking transaction after transaction to see if I could find a pattern. I didn't have much by the time I got home. Coleman's habits were pretty much what you'd expect from a young woman her age and income level. She'd bought a few more computer games than most and streamed movies almost every week. She transferred money to an account with her mother's name on it around the first of every month - presumably paying rent. She'd bought an iPhone the year before, and had jail broken it. I thought that was a little odd since most people who buy iPhones are perfectly happy staying within the Apple eco-system and not about to mess with breaking into the phone's operating system to run apps that aren't available in the Apple Store. It's not that hard to jail break an iPhone, but it takes some skill, and Tanya had bought a game that only worked on jail-broken phones.

I was so absorbed by my thoughts that I didn't realize that my subsonic fob hadn't worked until I tried to get into the condo and couldn't. Another damn failure to write up for Aileen. Fortunately, I have actual keys that can override my smart locks, which got me in without more than an annoyed curse.

I dumped my bag in the kitchen and got a pre-made meal out of the freezer. While it nuked, I got a glass of wine from the fridge and filled my water bottle extra full. Once the microwave dinged, I got a fork, napkin, my bag and my liquids and hauled it all upstairs. I looked at the thumb drives. They only had a couple of files of some bits of code, none of which appeared to be related to the others. Given that Coleman had abandoned them, I figured they probably weren't a priority. I'd try to contact Leon Cortez the next day, since he was better at reading code than I was. I pulled the thumb drives from the laptop, dropped them on the desk, and went back to Coleman's financials.

There were about five different restaurants that she seemed to like a lot, including the Taco Fuerte truck. I checked the truck's social media accounts to see where they'd been the past few weeks. Sure enough, the truck had been parking at the beach near the Wheeling Corp. Headquarters in Santa Monica around lunch time almost every day. That made sense. Unless someone was seriously paranoid - which, given that someone had killed Rios, someone was - there was nothing to suggest that there was a connection between Rios and Coleman. The truck was close, and it was popular, based on its Twitter feed. I even recognized the names of a few Wheeling employees, namely some of the higher-level guys who were considered important enough to list on the corporate website.

Just to be sure, even though I wasn't supposed to, I cracked the truck's bank account. The money deposited each morning led me to believe that it was pretty successful, with somewhat larger deposits on the days they parked near Wheeling.

All of this took time, by the way. You don't just click a few keys and you're in. I had to log every place the truck had parked on a map. Then look up the company's business licenses to find out where they banked. It was a big national one, and I'd cracked them before, so I knew the back door way in. I still had to find the account I wanted, compare the transactions to the location, and so forth and so on. I also had to feed myself, walk around every so often so I didn't get a crick in my neck, and by the time I logged out of the bank site, it was way closer to three a.m. than I'd expected.

Profoundly grateful that I didn't have to log in anyplace by eight a.m., I dragged myself to bed. It was a good sleep, and really, really annoying when a text alert on my phone woke me up. It was from Abe, who'd told me he was staying in town for a few more days before heading back to St. Louis. I blinked. He wanted me to go to lunch and asked me to meet him in his hotel room around noon. I texted back that I would and went back to sleep.

I got up in enough time to shower, decided that it would take just as much time to drive as to walk, and walked over to the hotel, a rather unremarkable box of floors with small balconies overlooking the street. I didn't really look at the lobby, which had several overstuffed chairs in neat conversation groups. And a flat panel TV that was flashing the end of a Wheeling Corp. commercial with the blue background and the reminder that Wheeling was thinking about me.

Abe's room was at the end of a long gray hallway, with numbered doors and bland art. I started to knock, but the door was cracked open.

"Abe?" I called softly because I didn't want to make too much noise in the hallway.

I didn't hear anything, so I texted him.

"Sure. Working on something, but come on in."

I went inside. Just beyond the bed, I saw his two bare legs lying on the floor.

"Abe, what are you doing on the floor?" I asked as I went over.

A second later, I ran from the room, screaming my fool head off.

Chapter Four

Doors here and there along the corridor opened as I fumbled with my phone, trying to pull up the dialer, but getting the text app instead. I sobbed as I finally got the dialer open and called 911.

"Nine-one-one emergency," answered a business-like voice that somehow sounded soothing at the same time.

"He's dead," I gasped. "He's been shot. I think, at least, I'm pretty sure he has, and he's dead!"

"I'm calling police and EMTs now," the nice dispatcher said, after getting the hotel's name and cross streets. "Can you go back into the room and check for a pulse?"

"There's a big, bloody hole in his forehead!" I cried, trying not to gag. "If he's alive, it's a fucking miracle!"

At least, the dispatcher didn't get on my ass about the foul language. He asked me to stay put, and then asked where, specifically, in the hotel I was. A few minutes later, the cops arrived.

I don't remember much about what happened immediately after that. It's weird how I can remember that 911 call, but not what all the cops did when they got there. The one guy in the uniform was really nice, but held me in the hallway while his partner went into the room. I could hear the voices crackling on their radios. Soon, a bunch more folks in uniforms showed up and a couple more in suits. The first detective, a tall Black man with a shaved head, walked into Abe's room and came out, shaking his head. He muttered something at his partner, a small Asian man, who then turned to the hotel manager, an average-sized man with dark hair, who stood there wringing his hands. The poor guy looked like he was about to burst into tears. I suppose having someone get shot in your hotel isn't good for the resume.

The Black detective gently took my arm and led me to the very back of the hall. The uniforms fanned out, knocking on the doors that were still closed and talking to the people who had opened theirs.

"I'm Detective Ismael," he said, gently, and opened his notebook. "Can you tell me what happened?"

"My friend, Abe. I was supposed to meet him for lunch," I said. "I came over and the door was open, so I texted him and he said come on in." I gagged and my eyes filled. "But he was dead, and there was a hole. Oh, my god!"

I couldn't help it. I broke down crying.

"I'm sorry," I gasped.

"It's okay," Ismael said, glancing at his notes. "Do you know why Mr. Pearlstein was in town?"

"We were, um, finishing up the probate on my grandma's estate, and he wanted to stay over to visit with some friends. He texted me this morning about lunch."

I looked down at my phone, and realized that the dialer had closed, but the text app was still open and on the screen. There was one final text from Abe.

"Find Coleman or your next."

Everything started spinning, and the next thing I knew, I was in the hotel security center, seated next to a bunch of video monitors and accepting a paper cup of water from the Asian detective, a man with graying temples and kind eyes named Steven Tran.

"Feeling better?" he asked.

"I think so," I said. "This is horrible."

"Who is Coleman?" Tran asked.

"Holy fucking crap," I muttered. "This is my fault."

"What do you mean?" Tran asked.

"Did they find Abe's phone?" I asked suddenly. "Please tell me they found Abe's phone. Please."

Tran went to the end of the room, where the hotel security person ran a video back and forth on her monitor. There was more crackling from the radio there, then Tran came back and shook his head.

"There was no phone in the room," he said. "Well, besides the hard-wired one."

"Shit. Fucking shit." I held my hand over my mouth. "I got played. Totally fucking played."

"What do you mean?" Tran asked.

"This morning. Abe texted me. That's when he asked me to lunch. I didn't think anything of it. I just texted back that I'd be there. Then, when the door was cracked open, I texted again. I mean, I called out first, but didn't want to be too loud, so I figured he hadn't heard me because he was in the bathroom or something. You don't want to walk in on that, so I texted him. And he said that he was working on something, but to come right in, and I did and he was dead!"

I started hyperventilating, so Tran told me to hold my breath for a minute. I got control again and nodded.

"Abe couldn't have sent me those last couple of texts," I said, then swallowed back more bile. "So the bad guy, he's got Abe's phone. He's got it. He may even have had it when I got the text this morning. Holy shit. I just assumed it was Abe."

"Why wouldn't you?" Tran asked. "Can you tell me who Coleman is?"

"Tanya Coleman. She's a person of interest in Manny Rios getting killed." I took a big gulp of water from the paper cup I still held. There was something seriously wrong with that text, but my brain was not functioning yet. "I'm on contract for Brent Mikkelsen. He's an agent with the F.B.I. cybercrimes unit. We're trying to find Coleman. But why would whoever..." I gulped. "Killed Abe threaten me this way? It doesn't make sense."

"No, it doesn't," said Tran.

"Got something," said the security person. She had dark, full hair pulled back into a ponytail and wore a tan polyester suit.

Tran went over to her. I pulled myself up and followed. She shook her head.

"It's just shadows," she said. "This one is good. They seem to know where all the cameras are and ditched them. But I got a couple shadows here, so I'm guessing they went through the back service bay."

Tran hit the radio, telling the uniforms to search the service bay thoroughly.

"What's the time stamp on your shadows?" Tran asked.

"Nine-forty-three," the security person said.

I looked at the text app. "I got the first text about lunch at nine-fifty-six. Oh, shit."

"We don't know the time of death yet," Tran said. "We don't even know if those shadows mean what we think they do."

The radio crackled again - someone had found something in the service bay - and I heard Ismael's voice say that he'd be right down. I looked at Tran, who shrugged.

"All right," said the security person. "I've got Ms. Miller here going into the hotel at twelve-eleven."

"I was running late," I grumbled, looking at my grainy form cross the lobby. I gasped. "Oh, my god. I know those two guys."

The security person stopped the video and ran it back a couple minutes to where I was crossing the lobby.

I peered at the screen, then pointed. "Those two. They were following me after I met Abe Monday afternoon. I gave them what for in the parking lot at the restaurant. They followed me again, and I sent them a nasty email and they took off."

Both Tran and the security person looked at me strangely. Well, I guess it did sound kinda garbled. I took a deep breath and explained about my dad and my work finding people, dancing around the fact that some of my methods weren't always looked upon favorably by law enforcement.

"So, that one," I pointed to the taller of the two men in the video. "The one talking on the phone. His name is Earl Johnson. I can't remember his email, but I found it. It's on my laptop."

I looked down. My laptop bag was gone.

"No phone in the bag," announced a young man in a uniform cheerfully as he entered the office holding my bag. "She's got some weird shit in it, though."

Tran glared at the kid as if he wanted to shoot him. Well, it was, technically, an illegal search of my property.

"It's okay," I said. "You had to check. And, yes, I am licensed for the taser." I could see Tran debating whether he should ask me about it, so I decided to help him out. "It kind of started with my dad's snooping, and some of the people I've been asked to find aren't always thrilled that I've found them. So, a friend of mine suggested I carry the taser just in case."

I didn't tell them that the friend had been Brent. I was hoping like hell we could avoid him entirely. No such luck.

Ismael came into the security room and whispered to Tran that they'd found a gun with a suppressor on it in the service bay trash bin, when Brent barged into the room in full bluster.

"Jannie!" he yelped, and went straight for me.

"Who are you? The boyfriend?" Ismael asked.

"Was the boyfriend," I said, pushing myself out of Brent's arms.

Both Ismael's and Tran's eyes narrowed at Brent, who simply whipped out his I.D.

"Special Agent Brent Mikkelson, F.B.I. Cybercrimes," he snapped. "We have an interest in this case."

"I see," said Ismael, tossing me a significant glance.

Brent winced. "Not that. Tanya Coleman."

"What?" I gasped. "How did you find out so fast?"

"Come on, Jannie," Brent said. "There's been an alert out on Coleman since she disappeared."

"I called it in when she fainted," Ismael said, jerking a thumb at me.

"She what?" Brent demanded and turned on me.

I put up my hands. "I'm fine, Brent."

I looked at the clock on the wall and realized I'd been there several hours already. It felt like time had slowed down and sped up simultaneously. I shook my head to clear it. Brent turned on the two detectives.

"So, what have you got?" he demanded.

"You mean on *my* case?" Ismael asked, an annoyed smirk on his face. He glanced at me. "What I've got appears to be a contract killing by a perp who enjoys playing games."

"Your consultant here," Tran said, with a nod at me. "Received multiple texts from the victim's phone, leading her here for a lunch date, all of which we suspect were sent after the victim was killed. The last one threatened her if she does not find Coleman."

Brent looked at me. "What? That's nonsense. Why would a contract killer want you to find Coleman?"

"Unless she's being set up for killing Old Man River." I looked at the two detectives. "I mean Manny Rios."

"That's a stupid way to do it," Brent snarled as he paced. "We'll be all over it. He couldn't believe you'd keep something like that to yourself."

I didn't say that I might have if I hadn't fainted. An uncomfortable thought nagged at the back of my brain, but then something else occurred to me.

"Maybe he's not worried about getting caught," I said.

All three men shook their heads.

"Everyone worries about being caught," Brent said.

"We found a gun in the trash bin," Ismael said. "You know ballistics is going to come back positive on it. People who aren't worried about being caught don't ditch their guns."

"No," I said. "He ditched the gun out of habit." I looked at Ismael. "If he killed—" I choked for a second. "If he killed Abe under contract, he's done this before. In fact, I'll bet he's the guy who killed Manny Rios. The first thing that killer did was ditch the gun. It's his habit, and if it's his habit, that may be why he's not so worried about getting caught. He used Abe's phone so that can't be traced to him. The gun, presumably, can't be traced to him if he got it on the Dark Web."

"Or from some other illegal supplier," Tran grumbled.

Ismael threw his hands in the air. "Hell, he probably brings them in by the carload from Arizona."

I looked over at Brent, not sure how much he wanted me to tell the detectives.

"There may be another reason he's not worried about being caught," I said, thinking. "The people who hired him."

Brent looked at me and cursed under his breath.

"What about those two fellows that you said were following you last Monday?" Ismael asked.

"Someone was following you?" Brent looked angry.

"It was my dad, Brent," I told him with a sigh. "They even admitted it." I looked at the video screen. "It's just that they were in the lobby when I walked in. I wonder if they were watching Abe to see if they could catch me."

"It's possible," said Brent. "What did you threaten them with this time?"

"Humiliation on Facebook," I grumbled, blushing.

"That doesn't sound so bad," said Tran.

"It may have involved disparaging comments on the size of their anatomy," I said. "And they were obviously the kind of dickless wonders who would be worried about that."

Ismael burst into laughter in spite of himself.

"Trust me, guys," Brent said. "You do not want to piss Jannie off."

Which, frankly, made me wonder why he did so often.

"I'll keep that in mind." Ismael grinned, then looked at me. "And you got a name on one of them."

"Yeah. Earl Johnson. I can forward you the email address if you'll let me have my bag back. I can get you the car rental information, too."

Brent chuckled, and Tran suddenly cleared his throat.

"Do we want to know how you got this information?" he asked.

I swallowed. "Um. Probably not?"

Brent sighed.

"But if you're okay with not knowing how I found out, I could probably find out where Johnson and pal are staying," I said.

Tran looked at Ismael.

"We'll get back to you," Ismael said. He looked at me. "You going to be okay?"

I smiled weakly. "I'll manage."

Like what the fuck else was I going to say? Brent rolled his eyes.

"I'm going to head home," I said, finally. "Brent knows how to get a hold of me."

Brent looked like he wanted to follow me, but I knew damn well he had to stay with the cops and do their thing with them. I hauled it out of there, yanking the strap to my bag over my head and across my chest.

As I walked home, it occurred to me why the bad guy wanted me to find Tanya Coleman. They were hoping I'd lead them to her. But they couldn't have known what I'd dug up so far. I was pretty sure no one had been following me when I'd gone out to Palms the day before. Besides, if whoever was after Coleman had followed me to her home, then they would have known I was looking for her and wouldn't have had to kill Abe to get my ass in gear.

That's when it hit me. How did they know I was searching for Coleman? Only Brent and his boss, Phil McCaffrey, knew that I'd been contracted for the job. But they didn't know that I'd already started looking. In fact, I'd been very clear that I was not looking for Coleman, never mind that I was. Which would explain trying to get my ass in gear.

Which also meant there had to be a leak in Brent's office. But that didn't make sense. For crying out loud, this was the Federal Bureau of Investigation. Feds aren't perfect angels, by any stretch, but they don't sell out very often. So, if there was a leak, it was coming from a direction that even Brent wouldn't have been able to spot.

Back home, I used the fob to unlock the door and, wonder of wonders, it actually worked. I also checked my Two-Factor Authentication device before going in, although I have friends who scoff at it. It isn't all that hard to hack the codes it provides, but like defeating biometrics, you do have to go to some trouble to do it. Something about being so shook, though, it made me even more paranoid than normal.

As soon as I had locked myself into my condo and closed the curtains, I settled into the big, fat recliner in my living room. It was the only piece of furniture in there, except for the over-sized TV, which I seldom watched. I'd bought it because I was going to catch up on all the movies I'd missed. It took just about a month to realize there was a reason I'd missed those movies in the first place.

I sank further into the soft leather of my chair and debated turning on Star Wars. It was my movie version of comfort food. Mom and I used to watch it together when I was little. But thinking of my mother made me think of Abe, and I started crying again. After several minutes of that, I wondered if there was a romantic comedy I could distract myself with, but that just made me think of Brent, which resulted in more crying.

I had already figured sleep was not going to be on the agenda. I couldn't concentrate worth spit. This was not good. I had a case to work. I had to find Tanya Coleman, preferably without leading some fuckhead right to her. But there was Abe. I'd really liked Abe and finding him like that...

I had to get my head in the game. I'd lost a full week after Grandma Schmidt had died the previous fall, and that was more or less expected. Abe's death was a whole other issue. The problem was, I didn't have a whole week to turn the world off and hide in my misery. I didn't really have a whole day.

I needed to eat something, not that I was hungry. I could have called for delivery, but I was really trying to cut back on that because of the waste issues. I had several meals in my freezer that I'd made ahead. Sadly, they were not going to come to me. On the other hand, I would have to get up and get the door for the delivery. The kitchen, it was.

I sighed, looking at all the neatly packed and labeled containers in my freezer. They were there because of Grandma Schmidt. The summer before, when I'd visited her for the last time, she'd made me promise to eat better. It was almost as if she'd known she wasn't going to be around to nag me that much longer. It was thanks to her that I'd bought a condo with four levels, so I'd have to get some exercise.

I blinked back the tears. Brent would have had a field day with me. I could just hear him making fun of my emotions. He'd been pretty sympathetic when Grandma first died, then got increasingly impatient as my grief took its sweet time working its way through me.

I grabbed a container from the top of the pile in the freezer. The last thing I wanted to be thinking about was Brent Mikkelson. I struggled with the container's lid before pulling it off and resetting it so it wouldn't explode in the microwave.

The problem was, Brent had been right. I had been wallowing to the point that it was only making things worse. If Brent's version of sympathetic goosing had been on the harsh side, it had, at least, been effective and gotten me functioning.

The food came out of the microwave scalding hot, and it hurt my tongue. That's when I got angry, and it was a good thing. Admittedly, anger isn't the best way to keep your head clear enough to think, but it can get you up and moving.

CHAPTER FIVE

The next morning, I got up around ten, feeling if not awake, at least not so muzzy-headed that I was fucked up. I'd had some icky dreams, but nothing really scary. I went downstairs to get breakfast, then brought my cereal and coffee up to my study and sat down.

I woke my laptop and looked over all the notes I'd made on Tanya Coleman. Why had the bad guy ordered me to find her? That didn't make sense. Nor did killing Abe over it. One of my dad's scarier cronies had once pointed out that gangsters didn't kill nearly as many people as one might think because killing people attracts unwanted attention, most of it from law enforcement. When the gangsters did kill, they did it spectacularly because they wanted people to be afraid.

Okay. Killing Abe certainly scared the shit out of me, but then, maybe I wasn't the person the killer wanted to be afraid. Given the connection to the group going after Wheeling and Coleman, maybe that's who the killer was trying to scare off. Now that made sense. You probably could get most hackers to back off by threatening to kill them. I would have thought killing off Old Man River would have been enough to do the trick. Except that they wanted Coleman, too.

The text! It may have landed on my phone, but it hadn't been for me. Brent had been right - of course, I'd tell the cops and they'd be all over it. And the first thing the cops would do would be to ask Coleman's friends if they knew who would have sent it, and then Coleman's friends would know and it would get around big time.

It wasn't the most efficient way to spread the word, but given how deeply hidden Coleman seemed to be, it was looking like the killer didn't have too many other options. I put on my VPN and launched a TOR pipeline. I don't use TOR very often. It's a loose network of computers that your information goes through that makes it exceedingly-ly hard to track your movements on the Internet, and I seldom need that kind of safety. But I needed to do some snooping in a few Dark Web chat rooms, and if you're going on the Dark Web, you need to do it via TOR.

I didn't find anything that looked like a bounty on Coleman. So, the goal was probably to scare everybody into inaction. The question now was whether I should try to find Coleman or not? In some ways, it seemed like she was better off in hiding.

I lurked for a bit in a few more innocuous chat rooms and there was plenty of chatter about the killing the day before. People were really mad, but they were also scared spitless. I didn't type in any responses, but I emailed Brent, saying that we needed a meeting. A minute later, he emailed back that he'd meet me at one of the restaurants that Coleman had spent a lot of time at.

I debated choosing another place to meet, but decided that I could sort of look for Coleman, and talk things over with Brent, and then decide whether or not to look for Coleman. So I sent the okay back.

I went ahead and took my car to the restaurant that afternoon just in case I needed to follow someone. The restaurant was over in Culver City, a suburb on the West Side of Los Angeles County and best known as the former home of MGM Studios, back in the heyday of studio films. Now it's all owned by Sony. The place I wanted was in the hip part of town and not quite, but almost, within walking distance of the Coleman house in Palms. The restaurant was Italian and an older place, reveling in its legacy status. It also had Wi-Fi, but did not advertise it. I just happened to notice it when I logged into my laptop. When I asked the server for the password, he frowned and had to go back and ask at least two other people for it.

I was booting up my VPN when Brent walked in. I could see him through the screen surrounding my booth as he looked around, then looked out the door. The host approached, and he waved her off. He waited a few minutes more, then looked around again, and then out the door. What he didn't do was ask the host. I finally relented and got up and waved at him.

"How long have you been here?" he asked. The tension rippled off of him, but it wasn't just me.

"Long enough to boot up," I said. "I told the host that I was waiting for you."

"She didn't say anything," Brent grumbled.

"Did you ask her?"

"Look, I don't have time for this," he snapped, his eyes dark with annoyance.

The server came up, and I ordered baked manicotti while Brent ordered spaghetti with meat sauce without looking at the menu. We both ordered iced tea. Brent gave him his credit card and asked him to ring up the order right away. Brent did that a lot, especially when he was in a bad mood. He claimed that he didn't know when he was going to get a call, but actually it just made it easier for him to storm out of somewhere when he didn't like what we were talking about.

"Thanks for lunch," I said, forcing a smile.

He shrugged. "Let's hope you have something."

"As you pointed out, this is one of Tanya Coleman's fave dinner spots," I said.

"So?"

Great. Brent wasn't just in a bad mood, he was in full obtuse mode.

"She wasn't just eating dinner here," I said, more smugly than I should have, given his mood. "She was connecting to the Internet."

Brent looked around. "How? Her phone records didn't show any hotspot activity."

"She wasn't using her phone," I said. "She didn't need it. You wouldn't think it, but this place has Wi-Fi."

That got him. "Seriously?"

"Yeah. It's perfect if you need to login and don't want the world to know you're doing it. Look at how deep these booths are, and with the screens, you can see someone coming before they can see what you're doing."

The server appeared with Brent's card. "Excuse me, sir, but I'm afraid your card was declined."

"What? That's impossible." Brent grabbed the card. "I just paid the bill and there was plenty of credit on it."

"I'll buy," I said, handing the server my card.

Brent glared at me.

"You want me to look up your account?" I asked. "I have the VPN on."

"I'll check it later. Let's stay focused. You think Coleman came here to hook into the Internet? All right. But it doesn't mean anything. We don't know that Coleman was into computers. She seems to be part of the hacking group, but there's no evidence to suggest that she was into code or anything like that."

"Oh, there's plenty of evidence," I said. "You just didn't dig deep enough. She was a total geek through high school, and then her first semester at Santa Monica College, she drops all of that and suddenly becomes a business major. It didn't make sense, and I asked her mom about it. Yvonne said she was surprised when Tanya did. She also let out that Tanya is still adept enough to secure her laptop against her brothers getting into it. So, the smart money is saying that she's up to her neck in that group going after Wheeling and has the chops to do it."

"Son of bitch." Brent shifted, the tension inching up another couple of notches. "I told her."

"Told who what?"

"Never mind." Brent shifted again. "I was told to tell you as little as possible, but that I could confirm anything you came up with, and you've obviously figured out that our little hacking group has picked up something pretty hot. What it is, I don't know, and I mean I really don't know. They're skittish as hell, and given what's happened, I'm not surprised."

"So, maybe we shouldn't be looking for Coleman, so we don't lead these assholes right to her."

"You think I haven't been worrying about that?" Brent groaned.

The server came by with our lunches and my card and we waited until he was gone.

Brent glanced around, then started cutting up his spaghetti.

"Look," he said around a mouthful of pasta. "I need you out of this or as far away from it as possible."

"Tough. I'm already involved."

"I'm trying to protect you here." Brent shoveled in another couple of bites as if his life depended on it.

"I get that. But I'm the one who gets to decide what risks I take."

Brent swallowed his food, then glared at me. "Jannie, this is way bad. Worse than I ever thought." He paused as if he wanted to say something else but couldn't. "We both know cyber crooks are thieves and scum. One thing they are not is violent. This is violent. We've got two stiffs, one of which was not even involved, except that someone wanted to send you a message."

"Or maybe they wanted to send the hackers a message," I said. "The text message has gotten around and folks are scared."

"Good. They should be." Brent grabbed another huge bite and talked around it. "It's Wheeling, Jannie. They're the scariest fucks I've ever run up against. They're everywhere, and they're collecting personal data like no one else. Addresses, passwords, banking data. Hell, even Facebook and the Chinese don't hold on to as much as Wheeling does. We can't prove it, dammit. But whatever Wheeling has got going on, and assuming it's them, it's bad enough that it's worth it for them to hire a contract killer. Jannie, do you seriously want to be dealing with that?"

"No," I snarled. "But I'm already dealing with it. One of my buddies from high school just bit the big one thanks to these fuckers, remember?"

Brent winced and, too late, I realized what had been driving his bullshit. He was ass deep in guilt for pulling me into the case, which meant he was past hearing anything I had to say. I looked down at my plate. The manicotti was seriously good, and I did not want to abandon it. I waved at the server.

"Can you box this for me, please?" I told him, handing him the plate.

He ran off.

"What?" snarled Brent. "You're leaving already."

"Yes." I glared at him. "As I have told you plenty of times before, I have enough shit in my life without taking on yours. I'm sorry you're feeling guilty about getting me involved in this and Abe getting killed."

"I didn't say I was feeling guilty."

"You don't have to say it." I turned off the Wi-Fi and shut the laptop. "It doesn't change anything. You couldn't see Abe getting killed any more than I could. And maybe if you spent five minutes thinking about how I feel instead of how guilty you think you are, we could get somewhere. Either way, I'm up to my neck in this shit. That's not your fault. It's not my fault. It's how it is."

I jammed the laptop into its compartment. The server showed up with my lunch gloriously over-packaged. I got up and grabbed the plastic bag.

"I'll see you around, Brent," I said and stalked off, hanging onto what little dignity I had left.

I got into my car with my eyes overflowing and my hands shaking. It took me a minute or three to get enough of a grip on myself so that I could drive with some semblance of control. When I'd finally shook the tears out of my eyes, I glanced around, trying to locate the parking lot's exit. And saw a black muscle car with red trim. Why I recognized the license plate, I cannot say. I also recognized the shapes of the guys sitting in the car.

As Brent had so kindly informed the Pasadena P.D., I am not someone you want to piss off. Which made me wonder again why Brent did it so often, although that didn't help at the moment.

I only waited just long enough for my hotspot to connect to my laptop, then fired off a Facebook post just veiled enough that it wouldn't trigger their compliance algorithm, but would get the point across pronto. And just for good measure, I tagged my father's account along with it.

Anger was not the best way to keep me thinking clearly, but it did get me moving. I got back to Pasadena without incident and no black car with red trim following me. By the time I'd gotten home, my dad had already sent me a private message deploring my lack of discretion and that if he was kind enough to send me some friends to make sure I was safe, the least I could do was be grateful. It was total horse shit, but did that stop me from feeling the guilt for several seconds? Of course not. Dear Old Dad had the Abuser's Playbook down cold. I took several deep, calming breaths and reminded myself several times over that it did not mean I had to buy into his crap.

Grabbing my laptop and my food bag, I got upstairs from the garage to the maze of paths that twisted around the complex. Ten minutes later, I had walked past the pool twice already and was completely turned around. It's not that my sense of direction is that bad. It's that all the condos look alike and the signs pointing this way and that are really small and hard to read. I'd gotten a big kick out of how hard it was to get around the complex when I'd first bought the condo. Getting lost had gotten old pretty fast, and three years in, I was still ending up at the pool instead of my place at least once a week. Being stressed and upset wasn't helping, either. I went back to the pool, took three deep, calming breaths, and made my way back to my condo.

I unlocked the door, then clicked on the hall and kitchen lights, while closing the blackout curtains on the front. At least, I was hoping that would happen. The hall and kitchen lights did come on and I heard the curtains closing. I manually set the locks on the door, then went up the stairs to the kitchen, and put my manicotti in the fridge. As I shut the fridge door, I heard someone on the stairs to the bedroom.

My heart pounding in fear, I braced myself and turned. A woman slowly came down the steps, wearing a khaki skirt, tan ballet flats, a blue short-sleeved shirt and a light blue blazer over it all. Her hair was cut to her shoulders and was mostly gray, with streaks of darker hair running through it. She wore glasses that seemed to emphasize how round her face was, which, in turn emphasized how round she was. I tried to scream but only got out a strangled yelp.

"I'm not going to hurt you!" she called sadly. "I'm so sorry. I didn't want to scare you, but I didn't want to be hanging around outside and your door was unlocked."

"No, it wasn't," I gulped, realizing that no, I hadn't heard the lock turn back when I'd come in. "Who—" I stopped. The woman looked so much like Grandma Schmidt, and there was something else unutterably familiar about her. "Mom?"

"Yes. I'm sorry, Jannie."

"Wait." I staggered and leaned against the half wall that separated the dining area and living room from the kitchen. "What's your full name?"

"Rae Ann Schmidt Miller."

I rolled my eyes. Anyone could have dug that up.

I took a deep breath. "What was our code?"

"Running away to Boston."

I had waited for so many years for this moment. I had planned it, imagined running into my mother's arms and her holding me tight and promising never again to leave me. But all of a sudden I couldn't move. I couldn't speak. I don't think I was even breathing.

"Maybe I shouldn't have come," she said nervously. "I can leave now."

"No!" I screamed. "You can't fucking leave me again! I won't let you!"

She stepped back, startled.

"I'm sorry," I gasped. "I just—" I gaped and swallowed. "Holy shit." I took my laptop bag off my shoulder just to be doing something as my brain slowly ground into gear. "Okay. Why..? What..?" I looked at her.

She stood, her eyes filled with tears and her hands rubbing nervously together. She was just as upset as I was, and scared, too. I wanted to ask her why she was there.

"Why did you leave me?" I asked, instead, in a tiny little voice.

"You were dead."

"Obviously, I wasn't." I snarled.

"I didn't know that." She shut her eyes and shuddered. "All I saw were your shoes and that white sheet with the blood stain where your head was."

I thought back to that horrible day when the tornado had hit my school, and Tiffany Klinger stealing my beautiful, wonderful shoes. To hiding in the cloakroom afterward and staying there as the sirens went off. I'd heard that Tiffany had refused to get under her desk as the winds hit. She'd wanted to see the tornado. I remember being at the funeral for our teacher, Mrs. Petty, who had died because she was trying to get Tiffany to take cover and hating Tiffany all the more for it. And now, Mom was saying that she'd thought Tiffany was me.

"I wanted to cuddle you one last time, but I couldn't get that close," she continued. "People were coming, and I didn't want anyone to see us alive. That was the plan. I was going to make it look like we'd died, even before the tornado. That way, your father wouldn't come after us and we'd finally be safe. Then the tornado hit and it was like a sign from God or something. Or a gift of some sort. I couldn't waste it, even with you already dead."

"Only I wasn't." I swallowed. "Why didn't you come get me when you found out I was alive? Or didn't you know?"

"I found out about five years later, when you were thirteen." She shrugged. "I took a chance on going back to Lee Creek. I wanted to be near you, or at least, your grave. Only I couldn't find it. So, I did some checking. Then I called my mother and asked her to tell you that we would be running away to Boston in that next week. My mother hung up on me."

I sank into one of the dining table chairs. "She never told me. Abe had to tell me on Monday."

"I thought you didn't want to come," Mom said. She looked even more lost and sad.

I waved at her to sit down, and she sank into the chair across the table from me.

"I tried asking her again to leave you the message about six months later, then tried again the next year."

"According to Abe, Grandma said you'd only called twice, once about two months after the tornado, and you were asking about my funeral, and then when I was fourteen. And Grandma told him what you'd said."

"I waited five days each time, and you just went straight home after school. You weren't looking for anybody. You just kept your head down and ran off."

"It was safer that way," I whispered.

She blinked and sighed. "After that third time, I thought you didn't want to go."

"Are you kidding? I would've been there like a shot. I wanted away from Dad so badly, it was all I could think about." Slowly, I got a deep breath as something dawned on me. "Grandma never told me about those phone calls."

"Really?" She frowned and again squeezed her eyes shut. "Fuck. It never occurred to me that she wouldn't tell you, even if only to point out how selfish I was."

"She did that a lot."

Mom looked hard at me. "You never knew that I'd come for you?"

"No." I sniffed. "I was mad that you hadn't, too."

"Oh, God," Mom said. "How can you forgive me?"

I was crying full out. "Well, apparently, it wasn't your fault after all."

"Jannie, my sweet, darling daughter."

And finally, finally, we were in each other's arms, holding on for dear life.

Chapter Six

I had my mom back. I couldn't believe it. I actually had my mom back. We talked, and we cried and we talked some more and cried some more. We couldn't quite let go of each other.

I opened my freezer for dinner and Mom picked out some lentil chili I had made, which I nuked for us. As we sat down to eat, with a great deal of irony, we toasted my grandmother with one of my best scotches. It was kind of weird, given that Grandma had done so much to mess us both up, but we came to the conclusion that we both still loved her.

It was also weird how many tastes we had in common in spite of all the time we'd been separated. I mean, that we both loved computers and reading code and that, that was a gimme because Mom had taught me to read code almost before I could read English. But things like our respective love for high-end scotch, we couldn't figure out how that had happened. It was not like my mom knocked 'em back in front of her eight-year-old kid. And, as she told me, she had liked whiskey, but hadn't really gotten into high-end scotch until later in life. So we spent an overly long time speculating on nurture versus nature.

Mom told me about her life and some of the jobs she'd held, and hinted but would not say that she'd worked for a certain government agency that specializes in collecting and analyzing intelligence data, and that she'd done it at least twice.

She'd changed identities every five years or so. In fact, she'd made quite the art form out of it. She'd even hacked the Social Security Administration to assign herself a new number every time.

"Oh, please," she said when I gasped. "It wasn't that hard back when I first did it, and by the time they'd hardened the system, I had full credentials and was able to keep access."

"Wow. And they haven't caught you?"

"Not yet." She smiled and shrugged. "Jannie, the trick with hiding isn't to make sure there isn't a trail, it's to make sure the trail isn't noticeable. When the Social Security Administration gets audited, they're looking for anomalies, someone amending a lot of records who shouldn't be. But one record among the thousands that get amended every year? No one is going to notice that. It's just part of the agency's regular operations. If someone in the HR department of a large corporation gets a request to confirm that candidate x, y, or z used to work there, they're going to look up the record and send the information on. They're not going to worry if they've never heard of the candidate because there are thousands upon thousands of employees coming and going all the time. Like they say, there's always a way in, and there's always a way around."

I frowned. "I wonder if that's why I couldn't find you."

"Probably. You were looking for someone who was hiding, not someone going about her daily business." She smiled weakly. "And I've gotten very good at fleshing out my identities."

It was getting a little too close to my sore spot, so I changed the subject. It turned out, we'd both gone to MIT for our undergraduate degrees, only I'd gone on to Caltech for my masters and she'd gone to University of Wisconsin for hers. She confirmed that she had paid for my education, too. We laughed over my condo full of advanced and almost useless tech.

"You even have a smart fridge?" Mom asked.

"It's a dumb fridge now," I said. "They apparently stopped supporting it six or seven months ago. Funny thing is, I didn't even notice that they had because I never used the apps that went with it."

I told her about how I'd found the legendary hacker and recluse Lester Margolis.

"I found him twice, actually," I said.

"That's impressive."

I shrugged. "The first time was pretty hard, but by the second time, I had his habits down and it was a piece of cake. Fortunately, the first time got me a lot of money and notice. The second time was just for grins and giggles, since he's way offshore someplace without extradition."

"Is he as big an asshole as rumored?"

"Bigger. He's basically an entrepreneurial shit who thinks the world owes him a living because of his genius. Still, I wouldn't have my dumb fridge if it weren't for him."

"Why did you buy it?" There was an odd look on my mom's face, as if she wanted to ask something else that would hurt a lot more.

"It's a good fridge." I looked at her. "I was suddenly loaded with cash and in my late twenties, so I did what most folks would do. I bought stuff. I like tech, so that's what I bought. I was just being young and dumb, I guess." I held up my subsonic fob. "I mean, it works a good chunk of the time. I was running out of here this morning and I guess I wasn't close enough to the hub for the locks to set."

Mom's face suddenly went grim. "You need to start setting your locks by hand, then." She blinked back yet more tears, then looked at me. "That's why I'm here. Jannie, you need to back off finding Tanya Coleman."

I sat straight up. "What? What do you know about her?"

"I'm the one hiding her," Mom said. "It's what I do." She smiled weakly. "I've been hiding people from persistent abusers for years now. I even hid your stepmother."

I gaped. "You hid Eileen?"

"I never actually met her, nor did she know my connection to your father. It's safer that way, you know. And when Manny got shot, Tanya came to me, not knowing that I hide people."

"How did you get involved with the Wheeling thing?"

"I've been involved from the start. But about Tanya..."

I made a face. "I'm not going to lead anybody to her."

"I know you won't, if you can help it. But that's not all of it. Tanya needs to stay hidden, and by looking for her, you have put yourself on Wheeling's hit list."

"Oh, come on. Nobody's coming after me except Dad, and all he does is send his goons to follow me around."

"Would I risk being seen by them and alerting your father that I'm alive if this wasn't deadly serious?" Mom leaned over and grabbed my hands. "Jannie, that's why I stayed away. I absolutely cannot let your father know that I'm alive or he will use you and hurt you to get to me. At the same time, there is something going on at Wheeling that is going to be so devastating that it is worth their while to kill people over. You've seen what these fucks can do."

My gut twisted as I remembered Abe's body lying on the floor of his hotel room.

Mom got up and started pacing. "Wheeling has been a bunch of bad actors for a very long time, and it's not just the viruses. It's the kids they've been recruiting to write them. The blatant racism and sexism. The skewed research."

"I've always thought they backed up their points."

"With some decidedly bad data. I know. You should have seen some of the stuff I was asked to put together for them."

"You worked for them?" I quickly filled my glass with more scotch.

Mom nodded. "Several years ago. Leon Cortez and I were griping about them one day. I was due for an identity change, anyway, which Leon never knew. But I thought we could take advantage of it, so we decided that I should go in to see if I could find anything on them."

"You know Leon Cortez?"

Mom smiled warmly. "Oh, yes. We've had a thing for quite a while."

"Eeeuw!" I grimaced, mostly because I sort of had a thing for Leon, as well. "I did not need to know that."

"Too bad." Mom slid back into her chair. "As for Wheeling, of course, they didn't let me near anything significant, and when it became clear they weren't about to, I left. But I got enough information so that we were able to set up a plan. Tanya, God bless her, volunteered to go into that miserable cesspool. Wheeling has to hire a certain number of Blacks and other minorities so that they don't get busted for discrimination, but Blacks already know they don't want to work there. Tanya played dumb about their rep and that's how she got in." Mom's eyes shut again. "That poor girl. She took so much abuse from them."

"I know. Her mom told me about some of it."

"I told her to leave that hellhole, that no one should have to take that kind of abuse. But she said no. She was going to take the bastards down if it was the last thing she did." Mom picked up her glass and sipped without really savoring it. "We didn't know at the time just how close it was going to come to that."

I thought about Abe again and shivered. Mom sniffled, then got another grip on herself.

"Tanya found something," she said. "It's definitely a virus of some sort, but it's not written like any we know. And we only have bits and pieces of it. That's all she could get off the company's closed network before Manny was killed."

I re-filled Mom's glass. "Why hasn't anybody been able to hack their way in?"

"Everything Wheeling does is on a closed network. Not even all the employees have access."

"Then how did Tanya get it? She's a clerk in Human Relations."

"She's also very good." Mom smiled. "She used some good old human engineering and spent quite a bit of time copying things off people's desks during their lunch breaks. But that's why we have bits and pieces of code and not much else. She also found a way into the system but couldn't take advantage of it from her desk because her desk isn't connected to that part of their internal network."

"There must be some way in." I frowned. "Don't people work from home?"

"Apparently not, and, yes, that is very strange. But you have to understand that there's a whole elitist culture that's part of being with Wheeling. It's incredibly attractive, especially if you're an under-appreciated White male who's pissed at being asked to share his privilege."

I rolled my eyes. "Yeah. I've run across a few of those."

"We all have, darling, and let's attempt some compassion or we'll never be able to deal with them effectively." Mom blinked suddenly. "There was a point that I was trying to make. Oh, yes, the closed network at Wheeling. Not being connected to the Internet makes it a lot easier to keep the wraps on projects that might be more controversial, shall we say, and the whole elite thing makes it possible to make people put up with a hell of a lot of inconvenience since it's in service to the greater mission."

"In other words, the place is a fucking fortress." I took a good swallow. "That means that Tanya has breached it to a lesser degree and is now out of commission, but has knowledge that we can use." I put my glass solidly on the table. "Okay. What can I do to help?"

Mom turned on me. "Jannie, I don't want you to be part of this."

"I'm already part of this up to my tits! My friend from high school just got killed and the only reason why is that he happened to know me. He was trying to be nice to me by coming out here to get some fucking papers signed, and gets his head blown off. And I got to see the bullet hole, okay? I'm in this, whether I want to be or not. And, believe me, I want to take down those Wheeling fucks at least as much as you do. Those kids they recruit? A lot of them are Blacks and Hispanics. They get caught writing a virus and they are not going to get their hands slapped. They are doing jail time, just because they don't have the right color skin."

"I know. It makes Leon foam at the mouth." My mother swallowed and blinked back more tears. "But I have finally, finally gotten to see you and talk to you and... and... I do not want to lose you."

"What? Like I'm not risking losing you? I had to grow up without you. I planned our meeting down to the last tear. If you're in, I'm in, because I don't want to lose you, either. Not now. Not when I finally have you."

We had somehow both gotten to our feet and had faced off. Neither one of us blinked for several minutes, okay, seconds, but it sure felt longer. Oddly enough, we both backed down at the same time. Mom took a deep breath.

"You know, Jannie, when you were little, you would get this shit-eating look on your face when you knew you were right."

"I did?" I asked with a giggle.

"I hated that look."

That did it. No matter what miserable scary things were going on out there, in my condo, Mom and I were together and reasonably safe and all was right with the world. We collapsed in giggles and soon after decided we'd both had enough scotch and both needed some sleep.

"Do you want to stay here?" I asked. "I can loan you some fresh underwear."

"I have underwear and a couple changes of clothes with me." Mom pulled a flip phone out of her pocket and checked the small window on the top. "The bunker is moving again, so I was going to have to find a place to stay, anyway. Good lord, is it that late?"

"What bunker?"

"The different places we stay. We keep changing the spot and not all of us are in the same place all the time."

We went upstairs. Mom got her bag from the study. I gave Mom my bed and got an extra blanket out so that I could sleep in the recliner in my living room.

"I fall asleep there all the time," I told Mom.

She stopped me as I turned to go downstairs.

"Jannie, give me a day or so. I need to get some things in place so that you—" She paused as she caught my glare. "Okay, we have someplace safe to go if things go sideways again."

"Okay." I looked at her and tried not to cry some more. "It's going to be okay. We'll get through this."

She chuckled. "I know. We were always pretty awesome together."

"Yeah." I sniffed.

We hugged, and I went downstairs.

Mom was up before me the next morning. As I cleared the sleep fog from my eyes and stretched, I could hear her upstairs talking to somebody. She did not sound happy. I worked the kinks out of my shoulders, then got up. She came down the stairs wearing the same shirt she'd had on the night before, but with a pair of jeans.

"Good. You're up," she said, without enthusiasm.

"Yeah. Need coffee." I staggered toward the kitchen.

"That will have to wait. We need to get going."

"Huh?"

"Are you still interested in helping our team take down Wheeling?"

"Yeah!" I turned toward her, suddenly wide awake.

"Then we need to get some stuff set up here and elsewhere and introduce you to the rest of the team." Mom followed me into the kitchen. "In the meantime, why don't you get cleaned up? Pack a couple changes of clean clothing in your laptop bag. And make it quick, but we need to think about securing your desktop up there."

"Okay." I looked at her, feeling bewildered.

It didn't matter. I still did what she said. As I stood in the shower, I tried to parse out all that I was feeling. I had expected to feel happy, and I was feeling happy. But I hadn't expected all the hurt and anger that I was feeling at the same time. I wondered how much of it was the potentially mortal danger thing. I got out of the shower and got dressed in jeans and a cute knit top. I'm not even sure which one, except that I had dozens of them. I really don't like doing laundry.

I got my favorite hiking sandals and debated adding a pair of running shoes. Running seemed really appropriate, but I hated wearing them.

"A couple pairs of panties, a couple extra tops and maybe a pair of shorts or jeans," Mom said when I asked what all I needed. "Oh, and your toothbrush. Just make sure that it will all fit in your laptop bag and that it isn't too heavy. We need to travel light."

"Okay."

"Let's go take care of your desktop."

I followed her up the stairs to my study.

"How many hard drives do you have in there?" she asked as she pulled the tower out from under my desk.

"Two solid state drives."

Mom glared at the case. "All right. Let's get them out of here. What's in your paper files?"

"Not much." I swallowed. The last thing I wanted to tell her about was the file I had on her. "Why?"

"We've got to leave as little behind as possible that someone could use to trace you."

"We're coming back, aren't we?"

Mom looked at me for several long seconds, then shrugged. "I hope so. But we have to be extra, extra careful. Get your life papers out of the file and bring those. I'll get your hard drives."

"I could just wipe them."

Mom shook her head. "It will be better to keep them with us."

"They're encrypted three ways to Sunday. Even if somebody tries to read them, they'd have to have crazy mad skills to make sense of them."

"Jannie, we are up against people with crazy mad skills and then some." Mom rummaged through my desk until she found a screwdriver.

"What about not being obvious about your trail? If someone finds those drives gone, they're going to know I bolted."

"That's good enough for me," Mom said, sliding the panel off the tower.

"But you said last night—"

"I know what I said last night. I wasn't planning on taking you with me then." She took a deep breath, then went back to poking around the interior of my desktop. "And normally, not leaving an obvious trail is the way to hide. It's like people protecting things with biometrics. The vast, vast majority of the time, that's enough because to defeat biometrics, you have to be close to the victim and really, really want what the victim has."

She grunted as she unsnapped the cords to the drives from the motherboard.

"So we're going up against folks with the skills to defeat biometrics. That is why I have my subsonic fob, you know."

"Which worked so wonderfully well at keeping me out of your condo last night. Here."

I jammed the two drives into my laptop bag, along with my extra subsonic fob, then rifled through my files to make sure they were mostly non-essential stuff like old school assignments, a couple of love letters. I left my mom's file. It hadn't helped me much.

"Are you ready?" Mom asked.

I nodded.

"Good." She smiled. It was a smile that I remembered down to my toes, the one I'd last seen as I laced on my beautiful new shoes with the bits of DOS commands in lavender glitter paint. "It's time. We're finally running away to Boston."

I gaped. "You mean we're really going to Boston? I thought everything was going on here."

Mom laughed. "Sweet, sweet Jannie. It was never about the city. It was about finding someplace safe."

"Yeah." I smiled happily. "Right."

That made an enormous amount of sense. From Mom, safety would be in getting away and hiding. For me, well, I had no idea what my safe place was.

We went down all four levels to the front door of the condo, and I couldn't help but pause and look around me.

"Come on, darling," Mom said. "Let's lock up your little fortress and be on our way."

I clicked the combination on my smart fob and smiled as I heard the locks grind into place.

Chapter Seven

Outside the condo, Mom had an older Android phone out and was panning the camera across the walkways and windows of the neighboring condos.

"Getting video?" I asked.

"Not quite," she said. "I've got the super zoom on the camera. It's more subtle than binoculars and almost as strong. Good. It doesn't look like there's anyone inside the complex watching us, but it's safe to assume that you are being watched. We'll split up."

"What?"

"Only for an hour or two. I promise. Where's your phone?"

"Here." I handed it to her.

She entered two phone numbers as we started along the labyrinth.

"These are both of my numbers." She handed the phone back. "They're listed under Eve. I'll call you in half an hour with someplace to meet. Why don't you head toward downtown L.A.?"

"Okay."

We paused where the walkway split off, one way to the garage, the other toward the pool and the back entrance to the complex. Mom gave me a long, warm hug and walked firmly off toward the pool. I went to the garage. It seemed deserted of people, and when I got in my MachE and got it going, no one pulled up behind me.

But by the time I got to the Pasadena Freeway, I could tell someone was tailing me. My phone was connected to the car, so all I had to do was tell it to dial Eve, and it did. It took a couple minutes for the phone to connect, and then it sounded like it was going to go to voice mail, but at the last second, it picked up.

"Hello?"

"Eve? Mom? It's me."

"I'm here," said her voice through the car's speakers. "What's up?"

I swallowed. "You were right. I'm being followed."

"Just a feeling, or can you see the car?"

"I can see it," I said, glancing back at my rear-view mirror. "It's a big light blue sedan. Looks like a Caddy or something else American-made."

"About two cars behind you?"

"You see him?" I almost swerved out of my lane and hit the brakes.

"Be careful."

"What are you doing following me?"

"What do you think? Ah. Did the blue car just change lanes and fall back?"

I checked my mirror. "Yeah. Is that you?"

"I'm afraid not. What about a white pickup truck coming up on your blind spot on the driver's side?"

I looked at the wing mirror. "Yeah. I see it. Oh, shit. I think it's one of Dad's goons."

"Hmmm. All right. I've got both license plates memorized." Mom's voice was perfectly calm and even soothing, which was good because I was ready to pee. "It looks like they're tag teaming you, which makes sense. It's a lot harder to tell that you're being followed. Next step will be evasive maneuvers. I'm sorry, but you're going to have to ditch your MachE for the time being."

"No! Shit." I sniffed because I knew she was absolutely right. "Can I hide it somewhere?"

"Possibly. If you can make it look normal that you'd be going there. And it would probably help if you can find a place to park somewhere with a crowd around and not a lot of spaces."

I slowed as the traffic ahead of me did. The white pickup fell back.

"The pickup just changed lanes and went to the right," I said.

"I see it. The blue sedan isn't quite in position, but I don't seem to see anyone else. Can you keep going for a while?"

"I've got 200 miles or so. Maybe more with regenerative braking."

"I don't think we'll need that many."

By that point, we were into the downtown Los Angeles area. A huge blue bus slowly rumbled past me in the next lane. It was one of those big, boxy luxury ones and had airplanes painted all over it.

"I just had an idea," I said. "There's a super secure long-term parking lot near LAX. They don't even let you into the garage. It won't take long to sign forms and everything and if somebody pulls up and gets out of a car, I'll be able to spot them right away."

"Excellent. I presume they have a shuttle to the terminals?"

"Of course."

"Then let them see you take it. They'll have to follow in the cars and won't be able to follow that easily on foot once you get off the shuttle. I'll stay on the line now, but if we get cut off, call me from whichever terminal you land in."

"Okay." I eased over several lanes and onto Interstate 10, which was moving better, but not by much.

"And turn off your location on your phone once you get to the parking lot."

"Oh, come on. It's my secret account."

"How do you think I'm tracking you?"

"Shit." I glanced through my mirrors and the two cars were still behind me. "You're right. Crazy mad skills."

"Yes, but we have crazy mad skills, too." I could almost hear the smile in Mom's voice.

"How are you staying so cool?"

She cleared her throat. "It's... interesting what kinds of skills one can pick up when working for the government."

"I thought they only collected and analyzed data."

"That's what they say." Mom chuckled. "Interesting. It would appear that there are only two cars on you. Better yet, from what I can tell, each car has only one driver. We'll run the plates once we're safe."

"I can do that," I said. "I don't even have to hack it."

"Really."

I snorted bitterly. "Brent set it up for me since I'm doing work for him and the F.B.I."

"Well, we can do that after breakfast."

My stomach gurgled. We bantered on for the rest of the half hour or so that it took to get to the lot off of Aviation. As Mom had predicted, there was no good place to park. Even the McDonald's lot half a block down was full.

Another thing I had going in my favor was that the private parking lot next to the airport already had me in their system. As soon as I pulled up, the nice lady in the office was calling the shuttle. Less than five minutes later, I'd signed everything that needed signing and the green shuttle van had pulled up. I made a point of making the MachE forget my phone and wiped as much data from it as I could. I also remembered to turn off the location setting on my phone, never mind that the gods of Google might send the data, anyway. Both they and Apple sometimes did.

As Mom had told me to do before I'd left the freeway, I took the shuttle to the terminal at the far end of the airport. Like most big airports, traffic at Los Angeles International Airport runs in a one-way loop around the terminals. Given the traffic, it was nigh on impossible to maneuver with any flexibility at all. In addition, the inner lane next to the terminals is reserved for shuttles and other public transport. Cars are not allowed and if one tries, the cops are all over it like white on rice. Even idling too long in the passenger pickup will get you ticketed in nothing flat.

I jumped off the shuttle and wove my way through a small crowd to get to into the terminal. In that part of the airport, the terminals are all connected, so unless there was someone on the sidewalk walking alongside the windows, no one was going to see me running past all the ticketing desks. I had to go outside to get past the Bradley International Terminal, but once on the other side, I went back behind the glass again. I looked outside and didn't see anybody headed my way looking for somebody, so I pulled my phone from my laptop bag and dialed Eve.

"Where are you?" Mom's voice demanded.

I looked around me. "Terminal Three. Delta is just ahead."

"Shit. I'm past there, but your friends are headed for the loop back into the airport."

I saw the escalator down. "Fine. I'm going down to the arrivals level and see if I can find a shuttle somewhere."

"Good idea. Get the first one with tinted windows and call me once you're on."

I did exactly all of that, landing on a shuttle to the Bonaventure Hotel downtown. I sat in an aisle seat on the passenger side near the front and kept an eye on the windows. Business was relatively light that morning. We only stopped at two other terminals. I'd called Mom, and she said she'd meet me at the hotel.

If anyone noticed that when I got off the shuttle at the hotel I did not go straight to the check-in desk, then they didn't seem to care. I hung in the lobby for a few minutes until I saw a silver Toyota sedan pull into the driveway. Sure enough, when I slipped outside, Mom was behind the wheel. As I opened the car door, she held up a McDonald's bag.

"Oh, thank God!" I gasped as I pulled my laptop bag from my shoulder and slid into the seat. "I'm starving!"

I grabbed the bag even before I got my seat belt buckled.

"It's probably cold, but I did the best I could." Mom put the car in gear and pulled out onto Flower Street.

"It's great," I said, stuffing the egg and muffin into my mouth. "Oh, my god. You even remembered how much I hate the cheese."

"That specific quirk was especially hard to forget," Mom said, rolling her eyes. Well, I had been known to throw a fit if there was even a hint of that awful goo on my fast-food sandwiches.

My immediate pangs satisfied, I sank back into my seat. "Not to sound like an ingrate, but there wouldn't happen to be coffee, would there?"

"Not yet," Mom said as she steered the car onto the 110 North. Traffic was crawling, as usual. "But as soon as we can find some. In addition to a dire need for caffeine, we need an Internet connection. I want to pull up those license plates."

"I know a great place in Silver Lake," I said.

Mom got into the lane for the 101 North, aka the Hollywood Freeway, but shook her head.

"We're not going anywhere you normally go or even sometimes go. We're in hiding now. In fact, are there any cops around?"

I looked. "I can't see any."

"Good. As soon as we get up to speed, I'd like you to turn off your phone and toss it out the window."

"What? That's a thousand-dollar phone."

"And it's a way to track you." Mom glared at me. "You'll still be able to access your contacts online eventually and as long as it's over a VPN and on TOR. And even then, it's a risk, but I'll accept it. We'll get you a new phone. It just would be good to dump yours in the meantime. And be thankful I'm asking. I didn't give Tanya that option."

I sighed and pulled my phone out of my pocket. I got it out of its case, sighed again, and rolled down the window. The hot August air burst in on me as Mom accelerated. I didn't just throw the phone out the window. I didn't want it bouncing all over the place and maybe cracking a windshield or hurting someone. I let it slide out of my hand onto the road below. I turned back to see bits and pieces of premium electronics scatter across the freeway.

Sinking back into my seat, I tried to make sense of what had just happened. I mean, there was a part of my brain that fully understood what Mom had asked me to do and why, which is probably why I didn't question it any harder. But I had liked that phone. It wasn't the greatest piece of tech I'd ever owned, nor was it the worst. It just was, and I'd relied on it. Now it was gone.

"Jannie," said Mom softly. "I'm very proud of you."

I shrugged.

"You handled yourself very well on the way to the airport and when you got there. And giving up your phone. That's not easy. I really appreciate how good and strong you are."

"Thanks," I muttered.

I wasn't sure how to answer that. One thing I'd always held onto when I was a kid and Mom was gone was that she had genuinely loved me. Not the controlling shit that my dad had called love, or my grandmother, for that matter. But real, unconditional love. Mom had always remembered to praise me when I'd done something right, and it wasn't just the bullshit generalized kind of "you're wonderful" thing, although she'd done that, too, sometimes. But mostly when Mom praised me, it was for something specific that she'd thought I'd done well. Grandma, by contrast, only seemed to remember that she was proud of me once in a while, and it was because she should say so. The rest of the time, it was all about how I could be better.

We were well into the San Fernando Valley when Mom finally pulled off the freeway. We'd ridden in silence, not a particularly awkward one, but not an entirely happy one, either. I think Mom sensed that I was trying to wrap my brain around everything that had happened over the past few days. It's not like I was having a lot of success at it, though.

I think we ended up in Encino, but can't be sure. Given how each part of Ventura Boulevard looks pretty much like every other part of Ventura Boulevard, it's sometimes hard to tell where in the Valley you are at any given point. Mom actually found a spot on the street to park. There were two coffee places on the street besides the Starbucks on the corner. The air was even hotter than it had been on the freeway. No surprise there. It was mid-August, and the Valley was well-known for being at least five degrees hotter than anywhere else in Southern California. Angelenos routinely complained or poked fun at it, depending on which side of the hills they were on.

We walked to the second coffee joint. It was filled with light colors and the art on the walls was tastefully modern and boring. The tables had blond wood tops and the legs and chairs were all stainless steel. Mom pulled her Android phone from her pocket and tapped it, then walked around while I waited in the doorway.

"Looks like the Wi-Fi signal is good and strong," Mom said, walking up to me. "They have cupping notes on their menu, a refreshing lack of syrupy bullshit, and it smells like they use their roaster and, better yet, know how to. Finally, the barista works with some care, but is not pretentious in the least.”

“Okay.”

I probably wouldn't have put that much thought into evaluating the place, but then, I drank lattes. On the other hand, my mother had just gone total geek shit over coffee, of all things, and I didn't bat an eye. I wasn't sure if that was a sign of just how fucked up my life was at that moment or a good sign that I was getting used to her.

I found a table while Mom put in our order. I could hear the espresso machine hissing, which probably was Mom's order. I had asked for a simple pour-over of the place's medium roast, which I sometimes did when I found a place that understood the concept of medium roast. The few other people in the place were scattered about, hunched over their laptops. I focused on getting mine booted up and signing into my VPN and launching TOR. Pour-overs take time, but fortunately, I was ready to go when Mom brought our cups over. I got up long enough to add a little cream and sugar to mine.

It was excellent coffee. I had to give her points on that. But once I'd sat back down, I wanted to stay focused on getting into the Department of Motor Vehicles site via my F.B.I. sanctioned account.

“Agent Mikkelson won't know you're doing this, will he?” Mom asked after a very satisfied sip from her cup.

“He won't know unless I tell him,” I said. “And even if he did, I can't see him caring.”

“It's always possible,” Mom said.

“Huh!”

Her eyebrows raised. “What have you got?”

"That light blue sedan? It's a Chevy Impala and was reported stolen this morning," I said. "It's registered to an Alessandro Martinez, with an address on South 110th Place, in L.A."

"Stolen." Mom nodded. "That makes sense."

"The white truck is registered to Wayne Overs." I turned the laptop's screen toward her. "Here's his driver's license, and that sure looks like the tiny dick-brain that's been hanging with that other goon, Earl Johnson. The weird thing is that he's local. Johnson presented a Missouri driver's license at the car rental place when I checked that."

"Could Johnson have gone home?"

I frowned. "Who knows? I could check his credit card, I suppose. I've got that data from the car rental info. The thing is, he was at the hotel when Abe got shot. Actually, both of them were. There's video of Johnson talking on a mobile phone right after I showed up."

"There is." Mom frowned. "He doesn't sound terribly bright. It sounds like he was working as a lookout, then."

"What the hell," I grumbled. I pulled the laptop toward me and went to sign into Johnson's credit card account, taking a chance that he'd get an alert that someone had signed in from another device.

Mom sipped again. "We know that the attack on Mr. Pearlstein was connected to Tanya's disappearance because of that text you were sent that got out. Which means it's part of the larger attack on the team trying to bring Wheeling down."

I looked at her as I waited for the credit card site to load. "Are we sure Wheeling is behind the attacks?"

"I suppose that's a fair question to ask," Mom said. "But who else could it be? We know Wheeling is up to something bad, something they've devoted quite a few resources to. They would be the ones most invested in stopping our little group from carrying out our plan."

"Finally," I grumbled, then typed in Johnson's email address and the password for his Facebook account, which I had already gotten. "What an idiot."

"Who?"

"Dad's goon, Earl Johnson. He used his Facebook password for his credit card account."

"I can't believe people still do that."

"Lucky for us, he did." I scanned the credit card entries. "Okay, here's a hold for six-hundred dollars placed by that business suites hotel in Pasadena, and I'm seeing a couple mini bar charges, including one this morning, but no final charges."

"He could have used another card."

"I suppose, but I don't think so. He's also got charges from Denny's, on Colorado Boulevard, over the past few days, and look, here's one from the International House of Pancakes this morning. And there's the car rental deposit, but no final charges there, either."

"That would probably mean he's still around, unless the final charges haven't posted, or he used another card to close those out."

"True." I switched tabs on my screen and pulled up Johnson's bank account, which I'd gotten from the credit card information. "Huh. Looks like Dad's paying him, all right. Here's a deposit from Dad's car dealership from a week ago today. Wait a minute." I switched tabs again. "Huh. I don't think he's using another card for this trip. The account was only opened that Friday, and it looks like..." Some more scrolling and opening a few more tabs.

"Whaddya know. This isn't a straight up credit account. It's one of those that you have to put money on deposit to use, and it looks like..." I swapped tabs again. "Yep. It's a payment from Dad's dealership again." I looked up at Mom. "Dad is fronting him."

"You just said that he's paying them."

"I know, but he doesn't pay up front, and he doesn't pay expenses. He'll fork over a retainer if he has to." I sat back, frowning. "So, now, all of a sudden, he's basically giving Johnson a free ride. Why? Just to follow me? I don't think so. There is something seriously weird going on here."

"That, my darling, goes without saying." Mom finished her coffee and set her cup down on the table. "Which means it's time for you and me to move on."

CHAPTER EIGHT

Mom drove us up to Burbank to one of those outlet centers there, and, after she parked, led me into the SpotCo store. SpotCo was not unlike Target or Walmart, in that they carried everything. They were also known as really good corporate citizens. Most of their employees were full time and had benefits. The company donated tons of money to local charities. And they were big enough to sell decent products at good prices.

"Why are we here?" I asked.

"Tanya needs some fresh clothing, and you need a new phone."

Mom sent me to the electronics department and went to pick up the fresh clothing, which turned out to be a package of underpants. She found me in the tech department a minute later.

"I hope I got the right ones," Mom sighed, then looked at me. "What did you find?"

"Exactly what you said," I said, pointing to the phone hanging on the rack. "It's got a pre-paid plan."

Mom looked at me and sighed even more deeply. "Are you going to be okay tossing it onto the freeway if you have to?"

I winced.

"There's a reason they're called burner phones," Mom said softly. She pointed to another phone. "This one has a decent range of features. In fact, we'll get two of them and some extra minutes."

We had to get the clerk to come get the phones off the locked hook. As she rang us up, a woman at the other register complained loudly that her card had been declined. The clerk shook her head.

"Another one," she grumbled. She looked up at us. "It's been happening all day."

Mom smiled at her and stuck her card into the reader. I don't know why I held my breath, but Mom's card went through okay and we were out of there in no time. From there, we headed to Oxnard, of all places, and stopped at a grocery store, where Mom got a lot of healthy snacks and several pre-made salads. Not what I would have chosen, but she was buying, with cash, too. She also added several tea bags to the food stash.

As Mom got us back on the 101 to Ventura, she pulled out her phone and voice dialed somebody called Leah.

"Hey, Mom," said the voice that answered.

"Huh?" I looked at my mother.

"Nickname," she said softly, then louder at the phone. "I just wanted to let you know that I'm about fifteen minutes out, and I have lunch."

"Real food?"

"Of course."

"You did not bring me a butt-load of that fucking rabbit food, did you?" The voice rose in pitch at least four octaves.

"It's healthy."

"Fuck that shit. I need comfort food!" The young woman was almost in tears. "What's it take to get a god-damned smothered pork chop and greens?"

"We do not want to attract attention."

"Oh, come on. Half the folks at Roscoe's Chicken and Waffles are White."

"I'm with her," I said.

"Who's that?" The voice grew anxious all of a sudden.

"Our new team member," Mom said. She glared at me.

"Come on. You ran through Mickey D's this morning," I said, softly.

"That was an emergency," Mom hissed back.

"This is an emergency!" cried the voice on the phone.

"We'll get some burgers and fries," I said loudly. "It's not comfort food, but is it close enough?"

"Better than rabbit food."

Mom rolled her eyes. "That's going to push our E.T.A. out a bit, but there will be burgers and fries."

"Thank you!" gushed the young woman.

They hung up.

"Tanya?" I asked.

Mom nodded. "She's getting a touch punchy."

"No shit. She's been in hiding how long?"

"Ten days, and don't think she's not counting." Mom pulled off the freeway.

"It didn't take me that long to go apeshit during the quarantine, and I like staying home."

Mom glanced at me and frowned. "Odd. Leon said you do a lot of your work on the go. That's why he suggested you join the team."

"He did? Why didn't I hear about it sooner?"

Mom shuddered. "Because I asked him not to. I told you I didn't want you involved. Unfortunately, that happened anyway."

"Or fortunately," I grumbled. I grinned when I saw an upcoming sign. "Oh! I like that place!" I pointed. Mom sighed. "I haven't been there in years."

"I see."

I don't know if Mom believed me or not, but she pulled into the old-school burger joint's parking lot, anyway. We got a burger, fries, and a fried pork tenderloin sandwich that I would be happy to eat if Tanya didn't want. Mom did not let me pay for lunch, and used cash again.

"Cards can be tracked," she reminded me.

She didn't get anything, saying that she had her lunch and was happy with it. We stopped at a nearby wine and spirits store, as well, where we stocked up on wine and some good scotch, which Mom paid for with cash.

"How much have you got on you?" I asked, incredulously.

"Not much anymore," Mom said. "We'll fix that later."

We got to the hotel. It was one of those large towers next to the beach. Mom went straight to the elevators, and I followed. Mom set her collection of bags down and texted something as soon as the elevator doors closed. Sure enough, as we got off, I could hear a door opening down the hall.

A young Black woman peered around a door well about three rooms down from the elevator.

"It's about time!" she hissed. "I'm starving."

I held up the bags, and she quietly clapped her hands. We hurried inside the room.

I dug through one of the bags and pulled out a bundle wrapped in yellow paper with the grease just starting to soak through.

"It's not a smothered chop," I said, holding it out to her. "But they had that fried pork tenderloin."

"How sweet of you!" she gasped and did a little dance. "I'll take it. Thank you!"

Tanya's smooth skin was somewhat darker than her mother's, but she had the same busty figure. Her full black hair was pulled back into a ponytail and she wore dark yoga pants and a baggy t-shirt celebrating some festival in Malibu. There was a small conference table at the end of the room, next to a set of sliding glass doors that led to a balcony. Sheer curtains were drawn over the doors. Tanya pushed aside the papers that had been strewn across the top of the table, and collapsed into a chair, waving at me to seat myself, as well.

Mom sat down on the end of one of the two beds and gazed at the over-sized television screen, full of computer code. The beds had been made and housekeeping had clearly been through the room.

"This doesn't make any sense," Mom grumbled.

"That's because there isn't one line that I can find that references a directory," Tanya said through a big mouthful of sandwich. She looked at me. "Is this Leon's friend?"

Mom seemed lost in the code displayed on the screen.

"Yeah," I said, and went over to the table. "I'm Jannie."

Tanya shoved more of the papers around, and I got the fries and my hamburger out, then got up to get some mineral waters out of one of the other bags.

"Oh, you're the one with the F.B.I. boyfriend," Tanya said with a grin.

"Ex-boyfriend." I glared at the bag of fries.

"Huh." Tanya looked at me strangely for a second, then at Mom, who blinked and shook her head.

"If you can't find that reference, then the rest of us won't be able to," Mom said, standing up and stretching. "Do you mind if I look at some local news as a temporary distraction?"

Tanya shrugged. "Whatever you want, Mom."

Mom flipped a couple switches behind the TV, and found the one L.A. station that broadcast news in the afternoon instead of Judge Judy or a soap opera. Dramatic music poured from the TV as an ad for some big show finished up.

"Welcome back," said the grave young blonde behind the anchor desk. "Traffic around Los Angeles International Airport is finally returning to normal after an abandoned car nearly brought the airport to a standstill this morning."

On the screen, police and Homeland Security agents swarmed around a light blue Chevy Impala.

"The car was abandoned just before the screening station on the departures level at the airport. Surveillance video shows a dark figure wearing a mask leaving the car, then running toward Century Boulevard."

"Holy shit," I whispered.

"They must have given up trying to find you," Mom said.

"It's way worse than that," I said, pointing at the grainy video of a man wearing a full-brimmed hat and a colorful medical mask running through the stopped cars trying to get into the airport parking. "Dollars to donuts, that's the same guy who shot Abe Pearlstein."

"Your friend," said Mom.

I swallowed. Tanya got up and came over.

"You know," she said, her face tight in consideration. "The guy that shot Manny had one of those medical masks on, and a big old hat."

"I remember that," I said. "Brent gave me the surveillance videos from that night." I looked at her. "I'm so sorry about your friend."

"Me, too," Tanya said softly. She blinked back some tears. "So why is this guy leaving a car at the airport?"

"He was following me this morning," I said.

"Fuck. Seriously?" Tanya looked at both me and Mom. "Why would he be following you?"

"We don't know," said Mom. "And it's only a supposition that it's the same person."

"It's more than that," I said. "It's his habit. He's good at evading cameras. After both shootings, the first thing he did was ditch the gun. He lost me, so what's the first thing he does? He ditches the car and in a way that's going to attract a lot of attention to the car and less on him."

"Could it be that Earl Johnson you were talking about this morning?" Mom asked.

"Nope. Earl was on the hotel video making a call when Abe was killed," I said. "Or at least when the hotel security video picked up some shadows near the loading dock. And that's where the gun was found. I should probably call Brent."

"What?" gasped Tanya.

"No. Don't." Mom said.

"Why not?" I glared at her. "I want to know what was inside that car."

"For Heaven's sakes, it was probably wiped clean."

"Fucking shit!" Tanya yelped loudly and pointed at the TV. "Look at that."

"In addition to the difficulties processing credit cards—" a reporter intoned. Behind him was a SpotCo storefront. "Consumers whose cards have not been declined are reporting that their cards are no longer valid at their banks or other places of business."

"It's point of sale!" Tanya said, flipping the screen back to the code windows. "It's an attack on point of sale devices. Look!"

Mom and I looked at the code Tanya was pointing to.

"She's right," I said.

"She usually is," Mom said with a slight smirk.

"Shit!" Tanya yelped again. She looked around the room frantically. "I've gotta find that thumb drive. The one that I didn't think had anything on it."

"What thumb drive?" My mom asked as Tanya began upending her laptop case.

"It's one of the ones that have the code I copied," Tanya said, going carefully through the contents of her bag. "There was a reference to some point of sale something or other. It didn't make any sense, so I thought it was actually for some other retail project they were working on."

"Why would Wheeling do retail projects?" I asked.

Tanya snorted. "They've got their fingers in everything. It's supposedly all security of some sort, but they do it for all kinds of companies. They do movie projects. Finance projects. Banking projects. Hell, they were finishing some construction project right before I had to leave. And they make so much noise about how they exist for the good of mankind and they're non-profit. Non-profit, my sweet ass. They're all about the profit. I can't tell you how many times I had to fire someone because he wasn't bringing in enough billables." She sat back in defeat. "It's not here."

"Maybe it's somewhere else," said Mom.

The two of them went through every bag and every drawer in the room and did not find a thing. Tanya blinked her eyes as she tried not to cry.

"When are Leon and Arturo getting here?" Mom asked.

Tanya shook her head. "They're not. Leon decided we should mix it up again, especially since Jannie knows him in real life. And I don't think he wants to be too close to her boyfriend."

"Ex-boyfriend," I said again.

"Either way," Mom interrupted. "Why don't I call Leon? Maybe one of them has it. In the meantime, I'll check my car."

The thumb drive wasn't in Mom's car. We had to wait for Leon and Arturo to get settled where they were hiding first. So, while we waited, we took Tanya out to dinner. The whole point of hiding in Ventura was that we were far away enough from Wheeling that Tanya could get out of the room and go a little less stir-crazy. However, that evening, Tanya was obsessed with trying to recreate the bits of code that had been left behind on the missing thumb drive.

"If I could just figure out what it did," Tanya complained on the way home.

Outside the car, I saw a SpotCo sign. "What if it's supposed to nobble credit and debit cards?"

"Why would it do that?" Mom asked.

"It's probably ransom ware, don't you think?" I said.

"We haven't even confirmed that what's happening at SpotCo is the Wheeling virus," Mom said.

"What else would it be?" Tanya growled. "We know Wheeling's virus is an attack on point of sale devices and they're having problems with their point of sale devices."

"It could be a coincidence," Mom said with a sigh. "If we jump to conclusions, we could easily waste far too much time chasing our tails."

"Wait," I said. "There are two things going on. One is that the point of sale systems are failing. Not a lot of them, but randomly, and so far, it's only SpotCo that's having the problem. Secondly, cards that have been used at SpotCo are getting declined elsewhere. That's it! Let's go buy something with that card you were using today, Mom. If it's declined, maybe we can reverse engineer it and see how this thing works."

"I am not going to give somebody a chance to track our whereabouts," Mom said.

"She takes this hiding shit pretty seriously," Tanya said to me.

"And you had better be thankful that I do," Mom said. "It's why you're alive, young lady."

"But we need to know if your card was affected by whatever this virus is," I said.

Mom had to concede that was true, so we drove north to Carpinteria, and we convinced Mom to take us through the MacDonalds off the freeway. The card went through with no problem.

"Maybe it happens after a random number of times," I said.

"That doesn't make sense," said Tanya. "People are tracing it to SpotCo, and if they're the targets, then Wheeling wants people to do just that."

"Yeah. You're right," I grumbled. "Wait. I know someone who has a card that got hit." I dug into my laptop bag. "And I can hack his account in no time."

"Make sure you have your VPN on," Mom said.

Tanya and I looked at each other.

"Yes, Mom," we both intoned at the same time.

Mom rolled her eyes, but could do little more because she was driving. Tanya was in the front seat, but turned toward me.

"So, what are you using to get the password?" she asked.

"I'm not," I replied, triggering the hotspot on my new phone. "I'm going in through the corporate help desk."

Mom chuckled.

I shrugged. "Sometimes you have to hack into people's financials, and this way, it doesn't trigger an alert that someone has signed into the account."

It took a couple minutes for the site to come up, then for me to get in.

"Arturo has this sweet bit of code that's almost as good as human engineering a way in," Tanya said.

"I'd like to see that," I said. "And here we are. Yep. Here's the SpotCo transaction. It looks just like any other, though. Wait. Isn't this the center about half a mile away from Wheeling?"

I held up the laptop for Tanya to see.

"Yeah. That's it." Tanya pointed to the transaction immediately below the SpotCo one. "That's that little Italian place I like in Culver City. What was he doing there?"

"Meeting me," I said.

"But you broke up."

"I know. But he also hired me to find you."

Tanya slumped into her seat. "Oh."

"And thank you for proving my point about not going places you've frequented," Mom said.

Tanya and I looked at each other and sighed. "Yes, Mom."

When we got back to the hotel, Mom got a call from Leon. They didn't have the thumb drive and had looked through everything they had.

"No!" Tanya groaned when Mom told us. "Well, that settles it. I have to go home."

"You can't go home," Mom said. "Do you really want to risk not only your life, but your family's as well?"

"But I've gotta get that thumb drive." Tanya sank onto one of the beds, tears dribbling down her face. "It's the only way we're going to break this."

"It's not the only way," Mom said, looking worried, nonetheless.

"You don't have to go home," I said, suddenly realizing something. "I do."

"Absolutely not." Mom turned on me. "You're not any safer than she is."

"We don't know that," I said.

"Wait. What's at your home?" Tanya bounced to her feet.

"Your thumb drives," I said. "Your mom gave them to me when I was there the other day. I left them in my desk, the same way you left them in yours. You'd left them, so I didn't think they were important."

"We don't need them," Mom growled. She folded her arms and glared at us. "We can figure out the missing bits from what we have."

"Yeah, maybe next year sometime," Tanya said. "But this thing has already been released in the wild. It's not going to get any better."

"But being out there will help us analyze it," Mom said. She looked over at me. "You've got that stubborn look again."

"Because Tanya's right, Mom." I flopped onto the bed. "My condo is safe enough. Once I get the locks thrown, no one can get in and I can get through the complex better than somebody who's only been watching from the outside. And my blackout curtains are closed, so no one will see me."

Mom looked at me curiously. "You really feel safe there."

"Yeah. Why wouldn't I?"

"Yet Leon said that you prefer to work on the go. In coffeehouses and on the bus."

"Well, sure." I shrugged. "If I didn't, I'd stay cooped up in my little cave twenty-four-seven, and that's not healthy. Besides, if I'm working on something really sensitive, it's a lot harder to track me if I keep moving."

Mom shook her head. "That's neither here nor there. I don't want either of you going after those thumb drives. That we're looking at a point of sale issue should be enough to crack it."

"But—" Tanya began.

"That's my final word." Mom checked her watch and yawned.

Tanya and I looked at each other and Tanya shrugged. It may have been Mom's final word, but it wasn't going to be ours.

Chapter Nine

Mom insisted that there would be no more work that night, either. So, we watched a movie and drank a little scotch. We flipped coins to determine who would share a bed, and Mom and I ended up together.

She was gone when I woke up the next morning.

"She's out getting some cash," Tanya said from the conference table.

There was fruit salad and whole wheat bagels on a tray.

I dragged myself to the shower and was feeling better, if under-caffeinated by the time I ate breakfast, such as it was. At least there was cream cheese for the bagels.

"You got my number in your phone?" I asked Tanya as I re-packed my laptop bag.

Tanya read off a phone number as I checked it against the phone I had.

"Great," I said. I pulled the bag's flap closed. "I don't care what Mom says. I'm going after those thumb drives."

Tanya grinned. "The only reason I'm not going is that I don't know where you live."

"Try and keep her here, will you?" I asked.

Tanya laughed. "Just like she kept you here. I'll try, but you know."

"I'm afraid I do."

I hurried out of the room and got out of the hotel without Mom or anyone else spotting me. It didn't take long to find a coffeehouse, and I got a second breakfast, coffee, and a ride-share to the Ventura train station. The train south was just coming through and I was able to get my ticket and get on it. We pulled into Union Station in L.A. around noon. I had to wait for a Gold Line train, but that was no big deal. I walked to the condo complex back entrance, looking for parked cars with people in them.

I got through the labyrinth and was pretty sure I hadn't been spotted when I tested the door to my condo to see if it was still locked. Fortunately, it was. I pressed the combo on my fob and was rewarded with the sound of the bolt sliding open and the lock clicking off. I pushed the door open into the condo. My curtains were still closed, leaving the place almost completely dark. What light there was came from outside.

As I stepped into the foyer, someone grabbed my arm and shoved me further in.

"What the hell?" I screamed as loudly as I could.

I was released to the sound of the door slamming shut. There was almost no light in the foyer, but the man behind me was familiar enough. He was tall with light brown hair, what there was left of it. His expensive suit, however, could not hide that his formerly muscular build was devolving into a paunch. Milton Miller had always been a good-looking man, and the expanding waistline only made him look more charming.

"Dad!" I yelped. "What are you doing here?"

"I'm getting you out of here and bringing you home." He looked around. "Where are the lights?"

"What? No!" I backed up the stairs as he slapped on the light switch.

"Aw, come on, honey-babe." His green eyes pleaded, and there was a sincerity in them that was hard to resist. "You know I only have your best interests at heart."

I was pretty sure he thought he did. But I knew better.

"No way." I folded my arms across my chest.

Dad rolled his eyes and advanced on me. "Jannie, for once, you're going to do as I say. Now, where's your bedroom? We're going to get you packed and out of here right now."

"I'm not going anywhere, and I'm certainly not going anywhere with you!" I backed into the living room.

I had half a plan in my brain, but Dad was in absolutely the wrong place for me to pull it off.

"That's where you're wrong, kid," Dad said, still advancing. "Can't you see? I gotta get you out of here or they're coming after my dealership. You don't want to do that to me, do you?"

I thought that him losing his car dealership couldn't happen to a more deserving prick, but didn't say so.

"Back off and get out of here," I said instead. I kept backing up and got onto the stairs to the bedroom.

"That is no way to talk to your father." Dad's voice rose as he followed me up the stairs. His face was getting a little red, but it wasn't the exertion. "Now, damn it, we're going."

He reached behind his suit jacket and pulled out a gun. I bolted up the stairs and up to the study. Cursing, he turned on the lights in the bedroom by hand.

"Jannie! Get your ass down here, you little ingrate." He went over to the closet and pulled it open. "Sheez! Can't you wear a dress occasionally? Where are your suitcases?"

I grabbed the thumb drives off the desk and stuffed them in my jeans pocket, then slid down the staircase, easing my taser out of the laptop bag that was still slung over my shoulder. Dad continued to trash my stuff, looking for a suitcase.

"Don't make me come up there!"

He turned, waving the pistol - an automatic, I suddenly realized. I didn't think he'd really shoot me. That wasn't Dad's style. But his rage was coming on, plus he was scared of something, so it was a safe bet the automatic's trigger would get pulled, even if by accident. Not that I had time to ponder the issue. I closed my eyes, a trick a friend of mine had taught me.

"Lights out," I hollered.

The lights turned out. I opened my eyes and could see just well enough to aim the taser at my father and pull the trigger. He jerked about and fell. I ran past him, the spasms still rocking him as I stuffed the taser back into my bag.

Seconds later, I was out of the front door. I locked it with my fob and heard the bolt slide into place. It wasn't going to last, but I could hope. I ran around the twisted paths two different ways before leaving through the back entrance.

I took the long way around to the Gold Line station, checking behind me every step of the way. The day had turned hot, well into the 90s, and I was panting as I searched for a bit of shade on the platform. The train south showed about ten minutes later, then I had a wait at Union Station to get on the northbound train to Ventura.

I definitely had too much time to think, and it did not help that the last damn thing I wanted to do was think about what had just happened. I put my VPN on and hooked up my laptop to the hotspot on the new phone, and aimlessly read blogs until the train north arrived, then looked at a few more blogs until I got to Ventura.

It was almost dinner time when the train pulled in. I texted Mom about meeting for dinner and got a reply to stay put. She'd pick me up.

I was relieved that Tanya was in the car. Mom insisted on a moratorium on what I'd been up to, and we ate at a nice little diner close to the mission. That, of course, only stalled the inevitable and probably escalated the blow up that happened as soon as we got back to the hotel room.

"What the fuck did you think you were doing?" Mom screamed at me. "You could have gotten yourself killed!"

"I know!" I screamed back. "Believe me, I got that better than you think. But I got the fucking thumb drives and, better, more news."

"You got the thumb drives?" Tanya asked.

I pulled them from my jeans pockets and handed them to her. She grabbed them like they were candy.

"What could possibly have been worth you risking your life for?" Mom yelled, not at all mollified.

Tanya had the drives plugged into her laptop and turned on the TV screen.

"I don't know about her life, but these are worth everything," she hollered as she did a happy dance.

"What?" Mom looked at the TV screen, then glared at me. "No. The bottom line was that you had no business going back to that condo. You can't tell me there wasn't some trouble."

"Oh, there was trouble all right," I said.

"No!" Mom's face paled.

"I'm good, Mom." I paced the room in the small space I had. "But it was fucking weird. Dad was there."

"Your dad?" Mom asked. The shock lowered her voice by several decibels.

"Yeah. You know, your ex."

Mom ran her hands through her hair. "I don't think we were ever technically divorced."

"Whatever!" My voice had lowered in volume, but was reaching new heights in octaves. "He was there to take me home. And the weird part, okay, it wasn't weird, but it was."

"You want to try translating that into English?" Tanya asked.

I took a deep breath. "He told me that he had to take me home or they were coming after his dealership. Which makes sense because he'd be more worried about his own ass than mine, but doesn't because who would give a fuck if I went home with him or not?"

Mom sank onto a bed. "Wheeling Corporation."

Tanya sat down next to Mom and put her head on Mom's shoulder.

"We don't know that," Tanya said. "But it sure looks that way, doesn't it?"

"How does Dad fit into all of this?" I asked, trying not to glare at Tanya.

"He hired those two men to follow you," Mom said. "And we strongly suspect that a third was involved with them."

"And he wasn't worried about me," I said, pacing again. "He was worried about himself. He even pulled a gun on me."

"He what?" Mom gasped.

"I tazed him," I said. Suddenly it all overwhelmed me and I flopped down on the bed next to Mom on the other side from Tanya.

Mom couldn't help laughing. I started crying.

"What kind of daughter tazes her own father?" I said.

Tanya sat up straight. "What kind of father pulls a gun on his own daughter? Man, that is a whole new kind of messed up."

"Actually, a very old kind, Tanya," Mom said. "Milt Miller is a classic abuser."

"You know the dude?" Tanya asked.

"She was married to him," I growled. "There's a reason I call her Mom."

"We all call her Mom."

Mom sighed. "But Jannie has more right to call me that than anyone else."

Tanya's jaw dropped open. "She's your real-life kid? Why didn't you say something?"

"I had my reasons," Mom said, looking away from us.

"What?" Tanya screeched. She bounced up off of the bed. "This is, like, too fucking weird."

"Tell me about it," I said.

It didn't take that long to explain to Tanya the weird history that Mom and I had. I have to admit, I was still having some trouble with the idea that Mom thought I was dead, although it made more sense than just about anything else in my life did. Tanya had plenty to say about Grandma betraying Mom and me.

"I don't even want to talk about how many ways that is messed up," Tanya declared.

"Then let's not," Mom said, getting up.

Tanya looked like she was going to talk about how messed up it was anyway, but she backed off. I was glad. I still hadn't sorted out my feelings about Mom coming back, and the odds that Wheeling had somehow gotten control over my father, and being in hiding. I didn't think I could take much more.

"I think the thing to do now is to chalk this little adventure up to all's well that ends well," Mom said, as she began pacing. She sure didn't look like she was about to do that particular bit of chalking up, but then she shook her head as if to clear it. "Now, what do we do with what we have?"

Tanya scurried over to the laptop on the conference table. "I've got code to analyze. If I can figure out what this virus is, then Leon can write something to stop it."

"I'm going to check out Dad's financials," I said, finally getting a grip on my fear. "Maybe I can figure out who has a hold on him, if it isn't Wheeling. Or maybe connect it to Wheeling."

"Excellent." Mom nodded. "I think I'm going to monitor his movements and see if I can find anything."

We fell to work. After a couple of hours, Mom had found that Dad had gotten a phone call the Friday after Manny Rios had been shot from somebody who did not appear to exist. Or, in other words, a burner phone. Dad had called Earl Johnson almost immediately afterward.

In fact, when we compared time stamps with the information I'd gotten from Johnson's accounts, the payments and the card account had been opened within minutes of the call to Johnson ending.

"So, who made the call?" Mom asked.

I shrugged. "I haven't the faintest. I mean, there's no question Dad's got some creative accounting going on here. But I can't find any connection to Wheeling or anybody else. He doesn't even have any liens on the dealership that somebody could call in. If anything, people owe him money. My guess is that somebody connected to Wheeling found out about his funny business and is using that to manipulate him. But why him?"

"You're the only person who's connected to both him and Wheeling," Mom said. She frowned. "When would Brent have authorized getting you hired to find Tanya?"

"I don't know. It could have been that Friday. Or maybe the day before. But Brent didn't sell me out."

"Are you sure about that?" asked Tanya, her face still directed at the TV screen.

"Yes."

"Honey," Mom sighed. "I know he's your boyfriend."

"Ex-boyfriend, and that's not it." I rubbed my shoulders to ease the knots there. "It's who Brent is. He's compulsively honest. Some waiter accidentally gave him an extra fifty cents in change, and when Brent found out, he had to go back to the restaurant, even though it was closed, and get them to open up so that he could return the change. He once had a melt-down when he'd accidentally brought home a pencil from the office. He's practically OCD about it."

Tanya got up and glared at me. "Yeah, well, Brent knew Manny and I were going to make that exchange that night. He said he'd set it up with L.A.P.D. to do surveillance, so we didn't trigger anything. I just don't know why Manny got it and I didn't."

I thought. "It's possible someone is using his honesty against him, but it's without Brent's knowledge. I'll stake money on that." I drummed my fingers on the table.

"Well, you could check Brent's financials again," Tanya said.

She had a point, so I did, and didn't turn up anything the least bit odd. I kept going back to my dad and the fact that he'd hired a tail for me and paid upfront. Goons don't come that cheaply, and as I noted earlier, Dad's habit was to avoid forking over a retainer unless he had to, and he preferred to hire his thugs local to me so he didn't have to pay travel expenses.

"Tanya, do you know what happens to the money coming in to Wheeling?" I looked at her over the top of my laptop.

"Not really. Why?"

"The same reason you asked me to check Brent's financials." I got up and glared at my laptop. "Follow the money. We know Wheeling is up to something and we have good reason to believe that they've hired a very good professional assassin to protect their plot. Where's the money coming from? Someone of that caliber is going to cost plenty, and it's not going to show up as a line item on a payroll sheet. And Wheeling's a non-profit, so anything they bring in must be rolled over into operating costs for the group, unless they're directly supporting a charity."

"I don't think they're supporting anybody," Tanya said.

"I don't recall that they are, either," Mom said from the bed where she was working on her laptop. "I wonder if I can get into their financials."

I shook my head. "Probably, but I'll bet you anything they'll be squeaky clean."

"Why?" asked Tanya. "We know they're up to something."

"Which is why the last thing they're going to do is risk a revenuer sniffing around." I began pacing. "No. I think we need to find out who is supporting them." I grinned. "And that is my specialty."

It was no small task. I sort of hit pay dirt almost immediately when I looked up one of the two companies that actually owned Wheeling.

"It's a shell corporation," I explained as I looked over the information on my screen. "I mean, I knew it was. But it looks like both of the companies that own Wheeling are themselves owned by still another shell corporation."

Tanya looked up from the TV screen. "A what?"

"That's not surprising," Mom said.

"A shell corporation is one you set up to hide who really owns your assets," I explained. "It's not illegal or even unethical. Celebrities use them all the time to make it harder for the paparazzi to look up their addresses and send drones over their place to get pictures. But shell corporations can be used to hide money for tax purposes. And there are other reasons a corporation might not want folks to know who owns them."

"So you're saying that Wheeling is owned by a company that doesn't exist?" Tanya looked skeptical.

"Oh, the company exists." I pulled out some paper and made a note. "It's just that its sole purpose is to hide who owns it. It's big business in Belize and a couple of other places. But you can eventually get back to the original owner if you're willing to dig far enough. And I am."

It took hours. The web of shell companies and regular companies surrounding Wheeling was incredibly complex, with overlapping strands. I had never seen anything so complex. Even Lester Margolis hadn't used as many layers to hide himself, and he'd used a lot more than most folks. I was so absorbed I barely heard Tanya's cries of delight.

"Leon got it," Tanya giggled. "He says he can definitely put this one on ice. All we have to do now is find out where to put it."

"And I think I've got that." My eyes watered as I scrolled down one last page. "The chain ends here. All those companies? They're all owned by Mrs. Goode's Marketplace, which is wholly owned by Jackson Goode."

Chapter Ten

We celebrated. After all, Tanya had discovered the weakness and sent the bits of code to Leon. Mom had a few ideas to try for breaking into the Wheeling system by way of one of the companies that I'd dug up. It turned out she'd worked for that company before.

The party didn't last long. It was well into the wee hours of the morning and we were all pooped. Tanya didn't even finish her wine before she fell asleep. I barely remember getting into bed.

Waking up to pounding on the hotel room door did not help. Mom snorted and rolled over.

"What time is it?" Tanya grumbled through the mushiness of sleep.

"Dunno." I staggered to the door and peeked out the peephole.

"It's Arturo!" The young man on the other side hollered. "Let me in."

"Arturo?" More awake, Tanya came over and looked through the peephole. "That's him."

I opened the door, and Arturo burst into the room. He was medium-sized, in his late 20s, with thick short black hair in waves around his round face.

"What's going on with you guys?" he demanded. "It's after ten. We've got work to do."

"We know," I said.

He stopped and looked at me. "Who...? Oh. You're Brent's girlfriend."

The disdain was tangible.

"Ex-girlfriend," Tanya said before I could. "We just had a little celebration, that's all."

"We don't have time for that."

Tanya got up in his face. "For the first time in weeks, I feel like I've got a handle on this shit. Fuck, yes, I'm celebrating!"

"Peace, children." Mom had gotten sat up in bed, but was still blinking the sleep from her eyes.

"That virus is already out in the wild," Arturo said. "We've got to get it stopped."

I scratched the back of my neck. "We could just hand everything over to the F.B.I. and let them deal with it."

"No way," said Arturo, glaring at me. "We have to prove that Wheeling's behind it or Tanya goes to jail for stealing proprietary code."

I winced. "And proof that's admissible in court, too. What a fucking pain in the ass!"

"Those are our constitutional protections," Mom said.

"Hey." I held up my hands. "Normally, big fan. But sometimes they get in the way."

Mom sighed. "Arturo, we need to get breakfast, but then you're right. We need to devise a plan for our next steps. Stopping the virus before it can do any more damage, then getting the evidence we need to bring down Wheeling and protect Tanya."

The four of us went down to breakfast. Arturo remained belligerent and antsy.

"We don't have time to waste," he grumbled after a waiter had gotten our orders. "We've gotta get these guys." He set his jaw. "I've gotta get these bastards."

I looked at him. It was as if he was taking Wheeling's virus personally.

"We know, Arturo," Mom said quietly. "But rushing to a bad solution will not help."

He glared at me, the anger rippling off of him. "Sitting around isn't helping Manny."

Puzzled, I looked at Tanya, who had begun weeping again, and Mom.

Arturo jerked his head at me. "What about her?"

"Leon trusts her and so do I," Mom said.

"I trust her, too." Tanya let out a defiant sniff.

"Mikkelsen called her to find you!" Arturo almost banged the table.

"And I found her first," Mom said. "Whatever good reasons we have to be leery of him, Jannie does have the benefit of knowing him better than any of us, including Leon."

Arturo bounced up and stomped away.

"What bug does he have up his ass?" I asked.

Tanya blinked and sniffed. "Manny was his brother."

"Oh, shit." I gulped. "I'm so sorry."

I got up and went over to where Arturo was kicking the wall.

"Arturo," I said as gently as I could. "I'm sorry. I didn't know Manny was your brother."

He sniffed and his jaw trembled a little. "We were both Old Man River. It was Manny's name on the account, but we both posted that way. We were waiting to see how long before someone figured it out. When they killed Manny, my mama just faded into herself. My sisters, too. They took out our whole family." He shuddered and jerked a thumb at my mother. "I know Mom is right. But I just get so angry. And scared, too. I mean, I can't get my card to work, either."

"Your card not working may be a good thing, actually." I paused. "Why are you all so down on Brent? I mean, he can be a controlling pain in the ass, but he is honest."

"It just seems like every time Wheeling has been one step ahead of us, it was when we've connected with Mikkelsen." Arturo shuddered. "Leon doesn't trust him. I don't know why he trusts you."

"Leon and I have been friends for years." I looked over at the others. "Come on. Let's get back to the table. We've got a plan to put together."

Back at the table, Tanya was eating pancakes and sausages while Mom ate whole wheat bagels with a touch of cream cheese. I had a pile of scrambled eggs and bacon waiting for me, as did Arturo.

"Alright," Mom said, getting out a steno pad and pen. "What do we know so far?"

"That the virus appears to be affecting the point of sale devices at SpotCo stores," I said. "How far it's reached, we don't know."

"Seems to be limited to Southern California," Arturo said. "At least, that's what I heard on the news, coming up here. Right now, they think that it's some bizarre glitch in the system and are trying to reinstall all the firmware on the devices."

Tanya made a face. "Which probably won't help much since the virus is being spread through credit cards with the malicious code on the mag stripe or the on-card chips. The cards compromise the banks, which then compromise the POS units the next time the card owner uses the card."

"What about contactless pay systems like Apple and Google Pay?" I asked.

"Those still involve credit cards," Tanya said. "Well, the code the cards send to the bank from the on-card chip. And the virus is set up to disable the cards at the bank level."

"You've got to be kidding," I said. "I've human engineered getting into an account or two, but this is full-scale hacking. Wouldn't the banks be hardened off on that?"

Tanya shrugged. "You'd think. But most of the banks' security is about protecting against theft, like money and identities. That's the scary part of this virus. It's not about stealing anything. It just fools the bank into doing something perfectly normal – decline a card for whatever reason. And it's using the POS systems to do it."

Mom tapped her pen on the steno pad. "We also know that Jackson Goode owns Wheeling via Mrs. Goode's Marketplace, as well as another of my former employers."

"Safest place on the Internet," Tanya snorted.

"It may be," said Arturo. "All sorts of folks are trying to crack that one and haven't done it yet."

"Someone will," I said. "It's only a matter of time."

"On the other hand..." Mom looked a little distant. "If Mrs. Goode's is actually part of Wheeling, then that might make it a lot harder to crack. And if they're inviting hackers by their advertising campaign, then they may be aiming the hackers right at their strongest defenses."

"That's right," I said. "But there's that company that you used to work for."

"PalmSci Systems," Mom said.

Arturo frowned. "Don't they provide data security?"

"That is their primary mission," Mom said. "Their clients are mostly city governments and school districts and a few federal accounts. I think the F.B.I. may be one." She made a note, then looked at us. "Is there anything we're missing here?"

"Leon says that we need to find where to put his fix," Tanya said.

"We should probably figure it will go on the top-tier servers," Arturo said. "Otherwise, we've got to distribute it to every point of sale device, and possibly every bank in Southern California."

"And that's assuming the virus doesn't spread to the rest of the U.S.," Mom added.

I looked at Arturo. "You said your card isn't working."

His eyebrows rose. "Right. We can reverse engineer it. I can get the chip reader."

"I should be able to hack into the bank systems if I can get into your account," I said. "Maybe if we can figure out what's going on at that end, we'll be able to stop things there."

Mom started writing furiously. "Tanya, once Arturo gets the chip reader, I want you and Arturo to reverse engineer the card and do the bank hacks. It will be easier for you to catch something if you're working both ends of it. In the meantime, Jannie and I will start trying to get into Wheeling through one of the Mrs. Goode's subsidiaries.

Leon is still working on the basic fix." She sighed. "I wonder how much time we've got."

"If it's just point of sale and credit cards, can't be that serious," I said.

"Are you kidding?" Tanya snapped. "Don't you remember how fast things went to shit at the beginning of COVID? If people can't buy stuff, the economy goes to hell. And if they can't get cash because the banks are fucked up, then no one can buy anything."

"Unless you're on the safest site on the Internet." I gulped. "This isn't ransomware."

"What do you mean?" Mom looked at me.

"Ransomware means that someone is looking to make a big score by holding someone's data hostage, right? In this case, you'd have to think that the target is SpotCo. But if this is coming out of Wheeling, and Wheeling is owned by Jackson Goode, who is already insanely rich, it isn't about a big score. That's not to say Goode doesn't want to get richer, but it's just a numbers game at this level. Having more money is not going to make it any easier for him to live. He can afford his own rocket into space if he wants it. And when you've got that kind of money, it's no longer about the cash, it's about control."

"As in, he wants to take over the economy," Mom said, then swallowed.

"Right." I looked down at my plate, my appetite suddenly gone. "How many times has he been quoted that he wants to beat Amazon at their own game?"

"And the economy is where the real power is," Tanya said, slowly.

"Which means that this is not aimed at SpotCo," I continued. "It's hitting the banks, too, and it's only a matter of time before other retailers start getting the virus, if they haven't already."

"Then we have work to do," Mom said. "Arturo, you and Tanya head up the coast further and find us a new bunker. I'll touch base with Leon, then Jannie and I will go to work on finding a way into Wheeling. In the meantime, everybody get as much cash as you can." Mom looked at all of us. "Let's get packed. I want wheels on the ground in ten minutes."

We were out of there in eight.

"How do you feel about San Diego?" Mom asked as we got on the freeway toward Santa Paula and Fillmore, a small agricultural valley between Interstate 5 and the coastal 101 freeway.

I shrugged. "It's as good a place as any." I looked at her. "I'm guessing you already got some cash."

"We'll get more when we get into Los Angeles."

"How am I going to get my money?" I shuddered. "I have one account that isn't obviously connected to me, but I can't get to it that easily. Given who we're dealing with, they have to be watching my other accounts."

"That's right." Mom suddenly smiled. "Maybe we should tip our hand a little."

"Are you kidding?"

"When people get worried, they're more likely to make a mistake, and we could use a couple mistakes right about now." She glanced at me. "Wouldn't you be a bit concerned if you were Goode and saw someone you know is involved in bringing you down suddenly pulling as much cash as possible from her accounts?"

"I would, but I'm normal." I shook my head. "I don't think Jackson Goode is. From what I've seen, he's got a lot of markers for sociopathic and narcissistic behavior. Of course, a lot of executives at his level do, so that isn't court-admissible evidence by a long stretch. But the thing is, guys like that don't get worried. So what if we've tumbled onto his little scheme? He's invulnerable, or he thinks he is."

"If he's operating on that level, then it should be relatively easy to find the proverbial chink in his armor."

"Not necessarily." I sighed. "That's what makes guys like that a challenge to find. They get that sense of invulnerability by making sure those chinks are very well-hidden. Lester Margolis was the same way. In fact, Dad operates that way a lot. He doesn't owe anybody money, so they don't have power over him. He plays the nice guy card with everybody else, so they're not looking for his weaknesses. He even tried it with me back in the condo. Said he had my best interests at heart, and it wasn't a lie for him. But when I didn't fall for it, out came the anger and the intimidation."

Mom shuddered. "With which I am all too familiar." She looked at me again. "You just said that you have another account that's not connected to you?"

I sighed. "Yeah. The problem is, I don't have that set of I.D.s with me. I'd have to get them out of my safe deposit box, which can be watched or traced."

"You set up an alter ego?"

"Years ago, when I realized that Dad wasn't going to stop following me around."

"He is determined to find me, isn't he?" Mom sighed. "So, why didn't you just disappear?"

I swallowed. "I guess I wanted you to be able to find me."

"Oh." Mom gazed at the road ahead, and the endless groves of orange trees on either side. "Well then. It's a good thing I did."

I looked at her. "Mom, why did you marry Dad?"

She looked at me, then back at the road.

"Why do any of us make the biggest mistakes of our lives?" Her voice was even, but somehow there was a deep sadness behind it. "I used to blame my mother. And it is true, she put a lot of pressure on me to keep dating your father and later, marry him. I had finally gotten a man with money and social standing." She glanced over at me again. "You have to understand, Jannie, the two most important things in the world to your grandmother were being liked by the right people and security."

"I kinda noticed that."

"So, when Milton Miller, son of one of the top business-men in town, started paying attention to me, she couldn't back off." Mom winced. "She coached me the entire time, telling me what I should and shouldn't say or do. There were times when I wanted to tell her to back off, but I didn't." She blinked her eyes. "I was scared of losing him. You've seen it. Your father can be very charming when he wants, and for some reason, he wanted me. I know now that part of it was that he needed to prove himself to his father by controlling the one girl in town that no one else could control." Mom sighed. "He also liked me because I was so smart. He's a very intelligent man."

"I know." I frowned. "I always hated it when he would put down certain women as dumb bunnies, then felt really icky because I thought the same thing."

"It's hard not to sometimes," Mom smiled. "Anyway, once I finally got away from your father, I kept looking back for the signs that I should have seen. And they were there, but they were also the more subtle signs, the sort of thing that's easy to overlook when you really want to be with someone. The truth is, Jannie, I really wanted to be with your father. I maybe even still do. Or maybe I just want to feel that rush when someone actually sees you as desirable."

"I know that feeling." Suddenly, I felt like crying. "It's like with Brent. He's so sharp and likes that I'm smart, too, and isn't always trying to act like he knows more than me, or that he has to know more. But he's so manipulative, and it's not his fault. His family is seriously messed up, too. Angry people. And they're all playing the martyr card. The worst of it is, Brent doesn't want to be that way, but he keeps falling into it, then gets mad at me because I won't play his game."

Mom sighed. "Honey, if I've learned anything over the years, and I hope I have, it's that there are a lot of very messed up people out there. But there are also some very good, healthy ones. The trick is to find the ones who belong to your tribe."

"That's some trick," I grumbled.

"Well, right now, we've got some good people that we're working with, and I am trying to stay focused on that."

There was a silence as I thought about Brent and having to leave that relationship.

"Why didn't you leave Dad?"

"That's the trouble, Jannie. I did. Twice before you were born, and then I tried again when you were three and took you with me. Each time, he found me and that last time, literally, dragged the two of us back." Mom's eyes filled. "That's why I had to go to such lengths to hide, and why

I had to be so careful when I found out that you were still alive. That last time, when he got us back to his house, he put his hands around your throat and told me that if I even thought about leaving him again, he would kill you." She swallowed. "The only thing that's been keeping you alive is that he wants to find me. That's why he keeps watching you. And if he finds me, he will hurt you or worse, and I couldn't bear that. The worst part of all those years was that the one person I should have been able to trust, I couldn't, and that was my mother. She didn't care that he was abusing me."

"I think she cared, Mom." I frowned. "I just don't think she understood it. He didn't hit me a lot, but there was this one time, he knocked me around pretty badly. I had bruises all over me and Grandma kept saying that he was actually a good man."

"That sounds like her." Mom sighed. "But, Jannie, the important part is not that everything was her fault, because it wasn't. We do make our own choices. I chose to marry your father. I chose to stay in hiding when I found out you were alive. I chose to trust my mother. Given the alternatives I had, especially after I got married, they seemed like our best options. Whether or not they were, I do not know. I do know that I have you back, and that's the most important thing right now." She slowed the car down as we got onto Interstate 5 south. "Now, where is your safe deposit box? We'll try to get some of your visible cash, too."

I told her where to go and we settled into silence as I tried to make sense of her words. The funny thing was, I had no trouble believing that she had stayed away to protect me. That was the only thing that made sense about the whole situation. Given what had happened to my first stepmother, Janelle, Dad obviously was capable of getting angry enough to kill someone. I wouldn't have thought that he would kill me until he'd barged into my condo after me. But perhaps I should have. He had kicked me around pretty badly those few times he had.

Which was why Mom had stayed away. I couldn't help wondering if the bits of code that I'd found when looking for her had been her way of signaling me, letting me know that she was still out there, trying to reassure me or something. I debated asking her, then decided that I didn't want to know if it wasn't. She was there. Finally. That was enough.

My safe deposit box was at the Glendale branch of a major bank chain. Mom dropped me at a mall about five blocks away, asking me to text her when I was ready. I hurried up the street. Fortunately, the bank wasn't too busy, and I was able to get to my box and my additional I.D.s without a problem. It was getting the extra cash that got me in trouble.

That took forever. By the time I left the bank, I could feel someone watching me. I hurried down the street away from the mall where my mother had left me. I didn't run. That would have attracted too much attention. But as I glanced behind me, I saw an all-too familiar dark hat with a broad brim on a tallish figure.

Chapter Eleven

It did not surprise me that Wheeling had been watching my bank. It was a logical place for me to go, especially to get nice, untraceable cash. I wasn't sure how I'd earned a professional assassin on my ass, but it didn't really matter. He was there, and I had to find a way to get rid of him, preferably before he shot me.

The good news was that the sidewalk was relatively crowded. We're not talking Manhattan crowded. Just five or six people strolling along the block I was on, but that's crowded for the L.A. area. It apparently was enough to keep the man in the floppy hat from putting a couple of slugs in me.

I reached for my taser, suddenly realizing that I hadn't replaced the wire cartridge after tazing my father. In fact, I wasn't even sure I had an extra wire cartridge. I had my pepper spray can, but that meant I was going to have to get way closer to the assassin than I really wanted to be. I grabbed the can anyway and ducked into a doorway covered by a brick addition to the building's wall that jutted out perpendicular to the sidewalk. It hid the glass door and most of the full-length plate-glass window next to the door. Drawn blinds covered the plate-glass on the inside of the building. I pressed my back up against the brick wall so that the assassin wouldn't see me until he was almost on top of me.

He approached the doorway at a saunter, his hand under his coat as if he was about to draw his gun. I whirled into him, spraying the pepper. As he fell back, screaming, his hand came out of his coat with the gun in hand and firing. I'm not sure how I wasn't hit. The glass door and plate-glass window behind me shattered. More screaming erupted along the street and inside the building, and I ran like crazy.

A bus stopped across the street, and I just barely caught it. I watched out the window as a police car pulled up next to where the assassin had fallen. I thought I saw the assassin's legs still on the ground, but couldn't be sure. In any case, I got off the bus several blocks away, and walked another two, just to be sure. I wasn't followed.

I texted my mother and went back to the outdoor section of the big mall complex where she'd left me. Mom texted back that she'd find me and check for another tail. If I saw her, I was not to acknowledge her unless she called or texted otherwise. I walked the perimeter of the shopping area at least twice before I got the all-clear text from Mom. She met me at a small dining table outside a pretzel stand.

"I want one of those," I gasped, pointing at the stand. "In fact, I'm getting the hot dog."

"Jannie, your eating habits are deplorable," Mom said.

I glared at her. "I just had an assassin shoot at me. I think I deserve a hot dog pretzel."

"What?" Mom pressed her lips together. "Who shot at you?"

"I don't know his name." I growled, then placed my order for two pretzel dogs and a large Coke.

Mom waited while I paid with one of my regular cards.

"Just seeing if it will work," I told her. "No point in not since Wheeling apparently knows I'm in the area."

"You could be spreading that thing."

I shrugged. "I haven't bought anything from SpotCo in a while, and I don't use this card when I'm there."

The card went through. The second my order was ready, both of us hurried away. Mom took a rather convoluted path back to her car, which involved going back and forth and around a lot of corners. But she seemed satisfied that we were not being followed.

Once in the car, she all but peeled out, and didn't say anything until we were on Interstate 5 heading south.

"All right," she asked. "What happened?"

"It's like I thought." I told her everything that had happened after she'd dropped me off.

"This doesn't make sense," Mom said.

"Could it be that he's following through on his threat if I don't find Tanya?"

Mom frowned. "That's not entirely unlikely, especially if the point of that text he sent you was to scare the larger hacking community. The only problem is that they are already sufficiently scared."

"Are they scared enough to give Tanya up if they find her?" I asked.

"It's possible. We're not going to take a chance on finding out, however." Mom gazed at the traffic as it packed in just after the Long Beach Freeway. "The question is, who specifically is behind all of this? Is it simply some group at Wheeling or does it go all the way up to Jackson Goode?"

I thought. "I was kind of assuming Goode was behind it, given all his statements to the press about beating Amazon."

"On the other hand, it could be someone in his organization manipulating him."

"Could be. We don't really know that much about Goode or his people."

Mom sighed. "That would be a good task to hand over to Mikkelsen."

"But you don't trust him."

"It's not that." Mom glanced at me. "Granted, I've never actually met him, but based on what Leon and you have told me, I'm inclined to agree with your assessment of him. So, if he's been compromised, we need to know how and how badly. Besides, if he is honest, the fact that he's official law enforcement will get us some information that we wouldn't be able to get otherwise."

"Like an interview with Jackson Goode." I made a face. "Although how much good that will do, I have no idea. Goode isn't going to roll over and confess the second Brent shows up in his office."

"No. But we should be able to get some impression of him as a person and how deeply into his organization this plot is running. We know from Tanya's work that a lot of different employees have been working on different bits of the virus. Do they know that they're writing a real virus rather than one for security testing?"

"Good question." I gazed out at the billboards along the freeway and saw yet another one reminding the world that Wheeling was thinking about us. "Wheeling is big on that whole emulated virus bullshit. If that's what their employees think they're working on, it's possible they don't know how bad this is. In fact, the emulated virus thing is how someone at Wheeling has been tricking young people into writing viruses for them. I'd say decent odds that not everyone knows that they're working on an actual virus rather than an emulated one."

"And given the culture there, the odds are also decent that not everyone would be opposed to taking over the economy at Jackson Goode's behest."

I got my laptop out of my bag, hooked it up to the phone's hotspot, then went to my VPN.

"Time to do some basic research," I said.

I did use the DuckDuckGo browser to do the search on Jackson Goode rather than Google's Chrome browser. DuckDuckGo makes a big deal of not tracking you. There were plenty of news and magazine stories on Goode, but there was a running theme that Goode seemed friendly. However, he was reserved at the same time. One writer stated that she'd caught Goode flat out in a lie, but that Goode charmed his way out of it. Sort of.

I changed over to some different Reddit threads. That was even weirder. Most of the posts were positive, claiming that Goode was a hard-worker and incredibly smart. A few folks complained that Goode was really difficult to work for, but also that he paid very well. The catch was that you had to play along with his agenda, to where he was almost paranoid. You could question him, but there was a very thin line before he got pissed off. I got the impression that people who did well in that organization were very loyal and already politically in line with his views.

There were also a few hints that people who did not like Goode - and who posted that they didn't like him - were getting harassed. I recognized the handle on one such post, Timon of Athens. It seemed like the post was making fun of people who had a complaint against Goode, and that they deserved what they got. Even someone who was as paranoid as Goode appeared to be would have a hard time trying to figure out if Timon was criticizing Goode or not. Even I couldn't tell and I knew Timon, and I mean In Real Life.

The guy was insanely spooky. But he hadn't stayed off of Reddit or the other chat rooms. He'd just made it really, really hard to tell who he was. I'd gotten the odd hint that he may have been working with Brent on some sort of sting. It's nothing Brent would have been able to tell me, either.

And I was back to thinking about Brent again.

There wasn't much more on Goode that I could find. By that point, Mom had pulled into a nice little B and B in La Jolla, and she checked us in as Virginia and Audrey Tiklow. It surprised me that she gave the clerk a card instead of cash, but had to figure it was a relatively untraceable one.

"So, why did you use the card?" I asked when we got into the room.

"Unfortunately, paying cash for a hotel room would raise too many eyebrows." Mom grinned. "With some exceptions, of course, but I wouldn't want to stay in any of those places."

I shuddered. "Neither would I. And what are the odds places like that would have decent Internet connections?"

"Well, that too."

Our room was fairly large, with a king-sized bed covered with an extra fluffy comforter featuring huge pink roses. There was a small antique armoire next to the door, and on the other side of the bed was a table flanked by two easy chairs. The lamp had a Tiffany-style shade on it, but it was obviously a reproduction, since there were two USB ports and a plug in the base.

We dropped our bags on either side of the chairs.

"What did you find on Goode?" Mom asked.

I shook my head. "Nothing I didn't expect to find."

I told her about the Reddit threads and the articles I'd found.

"The interesting thing is that I found this guy I know writing about Goode. Have you heard of Timon of Athens?"

Mom couldn't help laughing. "Oh, yes. I know him very well."

"In Real Life?" I asked.

"No one knows him that well."

"I do."

Mom's eyebrows rose. "I don't understand."

"A couple, three years ago, a kid named Alphonse Littlejohn contacted me. He was about to be in some serious trouble for writing a virus. Only he hadn't known that was what he was writing. I mean, he knew it was a virus, but he thought it was a joke or an intellectual exercise for a friend of his online. He also got paid for it. He needed me to trace where the money had come from so that he could point the Feds toward the real bad actor. Which sort of worked, except that I got the evidence illegally, and we couldn't bust them."

"You might want to think about your tactics, dear." Mom smiled at me.

I rolled my eyes. "I know. Brent gave me hell about it. Anyway, it was still enough to get the Feds off Alphonse's back and another woman's, too. But the source of the money was Wheeling Corp."

"Well, we know they've been setting kids up to do their dirty work."

"That's what got Brent so interested in bringing them down. And me, too. Here's the weird part, though. Alphonse is Timon of Athens. He picked up that avatar after we got him off. Timon has been going after Goode in this weird, subtle way that sounds like he's praising Goode, but it's just snarky enough that you have to figure Timon is tweaking more than supporting."

"You know, I think I've seen a couple of those posts." Mom's brow furrowed. "Could it be that Timon knows that Goode owns Wheeling?"

"I have no idea." I sighed. "I don't even know if it's significant or not. The hard part will be getting a hold of Timon. Surprise, surprise, he's gotten insanely spooky."

Mom thought. "I think Timon is someone to keep in mind, but perhaps it would be best to focus instead on our primary task, which is finding a way into the Wheeling servers."

Oh, yeah. The fun work. We spent most of the afternoon searching code all over Mrs. Goode's Marketplace and the PalmSci Systems site. It was the sort of tedious work that results in aching shoulders and necks.

After a few hours, I found something that made my blood run cold.

"Brent was right," I whispered.

"What about?" Mom asked.

"Wheeling. They're collecting personal information. All kinds of personal information about..." I scrolled through the code I'd found on the site belonging to a Wheeling wholly owned subsidiary. "Almost everybody."

Mom got up and looked over my shoulder. "You're exaggerating."

"Maybe. But there are a lot of people here." I shuddered as I clicked through a couple links. "Oh my god, they've got practically all of Brent's office."

"That's tax form information." Mom pointed to my screen.

I opened a few more searches in different tabs on my computer.

"And work histories." I hit a button and pulled up the human side of the page I was looking at and landed on a search page. Just as a test, I typed in my name. "Look at this. Shit. They've been watching me for years. Ever since I first found the money connection to Wheeling. Oh, fuck. Look at this. A link to Dad's profile." I clicked on it.

"This may be how Wheeling got their hooks into him," Mom said.

I gasped. "Holy crap! Mom, they've got his social security number, his driver's license number, credit card numbers, bank account number, his home address, the dealership." I looked over at her. "What do you think they're doing with all this?"

"Spying on people, I would imagine." She groaned.

"Yeah." I shook my head. "How did they get all this? Half of this is stuff that no one gives out. I can't even get it that easily."

"As Wheeling says, they're thinking about us." Mom shuddered. "That probably explains how they knew where to find you."

"And where Abe Pearlstein was staying," I said, blinking back tears. I shook them off. "You know, there was that call to Dad from that burner phone right after Brent hired me to find Tanya. And Dad later said that they were going to take his car dealership. I wonder if Wheeling leaned on him to hire those two goons to watch me and follow me to Tanya."

"That would certainly explain it," Mom said. "Except that now they're trying to kill you."

"I disappeared and wouldn't go with Dad." I bit my thumbnail. "It must mean that I'm working with the folks trying to bring down Wheeling and Goode."

Mom sighed. "I'm so sorry I got you into this."

"You didn't get me into this," I growled as I searched on Virginia Ticklow, then Audrey Ticklow. "Brent did. Well, some good news. The names you used to check us in here aren't coming up."

"Small comfort," Mom said, then sighed. "Let's go get some dinner, then take a walk. We need to break things up so that we can find what we're really looking for."

Which is what we did. Back at the hotel, we went back to work, alternating between slouching in the easy chairs or working at the table. Our eyes watered from staring at our screens. Line after line of code, most of it not leading to much of anything except elsewhere on the same site. The only thing keeping us going was that there had to be a way in.

The truth of it is there is no perfect system. The best cybersecurity experts can do is harden a system off enough that it's not worth it to hackers to go after it. Since the vast majority of hackers these days are in it for the big score rather than bragging rights, making it extra hard to crack your site is enough to keep the hackers away. But if someone is really determined to get in, they will eventually, which is why Goode's bragging made him such a target.

Mom was right, though, in that he'd pointed the hackers right at his strongest defenses. The marketplace site was amazing in its complexity. It was easy enough to use - it had to be or people wouldn't shop there. But getting to the back end, where all the secured information was, was going to be a doozy. Fortunately, that wasn't what Mom and I were looking for.

It was coming on for eleven when we both yawned and decided to compare notes. That's when we found it - the bit of code that got us into Wheeling's closed system. That Goode was self-hosting all of his businesses' different sites on his own servers was no surprise. Most large companies do because it's safer for them to keep all the data that goes into making websites on their own machines, not to mention making it easier for them to maintain the sites themselves.

But if you can get into one part of a system, you can get into other parts of it, maybe not easily, but you can. Mom and I were a little surprised that the flaw we'd seen was so easy to crack. Then again, given how solidly Goode had hidden his relationship to Wheeling, it made sense. No one would be looking for a way in through the other sites.

Mom called Leon and told him how to crack the system, and he got into Wheeling in no time. Mom and I went to bed after that.

The next morning, Arturo called to say that he and Tanya had figured out how his card had been corrupted and could make some educated guesses as to how that was working on the banks' side of things. Leon called after that to let us know that he'd refined his fix thanks to what he'd gleaned from the portal Mom and I had discovered, plus what Tanya and Arturo had found. There was only one catch.

"I only have part of it," Leon said from the speaker on Mom's phone. "It's how the Wheeling servers are configured. Tanya says she knows how to work around it, but she can't tell me how without looking at the fix itself. The file is too big to send by email and I am not going to use a cloud service to transfer it."

"Of course not," said Mom. "Do we have a Secure Shell set up?"

"Would be nice," Leon grumbled. "But we didn't get it done before we all had to bug out."

Mom looked at me. "Can we set up a meeting? Maybe you and Jannie can find a way to connect that won't alert the Wheeling assassin."

Leon was good with that. We agreed to meet on the bus. Now, it sounds a little weird, but Leon and some other friends of ours used to play bus tag. It's this dumb-ass game in which two people try to catch the same bus at different spots on the line, which doesn't sound all that hard, except when the buses are running within minutes of each other. You can't use location apps, either. Just bus schedules and you can text each other, which was perfect for our situation. The idea was to find the other person, then post a photo of the two of you together with some sort of timestamp, and the more creative you got that way, the more points you scored.

Leon and I had won catching buses on Wilshire Boulevard, and given that they're running every three minutes and even leap-frogging each other, that can be tricky. The two of us decided not to push our luck. I wasn't sure where Leon was hiding, but he talked Mom and me into driving back to the L.A. area from La Jolla.

We chose to take a bus along Colorado Boulevard in Pasadena. It's not too crowded (another thing that makes it easy to miss someone), just crowded enough that we'd have cover from any assassins. After all, who wants to kill somebody in front of witnesses? Finally, there were plenty of places along the line where we could each get on.

So, Tuesday morning, Mom dropped me off at the corner of Colorado and Hill, then headed somewhere else to wait. She didn't say where. I stood on the corner until I got a text from Leon that he was ready to go. The bus was just pulling up, and I got on and found a seat on the driver's side just behind the Seniors' seats. Several of us had medical masks on, so when Leon got on near Lake Avenue, I didn't think anything of it that the guy getting on behind Leon was wearing a mask, shades and a black baseball cap with a logo on it that I did not recognize. I was also trying not to focus on Leon. My messenger bag sat on the seat next to me, which was on the aisle. Leon walked past to the back of the bus. I picked up the flash drive he'd dropped next to my bag and put the drive into my jeans pocket. Leon got a seat, but I didn't see where. The guy who had gotten on with him stood in the rear door well.

Three stops later, we were at Colorado and Fair Oaks, where I was going to get off. I got up and picked up my bag, then turned, bracing myself as the bus slowed.

The bus had just stopped, and the doors opened when the guy in the rear door well pulled a gun from the back of his pants and fired straight into Leon's face. The man dashed off the bus and disappeared into the crowd on the street.

Chapter Twelve

I had thought that seeing the bullet-hole in Abe Pearlstein's forehead was the most horrific thing I could ever see. I was wrong.

As the bus riders screamed, I sank into my seat, shivering and trying not to barf. Someone else did. Or maybe more than one person did. I couldn't really tell. I could just hear it happening, then smelled it.

It seemed like the cops were there in an instant, although someone else kept whining that they were taking forever to arrive. Then Brent was there.

"Were you hurt?" he asked gently.

I shook my head. "Leon."

"I know." Brent winced as if Leon's death had physically hurt him. "Come on, honey. We've got to get you off the bus. You're the last one on."

The police had corralled the eight of us who had been on the bus in front of the J. Crew store on the corner. A trauma team had been dispatched, and was busy holding hands and dispensing hugs, while workers from the restaurants in the area brought us hot coffee.

Detectives Ismael and Tran were on the scene, first talking with Brent, then with the other officers. Then they split up to talk to the other riders individually. Me, they left alone. I'm pretty sure they knew that I was up to my hips in what was behind the killing, but Brent had prevailed and eventually insisted that I go with him.

I don't know why I did. I think it was because I wanted to beat the living shit out of him, but didn't want to do it in front of the cops. I'll spot Brent some points. He was smart enough to get me in his car and got it going before I could start whaling on him.

"This is your fault, you lousy fuck!" I screamed at him as he pulled into the traffic on Colorado. "And why are you going to my place?"

"Where else are we going to go?"

"It's not safe at my place," I told him, the tears flowing freely.

Brent cursed some more. "Listen, Jannie, I am so sorry I got you into this."

"Fuck that!" Still sobbing, I glared out the window. "It's your fault that Leon is dead. That has nothing to do with me being involved. The assassin didn't even see me, and I've had him on my tail."

"Why didn't you say so?" Brent screamed.

"Because, you fucking idiot, you've been compromised." I was hyperventilating. I held my breath.

"Fuck," Brent sighed, then looked at me.

"These bastards have been one step ahead of you every time," I got out between gasps.

"I know." He looked at me. "It's not me. You believe me, don't you?"

"I don't know. I just know that Leon's dead and it has to be your fucking fault, because he wouldn't have said shit to you. I just can't figure out how that assassin knew we were going to be on the bus, except that you found out and sent him there."

"I didn't send anybody anywhere."

"Then how did you know where Leon was going to be?"

"Alphonse," Brent whispered.

"What?" I gaped.

"Alphonse Littlejohn told me about the bus meeting. He was set to get on the bus just after Fair Oaks, I think. He wanted to meet Leon because he'd found out who Beefsteak is and thought Leon would know what to do about it. Apparently, Leon was pretty excited by the news and wanted to talk to Alphonse directly and set up the bus meeting. Only Alphonse got worried because of all the other violence and called me to provide some protection."

"Why would he call you?"

"Hello? I'm F.B.I. You know. Law enforcement."

"Yeah, except that Wheeling's bad guys are one step ahead of you at every turn." I folded my arms and leaned back in my seat.

Brent pressed his lips together. "All right. Let's go back to my office."

"Oh, yeah. That'll be really safe."

"It's the safest place on the planet." Brent drove onto the 134 freeway. "It's an F.B.I. office in the middle of the fucking Federal Building."

"Except that it's compromised." I glared at him. "Unless you're the one working with these Wheeling fucks."

"I'm not." Brent swallowed and looked out at the traffic ahead. "Honestly, Jannie, I promise you, I'm not." He cleared his throat. "I'm not surprised you figured it out. We've known for a couple months now that there was a problem. We don't know who and can't figure out how it's happening. Our systems are clean. We've tried locking everything down and scrubbing it, and they still get our information. The only thing we can figure is that somebody hacked the email. But we've changed passwords. We've changed addresses. Half of us have brand-new machines in our offices. Nothing's helped. I even called Alphonse on a secure mobile phone when he emailed me to let me know about the meeting with Leon. Whoever is doing this is insanely good and has reach like nobody I've ever seen before."

"Like Wheeling?" I sniffed back still more tears.

"Like them." Brent shuddered. "I have no idea how these Wheeling fucks are doing it, but they somehow found a way to spy on our email and a few of our phone calls, and it's gotta be coming from the outside because our network has been cleaned too many times. There are too many different leaks from too many different places." He glanced over at me. "But that's why I gave you that video and info on Coleman on a thumb drive."

"Shit," I grumbled. "I should have figured."

"Still, even with the leak, there's only so much Wheeling can do, and sending an assassin into an office filled with F.B.I. agents is a pretty poor risk. Which is why we're going there."

I sighed. "We may as well go. Maybe we can figure out how those bastards are onto you."

Brent took the freeways through downtown L.A. to get to Interstate 10 and West Los Angeles, where the Federal Building is. We got off the freeway a little early and went through a drive-through for lunch. The food helped my tummy a little, but didn't do much for my nerves. Brent wasn't in much better shape.

When we got to his office, I was glad that no one seemed to notice me. Brent let me into the tiny room, then had to leave almost immediately. Brent's office was on one of the outside walls of a cubicle farm. The office had glass windows over dark panels and a door that shut, which said a lot about Brent's status there. I could see to the other side of the farm, to Phil McCaffrey's office, where Brent was headed. McCaffrey was not happy, either.

I looked away and flopped into the chair in front of Brent's desk. The top was littered with files and binders, with bits of paper and sticky notes scattered around. Two broken pencils sat on top of a stack of paper near the left edge. Brent was not the neatest person ever, and especially when he was working a difficult case, he preferred what he called creative chaos in his workspace.

I honestly think that the only reason I spotted the possible source of one of the leaks was that I was looking at the back of Brent's computer for so long. The desktop unit had been connected to the office network via an ethernet cable. I had to wonder why the darned computer was still connected to the rest of the network, although Brent had made a very compelling argument for the office network being clean. The ethernet cable to the office network was plugged into a tiny, flat black box that was really hard to see, and the box was plugged into the back of Brent's computer. The box had twisted with the cord, but I could make out a diamond-shaped logo on the box's far side with the letter P on it. There was something wrong with it, of that much I was sure.

Brent made his way toward me between the cubicles. I hurried out of the office and shut the door.

"I found it," I hissed.

"Found what?" Brent demanded, snarling.

I put my finger to my lips. "Shh. I don't know if it's broadcasting or not." I checked a computer in a nearby cubicle. "It's how Wheeling is keeping tabs on you. I'm not sure, exactly, but there is a box on the back of your computer that shouldn't be there. My guess is that it's a wireless modem."

"It's not." Brent glared at me. "It's a firewall and data tracer. The IT guys installed it a month ago."

"They did?" I shook my head. "There's something about that box that's wrong. I don't what it is, but it's wrong."

Brent put his hand on my arm. "Jannie. You're not thinking straight right now and small wonder."

"I know!" I pulled my arm away and looked at the back of Brent's computer. "But I'll bet that box is broadcasting and it's going straight to Wheeling. I don't know why, but I'll bet that it is."

"We can't say for sure that it's going to Wheeling," he said. "I told you, the IT guys put it there to try and trace what's going on."

"It's Wheeling's. I'll prove it to you." I went into the office. "I'll meet you tomorrow at the coffee shop in Silver Lake. Around noon. Oh, and be careful. There's an assassin on my ass."

I stalked off.

"Jannie!" Brent yelped.

I don't know why he didn't chase me down. I just got the hell out of there as fast as I could. Terrified, I got on an eastbound Wilshire bus because there was no other way out of there. Setting up that meeting wasn't the smartest thing I've ever done. Okay, it was pretty damned stupid, but it was all I could think of at that moment.

My phone buzzed with a text from Mom to get a new phone immediately. I rolled my eyes because I was already on my way to the nearest SpotCo to do just that. I wondered where she was. She had to have been close enough to the bus to have found out about Leon. But I didn't get to find out more. The bus I was on stopped and as soon as I got off it, I junked the phone I had by tossing it into the street. I bought the new phone and got it set up, only to realize that I didn't have Mom's new number in it. I tried texting the old one, but never got an answer back.

That's when I lost it. I hid in the back of a dark bar and cried for at least half an hour. After that, I decided the only sane response was to get good and shit-faced. I had the presence of mind to get a couple bottles from the nearest wine store, got some dinner, then took the bus all the way to Hollywood, where there was a surprisingly nice and reasonably priced motel.

The next morning, I did not feel good, but I pulled myself together enough to check out of the motel and head to Silver Lake well before the time I'd told Brent in his office. The same black, white, and gray abstracts were on the walls and the place wasn't terribly full. I conned George, the barista, into letting me hide behind the door into the back room. I shuddered. So far, the assassins hadn't hit anybody they hadn't wanted to, but it had suddenly dawned on me that didn't mean that collateral damage wasn't going to happen.

My head throbbed, and I shook. Damn it, I had not been thinking clearly the day before and it sure seemed like I still wasn't.

About half an hour before I'd asked Brent to show, my dad's goon, Earl Johnson, wandered into the shop. He ordered some stupid whipped concoction, then took the cup to a table near the door and sat down next to the front plate-glass window. After glancing through the window, he pulled his phone from his pants pocket. He must have been playing look out because he was texting somebody.

I went back to wondering when Brent would show. Or even if he would show. I wasn't sure what I'd do if he didn't, but ultimately, it didn't matter. Brent came and stood outside the door. He waited for a couple minutes, then had the sense to come into the shop. George caught his eye and beckoned him to the bar.

I slid out from my hiding space and went over to Brent. Johnson looked like he was texting again.

"You showed," I told Brent, leading him toward the back of the shop.

"I wish you hadn't run off like that," Brent grumbled.

The corridor to the restrooms was pretty narrow, which is what saved my life. I almost didn't hear the gunshots. I did hear the plate-glass window shattering and Brent's grunt as he fell on top of me, knocking me to the ground. I shifted.

"Stay down," Brent ordered.

There was more shooting, but it sounded like it was outside, and a car's tires screeched as someone peeled out. Brent finally rolled off of me and winced.

"You okay?" I asked.

He got up, then helped me up with a slight groan. "Okay enough."

The shop filled with F.B.I. agents, maybe three in flak gear, the rest in regular suits. Brent turned, and I screamed. There was a gaping hole in the middle of the back of his jacket.

"How are you alive?" I yelped.

Brent looked back at me. "Bullet-proof vest."

I barely heard him. Along the side wall next to the door, Earl Johnson lay in a pool of blood.

I simply could not take any more. I turned and ran to the back door, slammed it open, and horked all over the brown, dry weeds and broken glass in the alley behind the shop. Brent caught up with me a second later and held me as I heaved.

He brought me back into the shop, where, fortunately, someone had covered up Johnson. Brent held me firmly next to him. I'd like to think he was being supportive, but I had a bad feeling he didn't want me taking off again. Or maybe it was both.

There was some good news. Johnson was the only casualty.

"Poor guy," said a woman agent with blond hair. I later found out her name was Donner. "Bad time to be sitting right in front of the window."

"He was texting," I gasped. "He must have been watching for Brent or me."

"What?" Donner frowned and looked at Brent.

"Person of interest," he said to her.

"He knew this was going to happen? What a dumb-ass."

"We've established that," I grumbled, then gave a shaky smile to George, who brought me a latte.

"But why do a hit and run?" Brent asked. "It's all been direct attacks so far."

"They knew we were here," Donner said, grimly.

I sobbed. "It's my fault. I set this up."

"It's okay, honey." Brent squeezed me.

Another agent, an average-sized Hispanic guy with short black hair, walked up.

"We found the gun next to where the car was parked," he told Brent.

"Okay, Orguello." Brent sighed. "Can you liaison with L.A.P.D.? I've got to get the witness settled."

"Wait," I said, and looked at Orguello. "You found the gun? It had been abandoned, right?"

"Looks like," Orguello said.

"Honey, this is not the time," Brent said.

"Don't give me that." I glared at him and took a deep breath. "I need to know. Did they find a gun outside the bus?"

"Bus?" Orguello asked.

Brent waved him off. "You mean Leon? No, they didn't. They checked all over, too."

"Leon was killed by someone else. Which means Wheeling has two assassins running around."

"You don't know it's Wheeling."

"We don't have proof that it's Wheeling." I swallowed. "There's a difference."

"I got that." Brent cursed as Orguello wandered away to talk to someone else.

"It's gotta be that wireless modem on your computer."

"Assuming that's what's on there." Brent squeezed me. "Although, I have to say, there's probably a mike of some sort."

"I'd say we proved it." I sniffed, then tried to clear my head. "You're here with a bullet-proof vest on and all your friends."

"But how can Wheeling get into our system with a bug?"

"It's got to be that box. I'll bet it has a wireless modem."

"I told you IT put it on."

"Then Wheeling found a way to corrupt it."

Brent sighed. "I'll have IT put fresh boxes on. But that's assuming Wheeling can use something like that to get into our system."

My voice got cold and even. "There's always a way in, Brent. You know that. That wireless modem can probably go to whatever server you're hooked into, plus any other servers that are connected to it. Not to mention the internet. It's for all intents and purposes hard-wired into the system."

"Look, we can talk about this later." Brent squeezed me again. "I'm taking you home with me."

"No, you're not."

"Jannie, I don't want to argue about this. You're not safe."

"Like I'm gonna be at your place?" I rolled my eyes. "They got into your secure office and got your IT department to put a wireless modem with a mike on your computer. What makes you so damned sure they haven't bugged your home? Hell, I'm not even staying at mine, and you know how secure it is."

"Fuck." Brent looked at the front of the store. "Come on. We need to talk."

I finally pulled away from him. "I'm not telling you shit. You're compromised. You're not safe for me."

He looked hurt. "That's what you keep saying."

He followed me as I headed out the back of the shop. I stopped and looked back at him.

"Yeah, I know." I blinked back tears. "It's not just the leak. It's about us. It's about you and not asking, and when I call you on it, you call me passive aggressive."

"Well, you are!"

"That doesn't absolve you, and this is not about me."

Brent pressed his lips shut, then growled. "You can't just dump on me. That's not fair."

"No, it's not. But it's not fair of you to turn everything back on me when I call you on your shit. That's why you're not safe." I looked at the back door. "I've gotta get the hell out of here."

Brent grabbed for me. "You're a witness."

"One who wants to stay alive and I can do that best on the move."

"I could have you arrested." His hand clamped onto my arm.

I looked him in the eyes. "And what good is that going to do you?"

Slowly, he let go. "Fine. How do I get a hold of you?"

Brent's a pretty devout Apple person, so I told him about an Android forum where he could post a question.

"Ask about the best way to flash a ROM on your great aunt's phone," I said. "I'll find a way to send you a phone number. Just make sure you use a fake identity and a public computer, then sign out of the account when you're done. It's harder to trace."

"And I'll make sure no one's following me when I do."
He reached over and kissed my cheek. "Take care. Oh, and
I'll use a burner phone when I call."

"That's the safest way." I turned and ran.

I'm sure some of Brent's pals wanted to talk to me, but
if I wasn't going to talk to Brent, I sure as hell wasn't going
to talk to them.

Once on the streets, I ran up a couple blocks, then
down a couple of others. Somehow, I ended up on Beverly
Boulevard, which was good in that there was plenty of
traffic, not to mention plenty of buses. Not so good in that
I couldn't shake the feeling that I was still being followed.

I walked west, trying to act casual. Ahead of me was
Vermont and the Metro station there. The problem was,
all I could see in the back of my mind was that guy in the
bus door well turning and taking out Leon, and getting
off. Still, I dashed into the station and hid behind a pillar.

Sure enough, a tall man in a cowboy hat, face mask, and
shades ran past me and down the escalator. I ran out of the
station and across the street, where an eastbound bus was
just pulling up. I got on and sat in the wheelchair seats,
where I could see everyone on the bus.

I debated getting some wheels. The problem was, car
rental companies only accepted credit cards. On the other hand, I had my second identity. On the other hand
from that, wheels didn't mean I couldn't be followed. The
whole reason I didn't have my MachE with me was because
I'd been followed.

If my head hadn't been still hurting from the night be-
fore, I would have said it was time to get shit-faced again.
But given how badly things had gone since the day before,
I couldn't see how getting shit-faced was going to help.

"Fuck," I muttered.

I got off the bus in the middle of downtown Los Angeles, near the Music Center. There were several hotels in the area and I went ahead and used my fake I.D. to get a room at the Biltmore. I figured I could use the extra bit of luxury, plus the hotel was barely a block away from the Central Library. Both the hotel and the library had what I needed - public computers.

The thing is, if someone is trying to trace you through an IP address, namely the address to a specific computer, public computers are great because while you're at that location when you're using the machine, if you leave really quickly, it's going to be a lot harder to trace your location after that. The big disadvantage is if someone sees you using it, they can find what sites you've been using unless you find a way to clear the computer's cache before you leave, and sometimes the public computer won't let you do that. Also, library Wi-Fi can get a little pissy if you use a VPN because they don't want people looking at porn while hanging out in the kids' section, and trust me, people do.

I sucked down a couple shots of scotch in the hotel bar before going to my room and ordering in room service. I also spent some significant time thinking about whether or not I really wanted to find my mother and the others who were going after Wheeling. I don't mind admitting that I was fucking scared.

The problem was, I was also in it up to my hips and I seriously doubted that hiding would help. It wasn't even that. My grief was morphing into the anger phase. I couldn't help being pissed to hell about losing Abe, then Leon. I couldn't help being pissed that I couldn't go home to my beloved fortress of a condo. And the truth is, scaring the peewaddles out of people only goes so far before they start getting pissed, and then you've got trouble.

Well, with me you've got trouble. When it came to my father pissing me off, it usually meant going behind his back. But this wasn't about my father. It really wasn't even about my mother or her friends. It was about stopping somebody who apparently believed in his version of world order and didn't care who he hurt on his way to creating it. I'd already lost two friends to this megalomaniac. I did not want to lose any more.

But I had no way of reaching my mother. The plan after the bus meeting was for me to text her with my location when I got off the bus. Only I fucked that one up by getting rid of my phone before getting her new number on it. And if she'd been hard to find before, given the extra measures she was taking, it would be next to impossible to find her now. Which was the point when I thought about it.

I signed into the room Wi-Fi, then turned on my VPN within seconds. I shouldn't have, but given that I wasn't ready to leave the hotel, I thought that the VPN would be the safest.

I went to the hackers forum that I normally visited, and it was filled with tributes to Leon. Most folks were really upset, a lot were scared, but some were seriously angry, including someone who sounded a little like Tanya. That gave me an idea.

I got off the forum and cleared my browser's cache - or memory of where it had been - just in case. Yeah, I was on DuckDuckGo, but was in no mood to take chances. I created a new online identity using still another false name and the address to a mailbox shop that was part of another business that I knew of. I went back to the forum, registered, then selected Wishing4Boston as my avatar's name.

"I am devastated by Leon's death," I wrote in my post. "I can't help feeling so lost and alone."

Then I got a little stuck. How was I going to leave my burner number without it being obvious that I was leaving a phone number? I could have left it in binary or some other computer code, but most of the people on the forum could read that as easily as English.

I sent the post live, then went back to my settings and agreed to let people direct message me privately.

That was pretty much all I could do at that point. But the next morning, after I checked out of the hotel and found an open computer at the library, I signed into the forum. There was a direct message waiting for me. All it contained was a phone number.

Chapter Thirteen

M y heart pounded as I left the library, then dialed the number. I'd deleted the message and had to hope it wasn't still on the forum's server.

The phone on the other end rang once, then a soft voice answered in a grunt.

"It's Wishing4Boston," I said.

My mother's voice chuckled. "Looking to run away, are you?"

"Yeah, Mom." I sighed in relief.

"What the hell happened?"

"I got your text about changing phones, but killed the burner I had before writing down your new number."

"Honestly, Jannie."

"Come on. I'd just seen Leon..." I choked. "I'm sorry. I wasn't exactly thinking straight."

I could hear her swallow. "I can imagine. We're all pretty messed up here, too. Where are you?"

"Downtown L.A. Where are you?"

"In the Valley," she said.

"I've got a meeting place. Why don't I text it to you with an E.T.A.?"

"That should work."

I used Google maps on the phone to figure out when I'd get to the North Hollywood Metro station, then texted the time and place to Mom's phone. It only took a little over half an hour to get there. While I saw several scary folks on the subway, most of them had been living on the streets too long to have any social skills left and were not out to get me specifically. The other two had the decency to get off the train before I did.

Mom pulled up in the Toyota just as I got up to street level. Tanya and Arturo were both in the back seat. There was a lot of crying among the greetings, and Mom held off pulling out to reach over and give me a big hug and a kiss.

We went to lunch at a nice restaurant in the area, about a block or so down from the station, and mostly avoided talking about what had happened. Then Tanya wanted to find a place to stay closer to Wheeling's offices in Malibu. Arturo wanted to head east and out of Los Angeles entirely. Mom settled for the San Pedro area and found us a place geared for business travel with small suites and really good Internet.

Mom checked in, and from where Tanya, Arturo, and I stood in the lobby, I could see her frown and mutter what looked like a curse. I never did find out why. She was shaking her head as she led us up to the room.

I was still a mess. Mom made me promise to stay in the room, which I was all too happy to do, and left me there with Arturo. She and Tanya went to get food for the night. They already had plenty of scotch, tequila, and wine in the trunk of Mom's car. I had recovered from the previous day's hangover, but was in no mood to give myself another one.

The living room area of the suite was pretty spacious and had several chairs and an over-stuffed sofa all done in the kinds of pastels you usually find in major chain hotels. As you came into the suite, that's what you saw, but there was a kitchenette to the left, with a decent-sized dining table just beyond that, then the living room. The two bedrooms and the extra bathroom were to the right.

I wandered over to the sofa and sank down onto it, shivering.

"Are you okay?" Arturo asked.

"No," I snarled, then blinked. "I'm sorry. Didn't mean to be so pissy. I just don't know how much more of this I can take."

"I know what you mean." Arturo's eyes were filling, and he turned away so that I wouldn't see it.

To be honest, even Mom wasn't at her best. She and Tanya returned fairly quickly to find Arturo and me staring blankly at a bunch of cartoons on the TV.

"Have you slept at all?" she asked me as she put the salads, freezer burritos, and other pre-fab food away.

"Some," I said and shivered again. "What about you guys?"

That's when I noticed Tanya was looking pretty lackluster and Arturo winced.

"We're all still getting over our hangovers," Mom said.

"Yeah. I pretty much did the same thing that night," I said.

I did not talk about what had happened on the bus. I couldn't. But I told them everything I knew about what was going on with Brent, and about the coffee shop getting shot up.

"I suppose there's some comfort in one less goon to worry about," Mom said.

"Now what do we do?" Tanya said. "Do you have the fix?"

I pulled the thumb drive from my pocket. "Right here. Have you guys been able to get into Wheeling's system?"

"Sure," said Arturo.

"Then I guess we'd better get back to work." I pulled myself up from the couch.

"No," Mom said. "We need to grieve and we need rest." She put up her hands at our collective protest. "I know. We don't have a lot of time, but as I have said repeatedly, it won't help us if we rush into the wrong solution. I think the most sane thing we can do is watch a bunch of inane movies tonight, then start in fresh tomorrow morning and see what we have."

Which is what we did, only I had one bad crying jag, and Mom held me, weeping herself. Later, Arturo and I went out and got a pizza and a box of microwave popcorn. The junk food was soothing, and we all slept well.

I won't say we were recovered the next morning, but we all felt better. It just didn't last that long. Tanya hooked her laptop up to the TV, and what we saw on the thumb drive was discouraging, at best.

Leon had included several notes on his fix, and while Tanya and Arturo could probably install some of it re-motely on the Wheeling servers, there was one that we couldn't install anything on. It needed a special thumb drive and laptop to make changes.

Tanya sighed deeply. "The good news is that I have the laptop and can set up the thumb drive. We just have to figure out how we're going to get in there and get it done."

Mom sat back. "The problem is that none of us looks like most of the Wheeling personnel."

"You two come closest," Arturo said.

I looked at Mom. "Can we get away going in as women?"

Mom rolled her eyes. "There are plenty of women support staff. In fact, given the attitudes over there, no one will pay any attention to us." Mom looked at Tanya. "What's going on with the dress code there? It was all suits and ties when I was working for them, but that was several years ago and pre-pandemic."

"It hasn't changed," Tanya said.

"The only problem is that I don't have a business suit with me," I said.

"Nor do I." Mom shrugged. "We'll have to go shopping this weekend."

"Then I need to get a couple employee photos so that I can get the I.D.s made," Tanya said. She shrugged as Mom lifted her eyebrow. "I may have swiped a few I.D. blanks and parking stickers a couple weeks before I left." She swallowed. "It was Leon's idea, just in case we'd need to get someone else inside. And now that we can get into the servers, I should be able to set you two up as employees."

"That's right," I said. "You worked in Human Resources."

"And setting up employee I.D.s is a lot of what I did." Tanya grinned. "For my job, anyway."

"But wouldn't they have changed your passwords and verification codes when you ran?" Mom asked.

"Who says I don't know everyone else's?" Tanya said with a grin. "And before we heard about Leon, I was checking to see who was still there and tried a few of them. Guess what? They all work."

Arturo laughed. "In other words, they think they can't be hacked."

"It's a closed network." Tanya rolled her eyes. "When the offices were closed during the Pandemic, we had to modem in directly. No Internet. But we not only have the way in from online, we also have two modems, including that one you and Manny set up."

"We should probably install those, as well." Mom looked at me. "There's also something else that we haven't had a chance to talk to you about. While you were waiting to meet Leon, the three of us met in Pasadena and continued surfing the servers."

Tanya sighed. "I found a second virus on the special server that the credit cards are redirected to. That's why it lets the cards go through a couple of times. It's setting up a seed virus on the different bank servers that will let another, more damaging virus in."

"Ransom ware?" I asked.

"We don't know," said Arturo with a shrug. "Could be anything."

"And I found Goode's special file that will release the virus," Mom said. "Plus a lot of Goode's emails detailing the elements of his plan. I downloaded it all, and I'll make a point of deleting everything from the servers when we get in and hopefully slow down implementing his plan."

"Why wouldn't he have backed it up?" I asked.

"Oh, he did." Mom smiled. "On two different servers, not to mention the mag tapes. There are some emergency servers somewhere else which I cracked, but the trick will be to find their physical location, and that of the tapes. Goode is a little too paranoid to trust a storage service with the mag tapes. I think we can cause enough trouble to keep him from releasing the virus until we've either exposed him or crashed the other servers."

So, back to work we went. Tanya and Arturo worked on the code while Mom took me shopping at an outlet center in Long Beach, where we each bought a suit, two blouses and an extra jacket for the I.D. photo. We found several mace cans decorated with white and pink rhinestones in a gift shop and bought them. From the outlet center, Mom drove to a hunting supply store she'd looked up on the Internet. There we got some new wire cartridges for my taser, several stun guns, and four air pistols that shot balls containing pepper spray.

"Why not just buy a gun?" I asked.

Mom sighed as if it was obvious. "We have to register it. Besides, have you ever shot one before?"

"No," I said, taken aback.

"It's not as easy as it looks, and you don't have any training. Besides, guns attract attention, which is the one thing we don't want."

She was right, but I couldn't help feeling a little like I was being lectured at.

Tanya slid out the next day to go to a copy store to get the photos we'd taken printed onto labels for the I.D. badges. Between working on figuring out the new virus and how to stop it and scouring the Wheeling servers, Mom and I went over and over our plan.

Late Sunday afternoon, we decided we could use some extra cables, so Mom and I went to a nearby SpotCo to get them. Mom went to find a couple of extra burner phones just in case. I stood at the register while the clerk rang me up. Next to me, a man with light brown hair, glasses, and a square face snarled at the point of sale device.

"Alright," he grumbled and removed his key card from the machine. "All the drivers have been reinstalled. It should be good for at least a little while."

"Until someone reintroduces the virus," I said.

"A virus?" snapped the man. "That's impossible!"

I shook my head. "It's never impossible. Damned hard, yes. But there's a flaw in the chip reader that allows the virus in. Because it's not trying to read personal information or change it to someone else's, it got past you guys. What it's doing instead is creating a man in the middle attack, with everything actually going through a special server that shows up as the POS on the bank side, then as the bank on the POS side, with the POS sending a bad card code to the bank which causes it to cancel the card."

The man glared at me. "How do you know that?"

"That'll be nineteen fifty-four," said the clerk.

I handed her the twenty-dollar bill.

The man touched my arm. "Seriously, how do you know that?"

"That is irrelevant," Mom said. She put her hand on my shoulder. "Get that receipt and let's go."

I did, and Mom hustled me out to her car.

"Of all the stupid—"

"It's not stupid!" I sniffed as I got into the car. "We need all the help we can get. Why not let somebody else know what's going on?"

"Because it can lead the Wheeling people to us." Mom slammed her door shut and got the car going. "How do you know that man isn't a Wheeling spy?"

"I don't. But who cares? It's got to get out there what's going on."

"More likely, there's someone from Wheeling working on the point of sale devices ready to shut that very suggestion down."

"It will still get out there." I glared out the front window. "The one thing Wheeling is counting on is that it's going to take time to figure everything out."

"After we get the fix installed. We don't need anybody at Wheeling alerted that somebody is on to them." She sent a quick glare my way. "I don't understand. You know better than that."

I could feel the anger swelling up in me. "Don't treat me like a little kid. I am an adult and I got there without your help."

Mom swallowed. "I didn't—"

"I don't care!" I shrieked. "I don't give a flying fuck whose fault it was or wasn't. I grew up without my mother. I grew up wondering if she was alive, and if she was, why didn't she care enough about me to come get me? It doesn't matter what you were trying to do. I got screwed, and it hurts, and I'm tired of being hurt. I'm tired of it!"

"Do you want out of this?" Mom asked softly.

"Yes. No." I kept crying. "I'm stuck, no matter what. Given what happened with Dad."

"I'm sorry I got you into this."

"Brent got me into this."

There was an extended pause, then Mom opened her mouth and closed it.

"What?" I grumbled.

"Jannie, I know it doesn't help much now, but I am sorry." She swallowed as she kept her eyes riveted on the road ahead of us. "There was never a day I didn't think about you."

"You're right." I stared straight ahead as well. "It doesn't help."

God, I felt like an utter shit. But that's the problem with my kind of hurt. Sometimes it strikes out when it shouldn't. I didn't want to hurt my mom. I finally had her back. Still, with all the crap that had happened and my ongoing feelings of abandonment and whatever, I struck out anyway. It did not make me feel any better, and that just made me feel worse.

The problem was, we'd both been robbed, me when I'd been left to deal with my abusive father, her when she'd been lied to by someone who was supposed to be protecting both of us. That we were both reeling from the hurt was no surprise. Somehow, Mom seemed to be dealing with it better. Although, when I woke up in the middle of the night, I heard crying in the bathroom next to me, and felt even worse when I couldn't go in to her.

Mom insisted we break into Wheeling that Monday, late in the afternoon. She didn't say anything about what I'd told the guy at SpotCo. I still thought I was right about telling him what I had. At the same time, Mom had a point about possibly alerting the schmucks at Wheeling.

We didn't say much on the way over to the Wheeling campus. It was a huge, flat building of rough, dark brown brick, with several spots grown over with bougainvillea. There were about five or six parking lots, all filled with SUVs and cars, interspersed with dark-green lawn and willow trees. It was a little after four when we pulled up to the open guard station and were waved through thanks to the Wheeling parking sticker. We found a space at the edge of the biggest lot, and parked under the branches of the nearby willow tree. We split up from there. I had the laptop for the special server.

My heart was pounding as I walked in and bumped my I.D. card on the door reader. I probably could have just slid in. People were slowly starting to make their way out of the building, and no one paid me the least bit of attention. Wheeling Corporation wasn't massively huge, just big enough that no one was going to think anything of it if they saw someone they didn't recognize.

It took me a minute to orient myself, but both Tanya's and Mom's directions were pretty clear and I don't get lost easily, anyway. The cubicles were mostly full as I made my way to the staircase leading to the server farm, although there was that restless movement that meant it was close to quitting time. We had to be in and out of there relatively quickly. The idea was to leave between five and five-thirty, when the larger part of the employees would be leaving, as well.

The staircase led to a long hall with a windowed room on one side. Inside, the servers blinked as they sat on tall racks set up in rows along the one side.

I found Mom already hooked up to the main servers and installing the first modem. I nodded at her and went to work hooking up the laptop I had to the special server. It was easy to spot. It was at the end of a row, up against the wall, and on a rack that wasn't nearly as tall as the other servers were. I got in easily enough, but uploading the fix was going to take a few minutes. In the meantime, I found a corner at the back of the faceless machine and installed the second modem. Lights blinked, and my phone vibrated. Tanya texted a thumbs up, then texted a second one.

"We're live," I whispered to Mom.

"Are you ready to go?" she asked.

I looked at the laptop. "Just another minute."

Mom cursed under her breath. It took longer than a minute and felt like an hour. But soon the pop-up window on my laptop said that the files had been copied, and another half minute later, Tanya texted another thumbs up.

"Done," I told Mom.

She nodded and pressed a couple of buttons on her laptop. As she pulled the cables free, an alarm sounded.

"I was hoping we'd have more time," she grumbled. "Come on."

We ran like hell for the second staircase. Mom pushed me into the stairwell as men in dark suits rushed into the hallway from the staircase I'd come down. I ran hard upstairs, and straight into pandemonium, as workers jumped up and looked around, some rushing along the pathways around the cubicles.

"Act like everyone else," Mom said as she hurried me to the front of the building.

She suddenly pulled me back into a cubicle and we ducked behind a desk. The men in dark suits were everywhere.

"We're surrounded," I gasped.

"I know." Mom's hand gently grasped my chin. "I'm going to divert them. You walk calmly out to the car and get the hell out. Do you understand?"

"Mom?" I blinked back tears.

"Do as I say. Please." Her eyes filled as she handed me her keys. "And remember that I love you. I always have and I always will."

"Mom…"

She was off and running toward the nearest exit. The dark suits followed and as soon as they were clear, I slowly got up and walked out of the building.

I got to the car unmolested, but did not start the engine right away. I was too shaken, and I was hoping, praying that Mom would show up any second. But then there was little else I could do. I had to get out of there with everyone else leaving for the day.

The gate to the parking lot finally opened, and the guards began waving everyone through. They didn't look twice at me as I went past. I didn't know for sure why, but had a bad feeling I knew.

I somehow got back to the hotel in San Pedro. Tanya and Arturo were waiting for me.

"At least you made it back," said Tanya, trying not to cry.

"She could have gotten away," I said, sniffing. "Somehow, she could have escaped."

Tanya shook her head. "They posted the alert on the security office bulletin board. They got her."

CHAPTER FOURTEEN

W e knew what our next steps were. The special server hooked up to the point of sale devices had all its access codes switched around by the fix, so it was going to take the Wheeling people some time to re-image the server, and reinstall the program and data, and that was assuming they'd find the modem we'd hooked up. If they didn't find the modem, then they were going to be in a world of hurt because we'd be able to reverse anything they tried and switch the access codes again.

Mom had deleted the file that had the final bit of code for the secondary virus, and had written over the file addresses with a mini-virus that would create enough of a nuisance that Goode's software guys were going to be darned busy fixing all the bugs, especially once they installed themselves on the backup servers.

Tanya and Arturo had already remotely erased the phone Mom had been carrying. I took over monitoring the Wheeling servers while Arturo searched the servers, looking for any piece of the secondary virus that he could find. Tanya started analyzing the bits we did have. Around eight, Tanya had to leave the hotel to get some food for us. She brought back a huge sack of In 'N Out burgers and fries, and a tray of shakes. I wanted to get shit-faced again, but knew that wouldn't help.

It was coming on for midnight when she blinked and turned off the television, which had again been set up as a monitor. Arturo dozed over the two laptops he'd set up on the dining room table.

"That's it," Tanya announced. "It's time for bed."

"No," I said. "I'll keep working."

"Jannie, you gotta get some sleep, girl."

My voice caught. "I'm not gonna sleep."

"You gotta try." Tanya sat down next to me on the couch and put her arms around me.

"Trying won't help."

"What happened there?"

"They got her. You know that."

Tanya laid her head on my shoulder. "What happened?"

"She gave herself up for me." The tears rolled down my cheeks. "She told me she loved me, then ran off, drawing the security guys after her. And I was such a bitch to her yesterday. I yelled at her. I couldn't help it. I was just so tired of being hurt and then she goes and does this."

"She's your mother. Of course she would," Tanya whispered.

I tried to imagine my grandmother doing the same. Or my father.

"Not in my family. Only she did."

Tanya squeezed my shoulders. "That's why you need to get some rest. We're not going to be able to find her and get her out of there if you're a zombie from lack of sleep. Now, I've got a couple Benadryls to help you along."

"Shit!" Arturo yelped. "Look at this."

We hurried over to the dining table.

"It's Beefsteak," he said, pointing at one of the screens. "That lousy fuck just posted this."

"I thought he went underground," I said, leaning over him so that I could see.

"He did," said Tanya.

But there he was, or at least, someone who had signed into the forum on his account.

"Big upset at Wheeling with bad actors trying to break into their computers," the post said. "Wheeling's top exec says they have the person responsible. That's some bad luck."

"What the hell?" I asked and shut my eyes. "Oh, fuck. I just remembered. Timon of Athens found out who Beefsteak is." I glanced at the others and shut my eyes. "You don't want to know."

"As much as I'd like to beat the shit out of him, why do we care about Beefsteak?" Tanya asked.

I frowned. "I don't know that we do. But I don't know that we don't care, either. I'd better see what Timon knows."

Yeah, it was after midnight, but Alphonse Littlejohn, aka Timon of Athens, responded to my text almost immediately with a phone call.

"You saw the post from Beefsteak?" he asked.

"Yeah."

"We need to talk, but I don't want to talk on the phone. Can you get to my crypt?"

"Sure."

He hung up. A second later, a text message buzzed on my phone with a link to Alphonse's personal server. I only had a few minutes to enter the password, that only I knew, to find the message buried in the files. Anyone else trying to break the password would need some time to do it, so that was about as safe a way as any for Alphonse/Timon to leave me a message, then get it erased and overwritten.

Fortunately, I also knew where to look for the file, which was encrypted, but again, I had the password for it. I'd needed it back when I was trying to save his ass from the F.B.I.

I wrote down the details on the meeting, which would be late the next morning at a coffee shop in Inglewood. Then I cleared the phone browser cache.

Tanya looked at me in awe. "You got a meeting with Timon of Athens? Face to face?"

"Yeah. I've known him a long time."

"That dude doesn't trust nobody."

"I know." I blinked my eyes. "He's got good reason not to. It's a long story. Anyway, you're right. We should probably get to bed."

I took the two antihistamine tablets that Tanya gave me, and I slept for a little while. But when I woke up at seven, I couldn't get back to sleep, nor could I banish the image of my mother running away through the cubicles at Wheeling. I went back to work, monitoring the Wheeling computers while munching on some stale bagels. At least the coffee was good. Mom had, of course, bought premium beans and had kept them in the freezer, and there was a coffee grinder to go with the drip coffee maker.

It was almost eight when I saw an email go out from the security office. I opened it and read that the Wheeling servers had not been breached and that the person seen fleeing was, in fact, an employee who had been doing some unscheduled maintenance, and had tripped the alarm by accident.

Well, that was bullshit. But as I looked at the email, I wondered why the Wheeling people were pretending that nothing had happened, then realized they probably didn't want the F.B.I. or other law enforcement coming around. Then I also wondered about Beefsteak's post. Had it already gotten around on the forums that Wheeling had been breached? I scanned a couple of them and didn't see anything. The comments on Beefsteak's post seemed to indicate that no one had been aware of the breach. Now Wheeling was saying that it hadn't happened.

I had been considering blowing off my meeting with Alphonse, but suddenly I decided that I really needed to be talking to him. Tanya was just getting up when I pulled my stuff together. I gave her the keys to Mom's car.

"I don't want you guys with no way to get out of here quickly if things go to hell," I said. "I'm taking the airport shuttle, then the bus to the meeting. Okay?"

"I suppose." Tanya shrugged. "We should probably stay together as much as possible. Why don't you text me when you're done? We'll set up a meeting place and Arturo and I will come get you."

"Good enough." I reached over and hugged her. "Thank you for everything, Tanya. You've been a real rock."

"So have you, Jannie." She squeezed me tightly. "We'll come out ahead. Somehow."

I nodded, then hurried out. I got to the coffee shop right on time, but was not surprised when Alphonse showed up fifteen minutes late. He was a tall, Black man, with light-colored skin and a round belly. He wore baggy kelly green cargo pants with a grungy plaid shirt over a dark blue t-shirt that proclaimed, "There are 10 types of people. Those who understand binary and those who don't." A blue Dodgers cap covered his head. The only thing Alphonse loved more than code was his beloved Dodgers. The guy was also a walking encyclopedia and had been banned from several bars in the area for not just beating everyone, but leaving them in the dust during trivia contests.

He came right over to the table I'd gotten at the back of the restaurant where I could see the front window and the door. It was a small place with formica table tops, cracked vinyl seats and no White people except me. Alphonse sat down so that he could see the door and the front window, as well. We didn't say much, waiting to order our breakfasts, then for them to arrive.

"I hear you know who Beefsteak is," I said softly, after getting a bite of corned beef hash and scrambled eggs.

He nodded and slurped at some oatmeal. "He's Jackson Goode."

"What? Why was he cheering Manny on?" But as I said it, I realized the night before's post and Wheeling's pretend email almost made sense.

"I don't know. That F.B.I. guy, Brent Mikkelsen? He and I were trying to set up a sting on Beefsteak."

"Oh, shit. Were you emailing Brent about this sting?"

"Nope. Face to face. Like now."

"Good." I pressed my lips together. Brent must have emailed his boss about the meeting with Leon.

Alphonse looked at me. "Beefsteak was the one who set me up with that code thing. I don't know how Jackson Goode is connected to Wheeling, but he's got some in."

I sighed. "Actually, I know what the connection is."

"Did Leon know?"

"I'm afraid so. But that's not what got him killed. At least, I don't think it was. Have you talked to Brent since then?"

Alphonse blew out his breath. "No fucking way." He winced. "He was the only one I told that I was meeting Leon, and I know Leon didn't say anything." Alphonse blinked, then stared at his bowl. "Leon told me not to say anything to anyone about the meeting. The only reason I told Mikkelsen was that I was scared for Leon. I knew he had something going on with Manny Rios."

"Brent got compromised." I turned back to my plate. "It wasn't his fault."

"So, do I trust him now?"

"Hell, no." I looked at Alphonse, then made a face. "It's not that you can't trust him. I just don't trust Goode and anybody connected to Wheeling right now. I barely trust you."

"I got that." Alphonse smiled weakly.

"I really appreciate you coming out to meet me. Why don't you keep up trying to set up your sting on Goode? Frankly, the more distractions he has, the better. Just keep your distance."

"How do you know so much about this?"

I hesitated. "I'm on the team that's bringing down Wheeling. Only we're not trying to bring them down. We're trying to prevent something much worse."

Alphonse's forehead creased. "This have anything to do with the trouble SpotCo's having?"

"Why do you ask?"

"That puzzle I was supposed to crack? It was how to get into a highly secured system and set things up so that no one could change anything except Beefsteak. He told me he was having trouble with his insurance company changing his medical records so they wouldn't have to pay up. That's why I did it. He told me he'd set up a seed virus that worked with a magnetic stripe reader that would let my code into the system. Only since the SpotCo people started having trouble with their point of sale thingies, it occurred to me that they have magnetic stripe readers."

"And if you set it up so that no one can change a bank account record, then you can control who can buy stuff and who can't. And where they buy it." I groaned. "Alphonse, I'd take you with me, but I do not want to risk your neck. You know what happened to Leon. It's connected to what Wheeling's really up to." I bit my lip. "But I'm going to have to let a friend of mine into your crypt. Umm. Call them T-Rex. We need to see that code you wrote. With what you know, we should be able to fix this in no time."

"We can but hope."

I paid for breakfast with cash, telling Alphonse it would not be a bad idea to get as much of his as he could.

I left the coffee shop and grabbed a northbound bus, texting Tanya that I'd get back to her location on my own. Yeah, I'd been feeling pretty paranoid even before I'd talked to Alphonse. But since then, that icky feeling of some evil presence lurking over my shoulder had grown tenfold.

If Beefsteak was Jackson Goode, why had he outed Manny before killing him? It would have been much easier for Goode to kill Manny outright rather than tweak the hacking community. Unless he wanted to tweak the hacking community. Or maybe he just wanted to scare them - and lord knows, we were scared. But scared doesn't always last. As I have noted earlier, scared often becomes pissed, and that can overcome a lot of fear. Then I sighed. It can also make you do some pretty stupid shit, and I'd been proving that one a lot recently.

Tanya and Arturo were shocked about Beefsteak's real identity, but thrilled that Timon of Athens had some insight into the secondary virus.

"Yeah, well, don't get too excited," I growled at both of them. "If Goode was onto Manny, what else is he onto? How much does he know about us?"

"We've done everything we could," said Tanya.

Arturo gulped. "That doesn't mean he doesn't have some way of tracking us."

"He hasn't caught us yet," Tanya pointed out.

"But why?" Arturo asked. "Okay, the guy is a megalomaniac, but he's not stupid. He's got to have some sort of backup to that special server, and there's no reason to believe that his people won't find that modem or find a way around the access code changes Leon set up."

"They haven't so far," Tanya laughed. "From the emails I've seen, they're peeing their pants trying to figure out how to get it back up and running."

"And they caught Mom," I said darkly, my gut twisting at the thought.

I had no reason to believe that they'd been able to torture her into revealing secrets. There was something Mom had said about working for the NSA that led me to believe that she might have some way of avoiding that. But I could see no reason to keep her alive, either. I sank into a dining room chair, trying to catch my breath.

Tanya came over and put her arm around my shoulders.

"Hey," she said quietly. "We don't know that she's gone. We just have to believe that she's still with us, okay?"

"What good is that going to do?"

"It will keep us going."

I wiped my eyes. "There's that, I suppose."

Arturo snorted. "And we still have to stop these bastards, not only for Manny, but maybe for your mom, too." He grunted. "I would just love to call Jackson Goode out and tell him to his face what a bastard he is."

"That's what we need to do." Tanya grinned.

"What?" I gaped at her.

"We need to talk to Goode." Tanya thought.

"That'd be suicide," Arturo yelped.

Tanya shrugged. "Well, maybe not directly. But what about Agent Mikkelsen? Jannie keeps saying he's honest."

"He is," I said firmly. I don't know why I felt such a compulsion to defend him, but I did.

"And you know how to get a hold of him, don't you, Jannie?" Tanya folded her arms across her chest.

"His office is compromised," I said.

"But he can still ask questions." Tanya began pacing. "He can get in and talk to Goode in a way none of us can. And I'll bet you have a way to talk to him without going through his office."

I nodded slowly.

"It does seem like our best shot at finding something out," Arturo said.

I shook my head. "Maybe. But what are the odds Goode is going to let anything significant drop? He's not stupid."

"If he's Beefsteak, he likes tweaking people," Arturo said grimly. "Why do you think he posted about Manny?"

I shut my eyes. I wasn't surprised that Arturo had picked that part up.

"All right." I switched on my personal laptop and went to the forum I'd told Brent about, trying to think of the most secure way to get to him.

For once, things seemed to be breaking our way. Early that morning, a GemstoneMan had posted looking for the best way to flash a ROM onto his great aunt's older phone. I used the direct message option to send him my phone number. My heart froze when the phone rang ten minutes later.

"It's me," said Brent's voice.

"I told you not to use your work computer."

"I'm not even in the office." He sighed. "I bought a cheap laptop and am hiding at the UCLA Library for the time being. I'm assuming you saw Beefsteak's post."

"Yeah. And we know who he really is." I sighed. "He's Jackson Goode."

"Who?"

"Jackson Goode." I tried to keep the disdain out of my voice. "The guy who owns Mrs. Goode's Marketplace."

"I got that." Brent sounded utterly exhausted. "What the hell did you and your friends do?"

"You don't want to know."

"Damn skippy, I don't. Just don't do it again."

I took a deep breath. "Look. Can you talk to Jackson Goode? I mean, you've got an excuse to interview him. Call it an anonymous tip that you have to follow up on."

"He's not going to tell me anything. He's no fool."

"That's never stopped you from questioning someone. You've said it yourself. You never know what hint you're going to pick up."

He sighed deeply. "You're right. By the way, I've got an I.D. on that stiff from the coffee place. His name is Earl Johnson."

"That's the guy that was following me." I stopped. "Dad was paying him. Then he was on the spot when Abe was killed. Probably doing the lookout thing."

"Lookout. Why?" Brent asked.

"To be sure they got me, maybe." I bit my thumbnail. "And to be sure that I found Abe. We think that Wheeling initially wanted me to lead them to Tanya, but then I disappeared, and now they're out to kill me."

Brent cursed a blue streak. "But how did they get a hold of you? And why your dad?"

"You hired me," I said, then groaned after Brent. "You couldn't have known. You know what you said about Wheeling collecting personal information? Well, we found one of Wheeling's sites that had all this personal information on it, including mine and the fact that they'd been looking at me for years."

"Shit," Brent groaned.

"Yeah, but they also linked me to Dad and his creative accounting. Apparently, Wheeling decided they could exploit him and I've got the financials that show Dad hired Johnson, and he did it right after you hired me."

"It's an interesting point." Brent swallowed as if he was clearing his mind. "As for Johnson, he had a gun on him that looks like it's the one that killed Leon."

"You mean he was the guy on the bus." I pressed my lips. "That makes sense. He didn't ditch it."

"You're obsessing on that."

"It's the assassin's pattern, Brent. He ditched the guns when Manny and Abe got shot. He ditched the car at the airport. He ditched the gun again at the coffee shop. Patterns are how I find people. Remember?"

"Fine."

"Yeah, but why hire a second assassin?"

"The other one was busy. Or maybe he's just gotten too visible. Listen. If I'm going to tackle Goode, I'd better jump on it. I'll talk to you tomorrow."

As he hung up, it dawned on me that he hadn't asked if there was anything we thought he should be looking for. I debated calling him back, but my nerves were so shot that I didn't think I'd be able to call him on it and stay calm enough to get through to him. Assuming I could get through to him.

I set Tanya up to get into Alphonse's server and encrypted files, then took the car to get some tacos from a nearby restaurant for dinner. Okay, I got a salad for myself, for all the good it did. I picked at it as I went back to monitoring Wheeling's servers.

I looked for any hint, even the least suggestion that would lead me to what had happened to my mother, or even where she was. I pored over pattern after pattern. Or, rather, I tried to. I couldn't concentrate worth beans. All I saw in my head was Mom telling me that she loved me, that she always had and always would.

Nobody had ever said anything like that to me, at least, not in any meaningful way. My father had never said that he loved me. My grandma said it all the time, but usually as part of some criticism, as in, "I love you, that's why I'm nailing you." It usually felt as if she was saying what she was expected to say, not what she actually felt.

It's not as though I thought that my father and grandmother didn't love me. In fact, I was pretty sure that they did. But they couldn't express it, not in any way that made me feel warm and safe. Only my mom had been able to make me feel that way.

And now, even missing again, even though I'd treated her so badly, she'd made me feel that way once more.

Chapter Fifteen

I t was a fucking miracle that we survived the next morning. The night before, Tanya and Arturo pressured me into agreeing to move someplace else. I wanted to stay in case Mom escaped. They insisted that Mom would find a way to contact us. Gee, just like I had when I'd gotten separated from the group.

In between monitoring the Wheeling servers, we'd taken turns gathering the drying underwear from the shower curtain rods, wrapping cables, and consolidating our seven laptops, phones, and other devices, pulling together what groceries we still had. We were still traveling pretty lightly, so once we'd gotten up that morning and dressed, Arturo was able to take most of our stuff down to Mom's car in one load. That left Tanya and me behind to do a sweep of the room to be sure we hadn't left anything behind, identifying, incriminating, or otherwise.

As we were shutting the door to the room, Arturo texted Tanya.

"Shit," Tanya gasped.

"What?"

"Arturo says there's a man in a mask and cowboy hat at the front desk, and it looks like he's carrying a gun in his back waistband."

I felt my heart stop. "Could be anyone. On the other hand, I don't want to chance it."

We ran for the stairwell, then slid down the stairs as quietly as we could. The stairs opened into the elevator bay, which was a hallway with four elevators, two on each facing wall. Fortunately, the door to the stairwell was on the side of the bay closest to the hotel lobby. Unfortunately, the guy in the cowboy hat was in the elevator bay. He sure looked like the guy that had chased me down at the bank in Glendale. We waited for the elevator to ding, then I peeked out of the stairwell door. The elevator bay was empty.

I nodded at Tanya and we both slid out of the stairwell. I checked the lobby just in case. Nobody with any hat at all was in there. Tanya started to run, but I held her back.

"Just act normal," I said, walking between the sofas and chairs scattered about in front of the check-in desk.

"Like that's possible," Tanya grumbled.

The car was parked on the far side of the parking lot. I could see Arturo waiting at the driver's side. We were almost there, when his eyes opened wide and he dove for the ground. At least four shots cracked through the air, almost drowned out by the sound of glass shattering and a car alarm going off. My left shoulder burned as I fell face-forward. Tanya crawled between the parked cars to the top of the row.

I rolled over. I was between two cars, but it was in the row across from the one where Mom's car was parked.

Worse yet, the assassin was running up the lane between the rows, checking between the cars. I managed to sit up and got my taser out of my bag. The assassin leaned over the back end of a small sedan, his pale blue eyes glittering.

The next thing I knew, a puff of white powder burst over his chest and he reeled back, coughing and gasping. The pepper spray, although I didn't know if it was Tanya or Arturo who had pulled the trigger on the air pistol. I coughed, too, but wasn't immobilized. With the last bit of adrenaline in my veins, I pulled myself to my feet and hauled ass to Mom's car.

Tanya and Arturo were already inside, and Arturo had the engine running. I'd barely shut the door to the back seat when Arturo peeled out of the space and gunned the car down the lane toward the assassin. He was still bent over, but as we turned to get out of the lot, the assassin got himself erect and the car thunked twice as the bullets hit the side. Arturo stepped on the gas.

"Where the fuck do we go now?" Tanya gasped.

"How the fuck did he find us?" I cried.

Arturo glanced at me in the rearview. "Shit!"

"What? He's following us?" I gasped.

"No. You're bleeding."

Suddenly, my shoulder didn't just burn, it screamed. I gasped and cried with the pain.

"We gotta take her to the hospital," Tanya yelped.

"That's a bullet hole," Arturo yelled. "We can't."

"I'm fine," I somehow gasped. "I mean, it hurts like hell, but I'm fine."

I was, too, not light-headed or anything. I fumbled with my phone one-handed and dialed Brent's burner phone. He picked up in two rings.

"Where are you?" I demanded.

"Working, as usual." He sounded casual, but not quite.

"I need a safe meet-up spot and a first aid kit, stat."

"Sure. I'll call you back in about ten minutes."

I figured he was in his office and didn't want to say so. I was glad he'd gotten that much through his thick skull. At a stoplight, Tanya reached over the front passenger seat and helped me get my T-shirt off.

"Looks like it's just a bad scrape," she told me, wadding up the shirt and putting it on my shoulder. "Use this like a pressure bandage."

It stung like hell, but I held the shirt down. Tanya flopped back into the front seat and buckled up as Arturo got the car going again. Lacking anything better to do, we got onto the 110 North toward Downtown L.A. Brent called back within five. I fumbled the phone on with my left hand since my right hand was still holding the shirt on my left shoulder.

"What the hell?" Brent asked.

"Nevermind that," I said, my voice cracking. "Where? We need to be discreet. I've got a hole in my shoulder."

"Fucking hell! What have you been doing?"

"Where the fuck do we go?"

"There's a safe house in Hermosa Beach."

I muted the phone. "Arturo, Century Freeway, West."

Tires squealed as Arturo pulled a fast lane change to get onto the interchange between the 110 and 105 freeways.

I unmuted the phone. "Alright. What's the address and how do I get there?"

"I'll text it to you."

"No! I'm not using Maps."

Brent cursed under his breath, but gave me the address and the directions. I repeated it all back, watching as Tanya typed it into her phone, her two thumbs flying.

"Now, what the hell is going on?" Brent demanded.

"I'll tell you when we get there."

"Tell me who 'we' is."

"Not now. Goodbye."

I swiped the call off. I shut my eyes against the burning in my shoulder, but kept the t-shirt squeezed against it.

The safe house was in a block of condos three streets in from the beach and at the top of a slope. The buildings were all narrow and three stories high, although the exteriors varied. The condo we needed was deep steel blue clapboard with white trim. The garage door was open as we pulled up and I saw Brent's car inside. Brent also waited in the driveway. He waved Arturo into the garage, then as the car stopped, went over to the passenger side where the bullet holes were.

His face paled as he touched them, then wrenched the door open.

"What the fuck!"

"Feeling a little exposed here," I sniffed. "Can we talk inside?"

"I'll bring everything in," said Arturo.

"I'll help," Tanya said.

Brent all but pulled me out of the car, breathing heavily, as if he were both trying to be calming and trying not to break my neck.

The first floor had a wide open living room on polished dark wood floors, with a kitchen and eating area to the side, and it all looked like the guys at Ikea had designed it for a catalog shoot. Brent got me sat down in a chair next to the black lacquered dining table and pulled a red plastic box toward him. I gasped as he gently removed the t-shirt from the top of my shoulder.

"You got winged, alright," he grumbled. "But it didn't go deep, and it looks like it's stopped bleeding already." He pulled a white tube from the red plastic box. "This is going to sting like hell. I'm sorry about that, but we don't want an infection."

"No," I said sourly. "I don't."

Brent glared briefly, then went back to cutting gauze and getting me bandaged. Tanya and Arturo came in with everything we'd had in the car and piled it on the navy blue sofa. Brent cleaned the gauze and tape up, shut the red box, then sank into a chair next to me.

"Now, you need to tell me what the hell is going on here." He glared, but it was more out of worry than anger.

"Wheeling's assassin found us," I told him, blinking back tears. "How the hell did that happen? Did you talk to Goode?"

"I questioned him yesterday."

"What did you say to him?"

Brent got up and started pacing. "What the fuck does it matter?"

"Let's see. I almost got killed today by one of their flunkies at a hotel he shouldn't have known about."

Brent turned on me. "And why the hell were you there in the first place? Why can't you just do as I tell you?"

"Somebody's going up on 'Am I the Asshole,'" Tanya said, referring to the Reddit thread.

Brent turned away and gaped. "Who are you two?" His eyes narrowed. "Never mind. Go upstairs and get settled."

Tanya and Arturo looked at me, and I nodded. They grabbed the luggage and scrambled upstairs. Brent looked back at me.

"Well?" He held his hands out.

"What did you ask Goode about?"

"Beefsteak's post." Brent went back to pacing. "I told him that we'd gotten a tip that he might know what was going on at Wheeling, and he said he didn't know that anything was. So, I asked him if he'd heard of Leon Cortez. Surprise, he hadn't. Then I asked about Virginia Tiklow."

My heart stopped. "Why her?"

"She's a friend of Leon's. A couple months ago, Leon told me that if I ran across her, I was to trust her. You wanted to know who Wheeling has."

"I know who he has!" I screamed. "You idiot! You goddamn fucking idiot!"

"Don't scream at me like that."

I got up and advanced on him. "I damn well can. You couldn't ask what I was looking for. You couldn't ask whether it was a good idea or even safe to bring up those names. Which is why I nearly got fucking killed today."

"I didn't have to ask."

"Yes. You. Did. Because you didn't ask, you told Jackson Goode, the guy who's probably paying that assassin, exactly how to find us."

"I did not."

"He had her name and hacked her credit card and saw the hold on it from the hotel, then sent his assassin after us. It's the only way he could have known where we were." I strode around the room. "You and your fucking allergy to asking. You'd think a guy whose career is based on questioning people would be better about that. But, no. You have to be in control all the time."

"Asking is not about control."

"Bullshit. Control is exactly what it's about. When you ask, you give me the power to say no, to not tell you what you need to know, to make the decision. And that's the problem, Brent. When you assume you know what's going on and don't ask, you rob me of the chance to make choices, too. That's why it's so goddamned fatal when you do that. And today, it damned near got literally fatal."

"And every time I do ask, you throw up a wall. You don't let me near you, Jannie. You say I assume, and maybe I do, but you know what? You assume, too. You assume the absolute worst in me. Do you know what that feels like? Just because you got abandoned as a kid—"

"Don't go there!"

"Fuck that. You don't trust anyone, and you sure as hell don't give me a chance."

"I give you plenty of chances. And when was the last time you actually asked me anything?"

"When I got you into this. I asked you if you were busy that night."

"But you didn't ask if I wanted to go out."

"I didn't get a chance to. You got all over my ass about the rules."

"I'm not the bad guy here."

"No, you're not. But you're not helping, either." He put his hands up. "There's fault on both sides. You're right. I should have asked about what you wanted from Goode and why he'd be up on what Wheeling is doing. That's my fault. I acknowledge it and I'm sorry. Fat lot of good it does now, but I am."

I sank onto the couch, sobbing. All I could think of was my mother saying the same thing.

"Jannie, I'm not going to abandon you."

"But you try to control me."

He sighed. "I guess, maybe. But when are you going to give me a chance to get over it?"

"It's not that." I shook my head. "I know that you're trying."

"I am. But it's really hard when you run like a bat out of hell at the least hint that I'm controlling you."

"No, Brent. You don't understand. I mean, in a lot of ways, you do." I shook my head to clear it. "Your family is just as fucked up as mine. They're all so angry and defensive. That's why you can't ask, you know. They can't, either. Your mom plays the martyr. Your dad sulks, then explodes. Just like mine. But that's the problem. We let being angry drive us. That's what I did the other day. I was angry at my mom because she wasn't there and I ended up hurting her. But you know what? She gave herself up for me at Wheeling. After she told me how much she loved me. She gave herself up so that I could get out of there." I looked up at him. "We gotta stop being angry."

He closed his eyes and looked away. "It's not that simple, you know."

"Believe me, I know."

He blew out his breath. "This isn't getting us anywhere. And I've got a case to concentrate on. Wait." He turned and stared at me. "You said something about Wheeling and your mom giving herself up for you?"

I sank onto the couch. "Virginia Tiklow is my mother. That's the name she was using when she checked us into the hotel."

"Your mom is dead."

"Uh, no. She survived the tornado."

"And disappeared." Brent looked at me softly. "That's why you're so into finding people."

"No shit."

"How is she connected to this thing with Wheeling?"

"She's part of the team. She found out that you'd put me onto finding Tanya and decided she'd better put me off. Only I ended up joining the team, too. A day or two after Abe…" I choked. "It's a good thing I went with her. They were coming for me already."

"Yeah. Lee Conroy, it looks like."

"Conroy?"

Brent nodded. "Yeah. I did a search on his MO of dropping the gun. He and three others popped up. But he was the only one with suspected ties to one of the executives at Mrs. Goode's Marketplace." Brent studied me. "So, why would Goode go after you?"

"I'm not absolutely sure." I looked away and blinked. "I mean, initially we thought they were hoping I'd lead them to Tanya."

"Yeah. That text you got."

"Only my father sicced Johnson and his pal on me the day you hired me to find Tanya."

"You told me that, too. So we know that Wheeling didn't want you doing anything but leading them to Tanya Coleman, and had your dad hire Johnson to make it look good. But why they would go to that kind of trouble, I don't get."

"The best I can figure is that they didn't want me getting too close to what's really going on at Wheeling. Shooting Abe, then sending me that scary, taunting text message. It's

Goode's pattern with a hey nonny, and from what I can tell, Goode really knows how to scare people."

"So, what does Jackson Goode have to do with Wheeling Corporation? And what does that have to do with Wheeling suckering in kids to write viruses for them?"

"Oh, my." I couldn't help a sour laugh. "Goode owns Wheeling, and it's not just about suckering in kids to write viruses. It's the virus those kids are supposed to be writing." I got up. "Let me get the others. We need to talk this all out."

Brent put his hand on my good arm. "The others. I probably don't want to know, but that's Tanya Coleman up there, isn't it?"

"And Arturo Rios." I sighed. "There may have been some less than legal activity going on, so I don't know how much you want to know."

"Shit. I've got to be careful with that." Brent's sigh was profound. "But being in the dark hasn't helped."

"You're right."

He shrugged. "We'll figure something out."

I went upstairs and asked Tanya and Arturo to come down. Only Tanya held me back.

"We've got a massive problem," she said, pointing to the laptop. "The F.B.I. has put out some big bulletin that I'm wanted for embezzling a whole bunch of money from Wheeling Corporation."

I grabbed the laptop and headed downstairs. "Brent!"

"What?"

I set the laptop on the dining room table. "What the fuck is this?"

"Crap!" Brent looked up at me as Tanya and Arturo came downstairs. "Just so you know, I did not initiate this."

"I didn't embezzle, neither." Tanya added.

Brent looked at the three of us. "But I'm willing to bet you three hacked Wheeling's computer system."

"Not saying nothing," Tanya said quickly as Arturo and I looked guilty. "I'll give you access to my bank accounts. You'll see there's no extra money there."

Brent rolled his eyes. "BFD. I do not necessarily want to know what you three have been doing. In fact, it may be better if I don't know. The only problem is that if I don't know what you guys are up to, it's going to be a lot harder to protect you and build a case against Wheeling."

"Or Jackson Goode," I said.

"Or Goode." Brent sighed, then paced around the living room. "Damn, I've been wanting to nail these Wheeling fucks."

"We'll find a way to do it legally," I said. "The more important question is why did they decide to go after Tanya like this now? The only thing I can think of is that they're trying to distract everyone from the critical issue of them writing viruses destined to fuck up the economy."

"Are you shitting me?" Brent glared at me.

I shook my head. "The SpotCo thing. We isolated the virus and installed a fix on the Wheeling server dedicated to it. That doesn't mean they won't find a way around our fix."

"But it explains why SpotCo's point of sale devices are working again," Brent said.

Tanya's eyes lit up. "They are? Hot diggety."

"Except that you're wanted by the F.B.I.," I grumbled.

Brent picked up the cordless phone installed on the kitchen counter. I glared at him, but he put his finger to his lips and dialed, then put the call on speaker.

"Thompkins," growled a female voice on the other end.

"Elaine, it's Brent." He smiled at me. "I just saw the wanted notice on Coleman. When did you put that out?"

"What wanted notice? Hold on." The clicking of computer keys came through the speaker. "Son of a bitch. I didn't put this out."

Brent glanced over at us. "Can you do me a favor and find out what the idiots who did have on Coleman? I know for a fact that she hasn't set foot on the Wheeling campus since the Manny Rios killing."

"Do you know where she is?"

Brent looked at me and Tanya. "I can't say. I'm pretty sure she's being set up."

Thompkins snorted. "You got evidence?"

"Okay, it's just my gut feeling right now. Any way we can keep from acting on it?"

"I don't know, Brent. You're asking for trouble here."

"I know." Brent's lips took on an odd sort of smile. "I appreciate it, Elaine."

He hung up the phone. I took a deep breath as Tanya played with the laptop on the dining room table.

"I'm trying not to sound strident here," I said as calmly as I could. "But what the fuck are you doing?"

"Thompkins is the supervisor over McCaffrey, then me." Brent almost grinned. "As you have pointed out, the office is compromised. Now, whoever is listening in on us thinks I'm playing games, not to mention in the doghouse and less effective."

"Shit!" Tanya screamed and pointed at the laptop. "Those fucks! Look at this."

Tanya had pulled up her bank records, and, surprise, surprise, there was over a million in her account.

Chapter Sixteen

T anya was hyper-ventilating and began pacing furiously around the dining room table.

"They're out to get me! They're gonna fuck me! I'll never be able to go home!"

Arturo grabbed her and held her close.

"Hold on," I put my hand on Tanya's back. "This is my department."

I took over the laptop and within maybe an hour, I'd traced the deposits into Tanya's accounts, and it was pretty obvious she hadn't generated them.

"The money's from Wheeling, alright," I said. I ran the cursor around the screen and clicked. "But not from an account owned by Wheeling."

"What?" Puzzled, Brent looked over my shoulder.

I pointed to the account information I'd pulled up. "It's from MagikOne Corp., and the account is at a bank in Belize."

"Weird," said Tanya.

"Not really." I made a face. "MagikOne partly owns the company that partly owns Wheeling Corp."

"Shell companies?" Brent asked. "That's convoluted as hell, even for that kind of setup."

"That's kind of the point," I said. "They're counting on people not being able to follow all the threads. The deposit may say that it's from Wheeling, but the money didn't come from them. I hope that's proof enough that Tanya didn't do this."

"Unless they're going to say that Tanya has the skills to pull this off." Brent winced. "And she sort of does."

I shook my head. "That's if she'd known to look, then been able to follow all the threads, then crack the bank. And there's no reason to believe that anyone would know to look to begin with, especially as employees."

"Well, it's enough to ask for better evidence." Brent stood up as Tanya sniffed loudly.

I didn't really pay attention. I was kind of puzzled. It had been relatively easy to trace the money to Wheeling. Almost too easy. Then it hit me.

"This isn't about putting Tanya in a bad spot," I told her, Brent, and Arturo. "It's about intimidation and fear."

"I don't get it," Arturo said.

"Wheeling and Jackson Goode want us to be afraid of them," I said and took a deep breath as I shook my head.

"That part's working," said Tanya.

I nodded. "Yeah. But the idea is to get us so scared we're either immobilized or do something stupid."

"Or maybe it's directed at the rest of the hacking community," said Arturo. "Look at these posts."

He flipped his laptop, which he'd brought downstairs, around so that we could see the screen. Sure enough, the bulletin had lit up the forums. There was a little support for Wheeling, but oddly enough, the vast majority of the people posting did not think Tanya had done anything. In fact, most of the posts were about how the posters did not want to go up against the think tank.

"I have to wonder what this Coleman really did," read one post. "We know how hard Wheeling's servers are to crack. How is a human resources secretary supposed to, even from inside? If they're coming after her like this, what will they do to any of us?"

Brent frowned. "I don't think Wheeling knows who's coming after them. And I'm willing to bet they've dismissed Tanya. It's like we said about that text from when your friend Abe was killed. It wasn't aimed at you or Tanya. It was aimed at the other hackers."

"Then why go after Tanya for embezzlement?" I asked.

"Distraction." Brent got a sardonic smile on his face. "Also, it makes them look like victims."

"One of the first things an abuser does when called on their shit," I said with a sigh.

"This is actually kind of good news," Brent said. "It will make it easier on me not to turn Tanya in." He looked at her as she gasped. "Not that I would."

"Really?" I said, my eyebrows shooting into my hairline. "You're all about the rules."

"No, Jannie," Brent shook his head.

"You can't even filch a pencil from the office."

Brent rolled his eyes. "That's not about the rules. It's about justice."

"What?"

"I got into being a Fed because I want to see justice done." Brent began pacing. "Okay, it sounds corny, but that's what is most important to me. I don't take pencils from the office because it's not fair to the taxpayers who pay for those pencils. I got Alphonse and your friend off on that virus thing because they'd gotten conned and it wasn't fair to bust them. Yeah, I get a little anal about some of the piddly stuff, but it's not fair to assume that those little things don't add up or are not important. It's about respecting other people, you know?"

Tanya snorted. "Well, that all sounds very nice, but you're not the one who's going to be spending her life on the run."

"You'll be fine," Brent said. "We'll find a way to fix it."

"So, what do we do in the meantime?" Arturo asked.

I shut my eyes. "I want to find out what happened to my mother. But there's also the reality that Wheeling is probably going to find another way around our fix on the point of sale device thing."

"Plus the bigger virus," said Tanya, pacing again. "We gotta get ahead of that one."

"True." I shuddered.

"What bigger virus?" Brent asked.

Tanya looked at me, then Brent. "It's the real objective of the point of sale virus. Not only did that virus mess up people's debit and credit cards at the bank level, it apparently seeded all the different banks with a virus that will open up a back door for another more powerful virus that will cripple the banks and leave Jackson Goode in sole control of our nation's banking systems."

"Fuck." Brent's jaw dropped open. "And I'm guessing this isn't about ransomware."

"It's about Jackson Goode taking over and remaking the world in his image," I said. "At least, I'm pretty sure that's what it's about."

Arturo shrugged. "From the part we got a hold of, he's not about stealing the money. Just keeping people from buying anything without his okay."

"How's he going to make that happen?" Brent asked.

"It'll be automated, of course," said Tanya. "We don't know how yet, because that's not part of the bank virus."

"And we don't necessarily need to know that part," said Arturo. "Although it would help."

I looked over at Brent. "I wonder how much it would help to put the banks on alert."

"I think the bigger problem will be getting people to believe us," Brent said. "Banks have a lot invested in keeping their systems secure. They're not going to want to believe that somebody has found a way in without some solid evidence."

"Then we get the point of sale people to talk to them," Tanya said.

I sighed. "That's assuming the point of sale people understand that it was a virus that caused the problem. The guy I talked to immediately dismissed the idea as impossible."

"I'm not surprised," said Brent. He pressed his lips together as he thought about it. "I think, however, that outreach will be my job. I can afford to be more visible. There's not a lot I can do on the coding side, either."

"I guess it's back to monitoring the Wheeling servers," I grumbled.

Tanya and Arturo went back to work on analyzing Alphonse's code, along with some of the bits they'd found on the Wheeling servers. Brent took over monitoring the forums. Not that there was much to be gleaned from that, but it saved me from doing it. Brent ordered dinner in from a local restaurant.

At about ten o'clock that night, he cursed.

"What?" I asked.

Tanya and Arturo instantly went on alert.

"Beefsteak," Brent said. "I think I know what happened to your mom."

"Really?" I yelped as I jumped up and looked over his shoulder, with Tanya and Arturo joining us.

There it was on the forum. The gloating practically floated through the screen.

"Can it get any crazier?" Beefsteak had written. "Wheeling has a hostage and the hackers have something Wheeling wants. What's going to happen next?"

Seconds later, a comment popped up condemning Wheeling. More followed. One person had the decency to ask how Beefsteak knew this, but Beefsteak remained silent.

"I need a new identity," I mumbled.

I opened up the DuckDuckGo browser on my laptop and cleared my cache for good measure. I set up yet another email address with another name and fake PO box, then paused, trying to think of a good avatar name. Outside the condo, an ice cream truck rolled by, playing a music box version of "Are you sleeping?" I shook my head and went with BrotherJohn.

"Alright," I said as I waited for the email approving my registration. "How do I respond?"

"Set up a meeting," Brent said. "We need to find out what they want."

"How about if I ask Beefsteak if he knows what Wheeling wants from the hackers?" I glanced back at Brent. "We probably don't want to give it away that we know who Beefsteak is."

"Good thinking." Brent grinned at me.

He'd always been good about saying things like that, and when we were hot on a case, I had to admit we were a damned good team. It was just otherwise that we had problems.

As soon as I could, I added the post. About five minutes later, I got a direct message from Beefsteak.

"I think I know what Wheeling wants," the message read. "Why do you want to know?"

I typed back, "Because I may have what Wheeling wants."

I glanced at Brent, he nodded, then hit Submit.

A minute later, the reply came back. "Wheeling says they'll send their representative to meet with you at noon tomorrow."

The address was for a restaurant in Westwood.

"No way. We've gotten shot at enough," I wrote back. Brent gave me another restaurant. "We'll do this one, and the least hint of a gun, I'm gone."

We waited.

The message page pinged. "Good enough. What does the Wheeling guy look for?"

Tanya held up something with an evil grin. It was a fisherman's cap with the Wheeling logo on it.

"The Wheeling hat."

"See you tomorrow."

I seriously doubted that Jackson Goode would be there, but it was interesting that he had slipped up a little. Brent rubbed his eyes. It was coming on for eleven by that point.

"What now?" Tanya asked.

"We don't know for sure that the hostage is my mom," I said. "We don't know for sure if he even has one."

"True," Brent grumbled and shook his head. "It's going to be tough to pull together a protection team in time."

"Maybe we want to tread lightly on that one," I said. "At least until we know what Goode does or doesn't have."

"And I want to have you in one piece," Brent said, then sighed. "I think I can get a couple of my friends to help out. That's why I want that restaurant. The sight lines are very clear and you can get a really good look at anybody coming in before they can see you. How about you wear a wire, too?"

"After the way you busted me over Alphonse and the illegal evidence?" I rolled my eyes.

"It's just to alert me." Brent winced. "Okay, it's probably pushing it on the legal side. But we won't be recording, so there won't be any illegal evidence."

"Alright." I was less than enthused about the wire, but if it would keep me safe, I was for it.

Brent's two buddies showed at the condo around nine that morning. They were the two agents I'd met at the coffee place where Earl Johnson had bitten it. Tanya and Arturo hid upstairs. Agent Damian Orguello looked a little grim. Agent Carla Donner, a medium-sized woman with blonde hair and a no-nonsense demeanor, seemed a little more upbeat. Both were wearing office casual khaki slacks and polo shirts. Carla helped wire me. Brent had apparently told them that we were working on a ransom demand from some kidnappers, which I suppose we were.

After I was wired and the radio tested, Brent and Carla went over with me all the protocols for dealing with a kidnapping. The big thing was that I was not to agree to do anything, nor was I to go anywhere with the person I was meeting. They could (and probably would) make all the threats in the world, but caving in would likely get the hostage killed. I was to hold onto the fact that I had something they wanted and wanted badly enough to hold someone hostage for.

Yeah, that really helped, especially since I did not, in fact, know what Goode actually wanted. But I figured I could tough it out for Mom. She'd given herself up for me. I could play a game I didn't think I could manage for her sake. If only I didn't feel like I was playing poker against a stacked deck for my mom's life.

"You okay?" Brent asked as he drove me to Westwood.

I shrugged. "As okay as I can get." I squeezed my eyes shut, then opened them. "I can't help it. I'm scared, Brent. I just found her. How can I lose her again so quickly?"

"You'll manage. And you've got this down." He glanced at me and smiled. "You're one of the smartest people I've ever met, and I get that you're feeling pretty worried right now, but you can play pretty tough when you want to."

I swallowed. "Yeah, I guess I can."

"I know you can."

It was good hearing that, but I sure did not believe it when I got to the restaurant over half an hour early. I did not order any booze, just a glass of iced tea. As Brent had said, the dining room was a wide-open space in a white room with dark green plants in sconces all along the walls.

The street was clearly visible from the huge plate-glass window across the front. Brent was right - I could see everyone coming in long before they could see me at the table in the back. The menu was trendy Italian, although there were several traditional dishes available. I opted for spaghetti carbonara and had the caesar salad to go with it.

Brent was at a table two over from me. Donner was on my other side at a table next to mine. Orguello had found a table next to the door. Brent was eating his usual marinara. Donner had gotten some fancy salad. I have no idea what Orguello was eating.

I'm not sure why, but I was not entirely surprised to see Earl Johnson's partner, Wayne Overs, wander into the restaurant, his eyes sweeping the room. Nor was I surprised that he was at least fifteen minutes late. He was wearing a black t-shirt that strained against his buffed-out chest and arms and his brown hair was still gelled to attention, just like the night I'd first seen him. The night I'd met Abe Pearlstein for dinner and he'd told me that Grandma had known Mom was alive. I choked at the memory.

I saw his eyes flit over my hat. He nodded, then came straight to the table.

"Shall I get you a menu?" I asked as he sat down. I was already halfway through my carbonara, which was so insanely good that I actually noticed in spite of my nerves.

"I'm not here for lunch." He grinned. "You're coming with me."

"Uh, no."

He looked a little surprised. "We have a gun to your pal's head."

"Got that. The only problem is that going with you means you're going to kill both of us."

"Yeah. No." He looked completely puzzled. "If you want to see your pal again, you'll come with me and we'll get what she hid."

"What she hid?"

Overs licked his lips. "It's in Boston. Her favorite spot there. Or someone's favorite spot there. She said you'd know."

"Me?" It took some considerable doing, but I kept my face straight. Or I hope I did. "Did she say specifically who would know this?"

"Uh," He blinked several times. "She said one of your pals would."

"She."

"Yeah. You know. The gal that got left behind."

"Behind what?"

Okay. It's probably not my most attractive characteristic, but there is a part of me that really loves tweaking idiots. Overs had clearly been told that I, or whoever, would cave the moment he reminded me how much danger my "friend" was in. Or maybe he just assumed that I would.

Overs gaped. "Your friend. Aren't you worried about her?"

Hell, yes, I was, but I wasn't going to say that to him.

"Seriously, asshole?" I said, instead. "Why would you think that I'd just roll over? I've got no reason to believe that you haven't already killed this person. I've got no reason to believe that you or your cronies aren't going to kill me once I hand over whatever it is that you want, assuming I can find it. Why the fuck should I trust you?"

It took both of his tiny brain cells to try to figure that one out, and even then, he didn't get it.

"We've got your friend. We're going to kill her if you don't do what we want."

"Got that. But you'll kill her even if we do, if you haven't already. So what incentive do I have to cooperate?"

He swallowed. "We'll kill your friend."

"You're going to kill her, anyway. So, again, what incentive do I have to cooperate?"

He looked panicked. I decided to show a modicum of mercy.

I snorted. "Okay, dumb-ass. If you or your pals find a way to show me proof of life, I'll think about finding whatever it is you think my friend hid. Again, assuming I can find it. Right now, you can either get the fuck out of here, or I can stick you with my bill. Your choice."

It took him a minute or so, but he finally got up and left. I waited until he'd left the restaurant to burst into tears.

"Fuckin' A," Donner said as she put her arm around my shoulders. "You rocked it, kid."

Brent supplanted Donner a minute later. "You handled that perfectly. I'm so proud of you."

"And I may have just killed my mother!" I yelped.

"No. You gave her the best chance she has at staying alive," Brent said, squeezing my shoulders. Then he sighed. "We just have to figure out how to get to Boston, is all."

I sniffed and dabbed at my eyes with a napkin. "No, we don't."

"What?"

"It's not about the city," I said simply. "I need to talk to Tanya and Arturo, but I'm pretty sure I know where this thing is."

"Okay. Why don't you call them and we'll go wherever this place is."

I shook my head. "No. This is something I need to do by myself." I looked at him. "Can you trust me, Brent?"

"Can you trust me?"

I took a deep breath. "I can trust your heart. But I need to do this one thing on my own." I smiled weakly at him. "Does that make sense?"

He frowned, but then nodded. "Yeah. It does. But, Jannie, there's an assassin out there trying to get you. You just gave the cold shoulder to someone else out to get you. Do you blame me if I'm worried?"

"No." I couldn't help laughing a little. "If it were you, I'd probably be freaking out right about now." I winced. "It's just that it's my mom, and something we shared that no one else did, and..." I closed my eyes and gasped. "It's just us."

"Okay." Brent closed his eyes, then opened them. "I suppose I have to respect that. So how do we make this as safe for you as possible?"

Because it was all about being safe. As Mom had said, Boston was never about actually going there. It was about finding that place where we felt safe from the abuse, from the criticism, from everything out there waiting to hurt us.

I called Tanya and verified that Mom and the others had been to my condo. They'd gone right after they'd heard about Leon, hoping that I'd go there and find them.

Brent drove me to Pasadena and, as we'd agreed, parked on the street. Donner followed me into the condo complex and waited outside while I went into my home, my fortress.

It was weird being back there. There was a stillness to the place, a calm that was utterly familiar and utterly foreign at the same time. I loved my condo. I felt good there. The only reason I left to work elsewhere was because I knew that my home was there, waiting for me, ready to shelter me from whatever rocked my world.

I walked up to the living room and saw my recliner. I sank down into the soft leather and closed my eyes for a moment. For the first time in days - or was it weeks - I felt relaxed, the tension sliding out of my shoulders and gut. I could breathe. I wanted to stay there forever, shut everything else out. But then, as I slid my hand down between the cushion and the arm, I felt what I had gone there to find.

I gasped for a moment, then closed my fingers around the thumb drive. In some ways, it represented everything that I was hiding from. But it was also the one thing that could save my mother.

The tears slid slowly down my cheeks. We had been separated for so long, and yet she still knew me like no one else. She remembered how much I hated American cheese. Such a dumb little thing, but it made a huge difference. She even knew how I felt about my condo and where to hide something so that I could find it right away without anyone knowing that I had.

I rested for several minutes more, drinking in the quiet. Then I got up, dried my eyes, headed for the door, went outside, and locked up the condo once more.

CHAPTER SEVENTEEN

Tanya and Arturo were ecstatic when they saw what was on the thumb drive.

"It's his entire plan," Arturo said. "Look at this!"

"I see it! I see it!" Tanya yelped.

"What do you mean?" I asked.

Brent had taken me back to the safe house, dismissing Orguello and Donner, but asking them to stay ready just in case. We stopped to pick up lunch for Tanya and Arturo. But as excited as Tanya was about the chicken and waffles - she'd sorely needed some comfort food - the various emails on the thumb drive were even better.

She'd hooked up one of the laptops to the big screen TV in the living room and Arturo had several emails open at the same time in a row of windows on the big screen.

Arturo grinned. "Goode was smart enough to give out bits and pieces of what he needed to all sorts of different people. No one person was going to know enough about the plan to mess it up."

"And look at this." Tanya pointed to several of the emails, one by one. "Each of these references what has to be that code that Timon wrote, but doesn't give any real hint as to what it is, and it looks like it's the lynchpin."

"So," said Brent slowly. "These emails mean that you can do... What?"

"We should be able to write the counter-virus from these," Tanya said, then sighed. "At least, I hope we can."

"What if I bring in some help?" Brent asked.

Arturo shrugged. "If you want. But Tanya can analyze code better and faster than anyone I know."

"And we have Timon of Athens for back up," said Tanya. "And since he wrote the critical part of the code, he'll know best how to counter-act it."

"Shit." Brent said, suddenly. He looked at me. "I want him to come here. Do you think you can convince him?"

"Why?" I asked.

"Jackson Goode knows that he wrote the critical part of the code and Timon's real name."

"How could he know that?" Tanya asked. "Almost no one knows who Timon of Athens really is."

"But Goode knows the real name of the person he conned into writing that bit of code," Brent said. "He probably doesn't know that person is also Timon. Or I hope he doesn't."

I had my phone out and dialed Alphonse's number.

"It's me," I said. "Have you had any trouble?"

"No. Why?"

"We've just discovered something that makes you a target as your real self."

"Fuck. What do I do?"

"Get out of your house now and meet me at that place we met the other day. You see any White guys going in there, hide and hide fast. Oh, and pack lightly, but bring some extra undies. You'll probably be hiding for a while."

I swiped the phone off and grabbed my bag.

"What the hell do you think you're doing?" Brent snarled. "You're just as much a target as he is."

"Call your pals and have them cover us." I glared back at him as I headed for the garage. "But we've got to get going now."

"I've got to get going." Brent strode ahead of me. "You're not going anywhere."

"He's not going to trust you. I told him not to."

I left the house and got into Brent's car.

"What did you do that for?" At least Brent got into the driver's seat.

"I didn't know he could."

Brent shot me a glare, then backed the car out of the garage. It took less than half an hour to get to the coffee shop in Inglewood, but Alphonse wasn't there. Brent had parked across the street and Donner sat at the end of the lunch counter. I ignored her as she ignored me.

My pocket buzzed with my phone's vibration. There was a text from Alphonse's number.

"Dude followed me. I'm hiding."

Before I could text back, another text, this time from Brent's number, came through.

"Lee Conroy walking down the street toward you."

Sure enough, the tall man in a cowboy hat and wearing a face mask sauntered in front of the coffee shop window. He appeared to be looking for something, but then he saw me.

"Gun!" I screamed, diving under the nearest table.

Glass shattered with the shots. Donner fell from her stool. I slid around under the table's sole metal leg, my back up against the booth's vinyl bench, trying to get my taser out of my bag. All I got was the stun gun, but I charged it anyway.

A pair of feet wearing cowboy boots under jeans walked past the table, then stopped. My heart in my throat, I jammed the stun gun into the leg, hoping I was hitting his knee and pressed the button.

Conroy crumpled, falling in front of the table. I scrambled out, but once clear of the table top, strong hands grabbed my shoulders. I screamed as my bullet wound burned, then reeled as a fist landed just above my ear. I don't know how I held onto that stun gun, but somehow I did.

Still holding onto my bad shoulder, Conroy got up, dragging me with him. I reached back, connected the stun gun with Conroy's side and pressed the button again. He knocked it away, but had gotten enough of a buzz to let me go and stagger back.

"F.B.I.!" called Brent from the door. "Hands up and stay where you are!"

Conroy bolted through the kitchen.

"Shit!" Brent yelped, then yelled into his phone. "Orguello! He's going out the back!"

Seeing Donner, Brent holstered his gun as he ran to her side, fumbling again with his phone.

"Oh, no. Is she…?" I gasped, crying.

Brent called for an ambulance, then grabbed a bunch of paper napkins out of the holder on the counter. The waiter and the two other patrons slowly slid out of wherever they'd been hiding.

"Jannie, see if there's anyone else hurt," Brent ordered.

I slowly staggered around the room, but it looked like everyone was fine. The waiter went back to the kitchen and returned with the news that no one in there had been hurt. I sank onto the edge of the nearest booth's seat, crying and gasping.

My phone buzzed again with a new text. It was Alphonse's number.

"I heard shots. You okay?"

I didn't dare answer it. Orguello came back through the kitchen, shaking his head at Brent. Brent had rolled Donner onto her side and was applying pressure on the hole in her back. Orguello gulped when he saw them, then ran back to the kitchen, coming out with several towels.

"I'll pay for them," I told the startled waiter.

"No. That's okay," she said, shaking. "They just trying to save her life."

Orguello took over for Brent, and a minute later, the paramedics showed and shoved both Orguello and Brent out of the way. Brent sank into the booth across the table from me. Shaking, I dug into my bag.

"I've got some hand sanitizer in here somewhere."

The waiter skirted the paramedics and brought Brent a large glass of water and another towel. He thanked her and went to work cleaning the blood off his hands.

"How bad is she?" I asked.

Brent shrugged. "She's breathing and there doesn't seem to be any blood coming up."

"Let's roll!" one of the paramedics suddenly yelled.

Orguello ran after them, presumably to ride to the hospital with them.

"Aren't you going to go?" I asked.

Brent shook his head. "Need to stick around for Inglewood P.D. Then I gotta get you back to the safe house. Do you know where the hell Alphonse is?"

"Just a text or two." Shaking, I showed him my phone. "I don't know if it's really him, though."

"Shit."

"Jannie!"

I looked up as Alphonse ran into the restaurant.

"You're alright!" I yelped.

"Hell, yes. I hid. You didn't text back, and I got scared he got you."

"I couldn't." I waved at him. "I'll explain later."

I scooted over on the bench so that Alphonse could sit next to me.

"I'm just so glad you're okay," I gasped.

He glared at Brent as he sat down. "I thought you said you couldn't trust him."

"We're working that part out," Brent grumbled.

"It's a long story, Alphonse," I said. "But Brent is helping us. It's his office that got compromised and he's not working from there right now."

It was another good hour or so before Brent got things squared away with the police. Phil McCaffrey called to check in and Brent held him off, promising to do the paperwork the next day.

As the three of us finally left the coffee shop, I noticed a white Ford truck parked on the street not far from the restaurant.

"Shit," I hissed.

"What now?" Brent asked.

"Let's hurry up, but keep your eye on that white truck."

We got into Brent's car, with Alphonse up front and me in the back. Brent peeled out into traffic, heading in the opposition direction from where the truck was facing. I looked back. The truck pulled out and nearly got hit as it made a u-turn in the middle of the block to come after us.

"Okay," sighed Brent, speeding up as much as he could in the traffic. "What's going on with the truck?"

"My father is behind the wheel," I said.

"Huh?" Alphonse asked.

"That settles it," I said, trying not to cry. "Wheeling has some hold on him and that the goons he sent to tail me are part of it. You know. Earl Johnson."

"That sounds about right." Brent's eyes flicked toward me in the rearview mirror. "That is not good."

"No shit," I said.

"Do I want to know who Earl Johnson is?" Alphonse asked.

"Was," I replied. "And you probably don't."

Brent ditched my dad pretty quickly, and drove around a little longer just to be absolutely certain that no one else was following us, either. And he was looking for multiple cars. We stopped to get dinner for everyone back at the house in Hermosa Beach.

When we got there, Tanya and Arturo took time off from analyzing and monitoring to focus on eating dinner with the rest of us.

"I can't believe you are Timon," Tanya kept saying.

"You know anybody smarter?" Alphonse finally growled at her.

"Yeah. Me."

There was a short burst of tension, then the both of them burst into laughter. After dinner, Tanya and Arturo turned on the TV and showed Alphonse exactly what they'd been working on.

"Oh, and we found this text file, too." Tanya clicked to open the file in full-screen instead of a section. "We're thinking this is the file that he needs so badly."

"Wouldn't he have backed it up?" Alphonse asked.

"We're sure he did," Arturo said. "But we've been through his system lots of times, and I think we got all the copies. Except for the thumb drive that Mom pulled together. She'd copied a lot of the code, and left it for Jannie."

Alphonse sighed. "We don't have any idea about when he's going to launch this sucker, do we?"

"No," I said. "We're kind of hoping that he needs this thumb drive to do it. Why else would he be keeping a hostage to get it from us?"

"Evidence, maybe?" Alphonse shrugged.

"Possibly, but it's illegal, so it can't be used in court." I sighed.

Brent, who'd been talking on the house's cordless phone, hung it up, shaking his head.

"What's going on?" I asked.

"Donner is hanging in there," he said sadly. "But it's still dicey."

"I'm so sorry," I told him softly.

"It isn't your fault."

I put my hand on his arm. "It isn't yours, either."

"No, it's not, but that doesn't make it any better." He shook his head to clear it, then looked at Tanya, Alphonse, and Arturo. "Alright. How do we get this bastard and bring him down?"

"The good news," said Tanya. "Is that with Timon—I mean Alphonse here, we can probably pull together a solid fix that can be distributed to the banks or even put on Goode's servers by Saturday night."

Alphonse sighed. "I wish we had Leon here. That man's code was pure poetry."

"But you guys can do it, right?" Brent asked.

The three of them looked slightly guilty.

"Ye-e-es," said Tanya. "With enough time."

"Which we're not sure we have," Arturo said with a pained look on his face. "The way Goode is shooting at people, you gotta believe he's itching to get this up and running. Look, I'm a hardware guy, mostly. I mean, I can write code, but it's not my strength."

Tanya sighed. "It's not mine, either. That's why I do the analysis. Nobody can beat me on that."

"I can do it," Alphonse said. "But writing code takes some time and I'm not nearly as fast as Leon was. He was amazing."

"He was a genius," Tanya added.

"We'll have to pull in some help," Brent started for the phone.

"What good is that gonna do?" Tanya snapped. "By the time we get any help updated and on top of things, this virus will be in the wild."

"Tanya," said Arturo. "We need all the help we can get. Now, or later."

Brent went to the phone. He made two different calls, neither of which made him happy.

"The software people are out of the office until Monday," he told us. "Friday's their extra day off. I called the emergency number, but that supervisor said he needs evidence that's actually legal to act on it. Damn!" He looked at Tanya, Arturo, and Alphonse. "It's on you guys, at least until Monday."

"Let's see," said Tanya. "Tonight's Thursday? We just have to keep Goode going for three more days." She rolled her eyes. "It's a walk in the park."

It might have been, if the walk was the one coming up from the bottom of the Grand Canyon. Still, all five of us went to work until our eyes were as dried out as that last piece of beef jerky in the aging tourist trap on the way to Las Vegas. Brent and I mostly monitored the Wheeling servers because for all Arturo protested otherwise, he was still pretty damned good at writing code. Tanya had parsed out the main algorithm for the virus and wrote it up on a whiteboard that Brent had produced from some storage closet. Sticky notes soon adorned the whiteboard.

By midnight, I called a halt.

"We're this close," Tanya complained.

"No, we're not," Arturo said.

"We gotta get some rest, guys, or we'll be good for nothing," I said.

The house had three floors and six bedrooms. I strongly suspect it had been intended as a vacation rental. In any case, everyone there had their own room. Only as I made my way to mine, Brent followed me.

"I can stay with you tonight," he said softly.

I tried not to groan. "Seriously, Brent?"

"This isn't about sex," he said. "Really. It's not."

"I'm going to try to take you at your word." I blinked because my eyes were so tired. Damn, it was tempting, though. I squeezed my eyes shut against the bit of warmth sliding through me. "I'm not ready for this."

"You've been having such a hard time. I want to be there for you."

I smiled softly in spite of myself. "Yeah. I believe you do." I shook my head. "I just don't know if that's what I really need right now."

"I suppose you don't." His chuckle was more than a little on the wry side.

I glared at him. "You're not suggesting that you know what I need better than I do?"

"Oh, hell no!" Brent grinned as he backed off. "I'm not a complete asshole, you know."

"You're not." And I knew he wasn't. "I've just got to get some rest and having someone else in bed with me probably won't help me do that."

"You've got a point there."

I tried not to roll my eyes. I mean, Brent probably meant it that it wasn't about the sex. It did not mean that he wasn't hoping for some. Or maybe he wasn't. Hell, I didn't know. I still went to bed by myself.

The good news was that I was so exhausted that I slept straight through to almost nine-thirty and probably would have slept later except that Tanya screamed.

"They found the modem!" she hollered as I staggered downstairs. "And they closed the backdoor we were using on the Mrs. Goode's site! We're screwed!"

Given that all of our nerves were frayed well past the breaking point, I couldn't fault her.

"You knew they were going to," Arturo said as calmly as he could.

"Not now, dammit!" Tanya prowled the living room. "We're this fucking close."

I stifled a yawn. "Which modem did they find?"

Brent landed just behind me on the stairs.

"The one on the main server," Tanya cried.

"But not the one on the special server for the point of sale handshakes," I said, moving into the living room.

Arturo nodded. "That one is still there, although I don't know why they haven't found it yet."

"So, where is Goode's mega-virus hiding?" I asked.

"All over the place!" Tanya groaned. "I can't tell you if he's going to launch it from the point of sale server or the other ones. There's bits and pieces of it and redirects all over the place."

Alphonse pushed past Brent into the living room and gaped sleepily at the TV screen.

"That fucking sucks," he grumbled.

"You're right," said Brent. "But you guys are good. Plus, you know the code. We can make this work. We just have to figure out how. It's a setback, but we can overcome it. I believe in you guys."

It was a good speech, and while it didn't completely overcome our angst, it went a long way toward helping us think clearly.

As it turned out, Tanya was right – our team was that close to having the fix together. We still had the modem on the special server, but we had a feeling it was being monitored. Actually, we were darned sure it was being monitored after I checked the forum where Beefsteak had been posting. Sure enough, there was another direct message from him that chilled us all to the bone.

"No more playing games. Funny how what I need got erased on my end. Bring me that file by five p.m. tonight or your friend dies. Oh, and no more backdoor tricks. They're so juvenile and quite annoying."

I took a deep breath and typed. "We need proof of life."

Five minutes later, my phone rang.

"I'm alive," said my mom's voice.

"Really?"

"A tornado couldn't do me in. What makes you think this guy will?"

I had to laugh. "I love you."

"Me, too." The call ended.

Chapter Eighteen

None of us were exactly celebrating. There was too much that could still go wrong, including Goode figuring out a way past his special code. Tanya, Alphonse, and Arturo went back to working on their fix. Brent and I went over all the different strategies that we could think of.

The big problem, as Tanya explained, was that the fix needed to be on the Wheeling servers before Goode launched his virus. It wasn't that the banks couldn't find a way around the problem eventually, even with our help. However, because of the seed virus that had been planted through the point of sale units, this second virus would spread almost instantaneously, permanently freezing millions of cards and accounts. It would take weeks or even months to get everything sorted out, which would cripple the economy in the meantime.

Brent wrote up a copy of our algorithms, but we had to find a discreet way to send them to the banks so that Goode wasn't alerted and didn't kill Mom. Not that the banks would be able to do that much on their end. It would take time to find all the seeds that had been planted, and it would only take a few seconds to spread the second virus everywhere.

Brent also wanted to set up a squad to go in and get Goode, but we weren't sure where he actually was. Worse yet, we didn't know where Mom was, either. The Mrs. Goode's Marketplace HQ was in downtown L.A., but Brent had called for another interview and had been told he wasn't there. Somebody else from Brent's office called and said that Goode's personal helicopter wasn't on the HQ helipad, either, and whenever he was in, the chopper was on the pad. Which, apparently, made sense since Goode piloted his own helicopter. I'm not sure how Brent found out that Goode wasn't at his home, either.

The other problem was how to get into the Wheeling servers. We didn't think our chances of physically getting into the building again were any too good. I pulled out my notes on the chain of shell companies that connected Wheeling to Jackson Goode.

"I wonder how fast I can get a warrant for the place," Brent said. "Just because you got his emails illegally, that only makes you a co-conspirator, whereas I've got a duty to disclose what I've learned."

"But can we get a warrant and get it served before my mom gets killed?" I spread the papers out on the table. "And will the warrant allow us to install the fix in time?"

"It's our best option," Brent said, going to his laptop.

I went back to looking through notes, then saw something that made me gasp out loud. The others froze.

"That box!" I yelped. "That goddamned box. I knew there was something wrong with it."

"Jannie, I told you IT put it on the desktop." Brent glared at his laptop screen. "We're trying to trace where the leak is coming from."

"What leak?" Tanya asked.

"The leak in our office." Brent sighed. "The only thing we know is that it's machine-related. Every potential suspect and even a few others have been checked and double-checked. Even Thompkins and me. We're all clean. But we've scrubbed the networks, installed extra firewalls, and the information is still getting out there. IT put a box on the back of the computer to trace all the data coming in."

"Yeah. But it's missing what's going out and for a damn good reason," I said pacing. "It's how Wheeling is spying on you." I put my hand up as Brent started to reply. "I know. IT put it there, but that doesn't mean Wheeling doesn't have control of it."

"How could they?" Brent asked. "We got them from PalmSci Systems. They're leaders in data protection and security."

"And owned by Jackson Goode!" I pointed to the paper on the table. "These are all the shell corporations connected to Wheeling and Goode. It's how we figured he owns Wheeling. I told you there was something wrong with that box. It had PalmSci's logo on it. I just didn't connect it to them because... I don't know."

"You were pretty upset," Brent said softly. "Understandably."

"I know." I blinked my eyes against the tears. But then I looked at Brent, the light dawning. "We can use it. The box hooks up to Wheeling, or possibly even Goode's personal computer."

Brent frowned. "Aren't the Wheeling people watching what's going through the box?"

Alphonse looked up from his laptop. "We should be able to anonymize the upload that will stop the virus. I think I've got an app here that will do it."

"Great," I said. "Now we just have to get Tanya into F.B.I. headquarters without getting her arrested so that these guys can use your desktop to upload the fix."

"That will be a snap." Brent rolled his eyes. "And I've got to convince Thompkins to mobilize a major takedown unit in just a few hours without alerting Goode." He took a deep breath. "Let's get to it, then."

Brent called Thompkins from the house phone to set up the warrant on Wheeling's servers. The others finished up by putting the code for the fix on three different thumb drives. I got one. Brent got one. Tanya kept the third.

"I just hope it works," Alphonse said. "We haven't fully tested it, at least not in a real world way."

"What are we going to test it against?" I asked.

"We can still test something," Alphonse grumbled.

"Probably," I said. "But we do not have the time."

Okay, maybe it was me worrying about my mother, but I really did not think that we did.

Brent made more phone calls, then shook his head.

"What?" I asked.

"Good news, bad news." Brent started pacing. "The good news is that we'll have the warrant and the personnel for the takedown. The bad news is that we won't have it until close to four."

"Oh, shit." The tears filled my eyes. "We only have until five."

Brent put his hand on my shoulder. "We can do this. We've got a crack team working on the fix. And we've got the best agents in the country backing us."

"What about Tanya?" Arturo asked.

"We just don't say who she is," Brent said. "And hope like hell no one decides they know."

It was close to noon when we left the safe house. Brent swung through a McDonald's, not that any of us had any appetite. When we got to the F.B.I. offices, Brent took us straight upstairs.

McCaffrey was waiting for us in Brent's office.

"What are you doing here with all these people?" McCaffrey demanded. He was about six feet tall, with a full head of brown hair that was graying at the temples. His glasses, which were attached to a black lanyard, sat on the top of his head.

"Working," said Brent.

He pulled McCaffrey around the rest of us into the corridor. In Brent's office, Arturo went right to work. I stayed in the doorway, both to watch Arturo and to watch the drama unfolding in the corridor. Brent spoke too softly for me to hear.

"We're safe to talk." McCaffrey rolled his eyes. "All radio transmissions in the building are jammed."

"Including the Wi-Fi?" Brent glared at him.

Tanya pulled out a router and hooked it up to the box on Brent's desktop.

"Yeah, believe it or not." McCaffrey glared back at Brent. "Do you have any idea how many pissed-off agents we have at the moment?"

"Some. But there's still the computer's microphone," Brent said through his teeth. "And there's a wireless modem functioning."

"Where?" McCaffrey demanded.

"I killed the computer's mike," Arturo called. "You're good."

"On the back of my computer." Brent pulled McCaffrey into the now-crowded office. "And probably several others in here."

"That's the PalmSci box." McCaffrey snorted.

"Corrupted by Wheeling," I said. "They own PalmSci."

"Son of a bitch!" McCaffrey gaped and started for the back of Brent's computer "I've got to get IT up here right now and get that thing off of there!"

"No!" Arturo and I screamed. I physically blocked McCaffrey.

"It's protocol!" McCaffrey grabbed my shoulders and I yelped as he hit my bullet wound.

"Wait!" Brent snapped. "Phil, Elaine Thompkins said we can leave it for a little while. We need it to get into Wheeling's servers. It's an emergency."

McCaffrey looked puzzled. "Elaine said it was okay?"

"She's pulling the warrant as we speak." Brent held his breath.

McCaffrey looked Brent over. "Okay."

We all started breathing again. McCaffrey gaped at Tanya, then took a deep breath.

"Do I want to know who you are?" He asked.

"No, you don't," said Brent. "At least, if you want this virus stopped, you don't."

"Fine," McCaffrey swallowed. "By the way, I didn't issue that wanted notice. It was another office."

"Could there be more than one box modem?" I asked. "Or is Wheeling in your servers?"

"I'll check it out," said Arturo. "Where's the office that issued the wanted notice?"

McCaffrey pointed and Arturo ran to an office three doors down.

The rest of us took a deep breath as we looked at each other.

"Now, what do we have?" McCaffrey asked Brent.

"We've got a hostage situation that's essentially at a stalemate between us and Jackson Goode."

Arturo came back, shaking his head. "That office has the box, so that may be how the Wheeling people put out the wanted notice."

Brent took over explaining to McCaffrey some of what the situation was while Alphonse took over getting the cloaking app working on Brent's computer, then testing to see if we could get into the Wheeling servers.

"But where's your hostage?" McCaffrey demanded.

"That's the tough part," said Brent. "We don't know. Obviously, Goode has two sets of servers, and he's probably getting ready to launch his virus from one of those two sets. We know one set is at the Wheeling Corporation building. But the other is someplace else and we don't know where. As far as we know, Goode isn't at home or his headquarters downtown, and we're assuming that the hostage is being kept fairly close to him, for obvious reasons."

Tanya and I unspooled several ethernet cords and hooked them up to various laptops in the room. While testing my connection, I spotted another direct message from Beefsteak.

"The clock's ticking," he wrote.

"Shit!" I yelped. "He's getting impatient."

"Or just playing games with us," Brent said, looking at the message.

I pressed my lips together. "I know how we can find him." I looked at Brent. "I'll get my father to take me to him."

"Are you out of your mind?" Brent glared at me.

"Dad is working for them and he'll trust me." I swallowed. "Maybe. He sure as hell won't trust you."

"You know," McCaffrey said. "She could go in with a wire and a tracer on. Might help keep her alive."

I pulled Brent away from McCaffrey's earshot.

"And I've got another idea for insurance, too," I murmured. "How many thumb drives can you pull together?"

"It's going to take forever to upload the fix with this cloaking app," Tanya groaned from another part of the office. "Do you think you can stall him, too?"

I looked at her and shrugged. "I sure hope so."

It was getting on for four o'clock when I was finally ready. Arturo had the cloaking app on three different computers, which essentially gave them three more modems to sign into the Wheeling servers with. Brent was not happy, and as he taped the wire to me, I could tell that he really wanted to take Phil McCaffrey's head off.

I'd found out (admittedly with an illegal search) where my father was staying and had a large plastic zip-top bag filled with thirty numbered thumb drives. One of those drives had the fix on it, another had the file that Goode wanted so badly. Only I knew which numbered drive each was on.

Dad was in the lobby of the hotel in Santa Monica, talking on his mobile, and wearing chinos with a full blue golf shirt. He gaped when he saw me walk in, said something to the phone, then swiped it off.

"What are you doing here?" he demanded, striding over to me.

"I've got what Jackson Goode wants," I said calmly, never mind that I felt anything but calm. "You're going to take me to him."

"Yeah." He stepped back and swallowed. "Okay."

He grabbed my arm, and I yelped with the pain.

"You're hurting me."

"Yeah. Well, I wouldn't have to if you'd done what I told you to do."

I didn't say anything as he marched me to the white Ford truck I'd seen the day before.

"Why the hell didn't you go with me when I came for you?" Dad snarled at me as he pulled out of the parking garage.

"Why do you think?" I snarled back. "And how the hell did Jackson Goode get his hooks into you?"

Dad let out his breath. "Creative accounting. He leaned on me and I had to get you home. I had to do it. I had to keep you safe."

I snorted. "Safe with you? Just like Janelle and Eileen were safe with you?"

"You don't know anything about them."

"Bullshit. I heard the screams. I heard you beat the shit out of them. And I saw what you did to my mother."

"It wasn't like that. You don't know anything about me. You have no right to judge me."

"Maybe not." I shrugged and looked out the window.

"Hey, I had one hell of a lousy childhood, too, you know. You think I hurt your mom? You should have seen what my dad did to mine, and then did to me!"

"Did you have to repeat his mistakes?" I snapped.

"I didn't hit you that often. I'd like some credit for that." Dad was breathing heavily and I'm pretty sure the only reason he hadn't completely lost it was that he had to keep the truck on the road.

"Fine. You've got credit." I looked away, then looked at him. "I don't hate you, Dad. Yeah, a lot of the shit I deal with is your fault. But, see, it's always been about the anger. I got angry, too. Then I did something really rotten as a result, and you know what? The person I hurt still gave herself up for me when push came to shove." I shook my head, trying to hold the tears back. "I don't want to be angry anymore. I want to get past it, and that includes being angry at you."

"Shit," he muttered.

Of course, that was when we pulled up to the Wheeling building. The parking lot held only a few dozen cars, and I saw a sleek, black helicopter on the roof.

"Whose chopper is that?" I asked.

"Never mind." Dad slid the truck into a parking space near the front door.

I looked around at the mostly empty lot. "Why isn't there anybody here?"

"Don't know," Dad grunted, opening the truck's door.

I got out, and Dad got a good grip on my arm, just in case. It was probably just as well. I was so close to running like crazy. The only thing keeping me going was the thought of my mother telling me she loved me while drawing off the bad guys so that I could escape.

"Uh oh," Brent's voice muttered in my ear.

I'd forgotten about the wire and that I could hear him and the rest of the team. Brent's voice got really soft and said something about bomb-sniffing dogs. I really didn't want to know any more about that.

Dad swiped an I.D. at the front door and took me straight to an elevator. We went downstairs to a large office not far from the server room. Dad shoved me inside, then shut the door. It was a dark room, with a large desk facing the wall where three wide-screen monitors had been hung, but were dark.

Mom was there, and I ran into her arms. She didn't look any worse for the wear. At least, I didn't see any bruises on her. The jacket she'd been wearing that day was gone, but she was still in her skirt, the silk blouse coming untucked.

"It's okay, honey," she whispered. "It's okay."

"Son of a bitch!" Dad snarled. "Rae. So, you're alive."

Mom let me go and faced Dad. "You knew that."

"And I knew Jannie would lead me to you sooner or later. Good job, kid."

"And I can always hide again," she said. "You can't hold me, Milt. And why would you want to, anyway?"

Dad rolled his eyes. "We're still married, you know."

Mom smiled. "I'm sure Eileen will be quite relieved."

The door to the office opened and Jackson Goode stepped in. He was shorter than I'd imagined, and while his rangy, rugged face looked like down-home charm when he was smiling, he was not smiling at that moment and just looked threatening. His brown hair looked strangely fake, too. You'd think with his cash flow, he'd have found a better looking wig.

"Okay, Milt," he said, going over to his desk. "Looks like everything is in place."

"Stall him, Jannie," Tanya's voice hissed in my ear. "We're only ninety-eight percent uploaded."

Goode sank into a full leather desk chair, then turned and looked at Mom and me.

"I hope you have what I need," he asked, his dark eyes glittering.

"Yeah. But what I need is insurance," I said, keeping my voice calm somehow.

"Insurance." Goode snorted.

I held up my bag of thumb drives. "Your file is on one of these drives. Only I know which one. You let us walk out of here, then I text you the number for the right drive."

"You're assuming I'm going to let you walk out of here."

I shrugged. "You might want to. It's either that or try and open thirty different thumb drives. I understand that you're on a schedule. And let's face it. The F.B.I. is hot on your trail."

Goode laughed. "It doesn't matter if they're on my trail or not. After today, I'll be the one in charge."

He flipped a switch under the desk and the monitors began glowing. One had the Mrs. Goode's Marketplace site up. Another had several windows tiled across it. The third, some code.

Some of the tiles on the middle monitor flashed, then went blank.

"Oops," Arturo said quietly into my earpiece. "I guess we just crashed the backup servers."

"What the hell?" Goode glared at the monitor.

"Come on, you damn thing," Tanya hissed. "Load."

Mom glanced at me as Goode pulled a keyboard from the back of his desk.

"I thought I told you guys no more game playing." He slammed a few more keys, then shook his head. "It doesn't matter. I don't need them."

But then the first monitor flashed with an animated version of Denzel Washington blowing a raspberry.

"No!" Goode banged a few more keys. "What the hell?"

He grabbed a mouse and began clicking through the pages on the site. Almost every one of them featured some black actor or athlete blowing raspberries and calling Goode a racist. I was pretty sure Alphonse had written the code a long time before.

Goode bounced to his feet. "Milt, bring those two to the server room."

"Shit," Tanya's voice hissed. "We're only ninety-nine percent loaded. Can't you keep him busy, Jannie?"

Lee Conroy was in the server room, near a laptop set up next to the main server. At least, I was pretty sure it was Conroy. He was tall enough and had the icy blue eyes. Turned out his hair was blonde and he had a bushy mustache. He also had a huge automatic pistol in his hand.

"I'm done playing, kid," Goode snarled at me. "Give me that thumb drive or I'll kill you."

"Kill me and you won't find out which drive it is that you need without going through every single one of them, and the F.B.I. is on its way."

"Milt, kill them." Goode turned back to the laptop and glared at the screen.

"What?" Dad gasped.

"Kill the two broads. It won't take that long to find the damn file with the three of us working."

Dad pulled a medium-sized automatic from a side holster under his golf shirt. He looked at it, then looked at Mom and me.

"No." Dad swallowed. "They're my women. I get to decide what to do with them."

Goode glared at him. "Are you sure you want to take that attitude with me?"

"Yeah," said Dad, pulling himself up straight.

"Lee." Goode turned back to the laptop.

Conroy chuckled and raised his gun. A second later, Dad dove in front of mom and me, firing his gun at the same time as Conroy. Conroy crumpled, and so did Dad.

"Dad!" I yelped.

"It's okay, Jannie," he gasped as he held his stomach.

"What the fuck?" Goode strode over and grabbed Dad's gun. "I told you. I'm done. You tell me which of your fucking thumb drives has my file or I'll shoot you."

He pointed the gun at me and my mouth went dry. I gasped, trying to find words.

"Now! Tell me!"

I swallowed. "I... I..."

"It's up and running," said Tanya.

Goode put the barrel of the gun to my forehead. "Well?"

"Seventeen," I whispered, handing him the bag. "Number seventeen."

Goode grabbed the bag and pawed through it, cackling when he found the drive. He popped it into the port on the laptop that Conroy had been standing next to. Goode finished hooking up the laptop to one of the servers on the tall rack. Mom slowly pulled me back around to the other side of the server rack from where Goode was happily tapping keys on the laptop. Crouching low, we slid over to Conroy's body and Mom grabbed his gun.

"And I'm in!" Goode cackled. "All I have to do is get the hell out of here. And, ladies, don't worry. I don't have to shoot you now." He laughed again. "The place is rigged. C-four everywhere. The code not only set off the virus, it set off a timer. I've got seven minutes to get to my bird, and then boom."

"What?" I gasped. "Why?"

"Because I can," Goode said with a wild grin.

He scrambled from the server room.

"That was too easy," Mom said.

I followed her to where the laptop was, my ear filled with cheering.

"Nothing seems to be happening," Mom said, glaring at the code on the screen.

"They got the fix loaded," I gasped. "Just in time."

Dad moaned.

"Oh, shit!" I sank to my knees next to him.

Mom came over and sat down across from me. "Hang on, Milt. We'll get you some help."

He gasped. "I didn't mean to hurt you, Rae."

"I know. I forgive you."

"Thanks." He blinked at me. "You guys gotta get out of here."

Mom looked at me and I nodded.

"Help is on the way, Milt," she said.

"Thanks, but ain't happening."

"Dad!"

His eyes rolled back into his head and there was a rattle to his last gasp. Mom and I blinked at each other, then Mom got to her feet.

"Let's go," she said.

But the room was locked. Mom aimed the gun she'd picked up and blasted out one of the windows, and we scrambled through as carefully as we could. One of the jagged pieces of glass still caught Mom's arm.

"Good thing we know where we're going." Mom nodded at the set of stairs ahead of us.

"Mom, you're hurt!"

"We've gotta get out of here now or we'll be worse than hurt." She blinked and gasped.

Her face turned ashen in the glare of the fluorescent lights above us, and I practically dragged her upstairs. I could hear Brent yelling that there was confirmation on the explosives and that the choppers pinning Goode down should back off.

We got to the back door, but that, too, was solidly locked. I grabbed a chair and banged on it as hard as I could.

"How much time is left?" Mom asked.

"I don't know."

There was the sound of metal wrenching and the door creaked open. I pushed Mom through first, then scrambled out, myself, right into Brent's arms. As he hustled us to a nearby willow tree, I could hear the first rumbles of an explosion behind us. Brent whipped a huge, heavy blanket over us as the blast roared.

Then there was silence.

Brent tried speaking to me, but I couldn't hear. My ears started ringing. A minute later, paramedics swarmed us. Mom had fainted but was still alive. They took her to the hospital first, then checked me over and put me in a second ambulance.

My hearing came back while I was at the hospital. I gave blood, too, but then they released me and told me to go home. Mom would be okay, and I could visit her in the morning. Brent took me back to his office, where Tanya was surrounded by her family. Mrs. Coleman barely let go of her daughter long enough to give me a solid hug. Arturo's family were there, too, laughing and crying.

Brent finally brought me home to my condo.

"Are you going to be okay?" he asked as I unlocked my front door.

"I'll be safe," I said. "That's all I really want right now."

He nodded, waited just long enough for me to get inside, then left. I watched from my front window as he went through the paths. Then I hand-switched the lights on and pulled all the curtains closed.

Chapter Nineteen

Jackson Goode, who had been the pilot for his chopper, died in the explosion. He'd been pinned onto the roof by Sheriffs' and F.B.I. helicopters that had backed off just in time to save themselves.

The morning after the explosion, Mom called me on the burner phone I still had.

"They're releasing me from the hospital," she said.

"Do you want me to come get you?"

"I'd like that, but I have to go away for a few days." She paused. "I've got a few things to get squared away."

"Oh."

"But I'd like to talk to you later this coming week."

"Yeah. I'd like that. Are you keeping this phone?"

"Yes."

"Good. If I get a new one, I'll text you the number."

I spent the next few days hiding in my condo. Brent dropped by on Sunday to get a DNA sample from me, since that was the only way they'd be able to identify my father's remains. He also had some news. Turned out that

Goode had another reason for blowing up Wheeling. The firefighters had made the grim discovery of an entire office filled with bodies. Based on the location of the office (which Tanya had confirmed) and the list of missing persons, the coroner's office realized that Goode had blown up most of the guys who had worked on his precious virus. Brent figured it was Goode's way of tying up loose ends. The news made me feel terribly sad, but I managed to put the guilty feelings aside, and that was a good thing.

Wednesday, I went out to get a new phone. I debated getting the top of the line, brand-spanking new model, but realized I wasn't going to use ninety percent of what it could do, and bought a nice mid-range model that took good photos, had a butt-load of memory, and fit in my jeans' pocket. I set up my old accounts on the new phone, got my old phone number back, then texted it to Mom's burner phone. She called, and we set up a lunch meeting for that Saturday at a restaurant near my condo. Back home, I put my hard drives back into my desktop tower.

It didn't help. I called Brent from my new phone.

"How's it going?" he asked.

"It's going." I sighed.

"Would you like to meet me for coffee?"

"Yeah. That sounds nice."

We met the next day at a place in Eagle Rock. It was comfortably frowzy, but had big picture windows, which I really liked. My favorite barista Dina worked there, only she wasn't in that day. I got there first, having finally rescued my MachE from the airport parking lot. Brent arrived, looked around, then went inside.

I waved from the table where both of us could see the room.

"Hey," he said, coming up. "Um, I thought I'd buy, if that's okay."

"Sure."

"What do you want?"

I smiled. "How about a café au lait?"

"Be right back."

Several minutes later, Brent returned to the table with our coffees.

"So, how are you doing?" I asked.

"Pretty good." Brent settled in and sipped from his cup. "Oh, just so you know, the guys from IT are not in trouble, but they are really pissed about those boxes they'd installed. And PalmSci Systems is in a world of hurt. Every government agency they've worked with is suddenly questioning their contracts with them." He sighed. "Oh, and McCaffrey is also claiming that you didn't find Tanya, so we don't need to pay you."

"I did so find her." I snorted. "I may have had help, but I found her."

"Well, just so you know."

"You're not in too much trouble, are you?" I stirred a bit of sugar into my cup.

Brent laughed. "Thompkins gave me a commendation, believe it or not. I didn't just bring down Wheeling, I foiled Goode's evil plan and we don't have to bring the case to the courts because Goode got himself killed."

"And we're sure he's dead."

"So far." Brent shrugged. "We'll see what the DNA tests turn up, but several guys on the choppers saw him go up with the building." He paused, then looked at me. "I'm talking to somebody. About the anger thing and the controlling."

"A friend?" I asked.

"No." Brent chuckled sardonically. "A shrink. Had my first appointment last night. It was interesting. How are you managing?"

"Oh, that." I sighed and took a deep drink of my coffee. "Let's just say that I've got my shrink appointments booked for the next eight weeks."

"Good." There was an extended pause, then Brent took a deep breath and looked at me. "I'd like us to try again. Would you want to?"

"You're asking me."

"Yeah."

I pressed my lips together and blinked my eyes. "I want to honor that. I know how hard it was for you to ask. But I can't right now. I've got my dad's death to deal with, and whatever's going to happen with Mom." I looked up at him and winced. "Do you mind asking again in a couple months?"

"Not at all." He smiled.

We chit-chatted for a bit longer. Then he had to go back to work.

I emailed Thompkins and McCaffrey and reminded them that I most certainly had found Tanya and had brought her to the office, no less. I did eventually get paid. And the DNA tests turned up positive on my dad's remains and on Jackson Goode's. But that took a while. Before that, though, I had my lunch date with my mom.

We landed at an Argentinian restaurant in Pasadena on Green Street. It was a little joint, usually crowded, and we'd gotten a table outside. The end of August heat was just ramping up.

We waited until our salads had arrived before really saying anything.

"How are you feeling?" Mom asked.

"Better," I said. "As soon as we get Dad positively I.D.'d, I'll have his estate to work out. The dealership seems to be running on its own for the time being, so I don't have to think about that."

"Yeah. I may have set that up with your dad's lawyers." Mom smiled. "How is everybody else?"

"Great. Well, mostly. The agent that got shot is recovering, but it's going to take some time. Oh, and Brent pulled some strings, and both Tanya and Arturo are starting at Caltech this week."

"How wonderful."

"Yeah. Tanya's going to work on her computer science degree and Arturo is going into electrical engineering. Better yet, they're going to be working part time at the company the banks hired to find that seed code. Alphonse is already working there full time."

"I'm so glad." Mom smiled.

"What about you?" I asked.

"Well, I'm going back to my real name. Rae Ann Schmidt." Mom chuckled. "I debated changing my last name, but thought it was time to stop hiding. It's who I am. And I got Leon's job at the community college."

"Wow." I stopped and held my breath. "So, you're staying in the area."

"Yes." Mom looked at me. "I hope that's alright."

"Yeah." I smiled as I realized it was. "It's definitely alright."

Mom put her fork down. "Jannie, I may not have made the best decisions I could have, but I did the best I could."

"I know, Mom." I blinked back tears yet again. "It was something Dad said right before..." I took a deep breath. "He was looking for you and it could have been fatal if he'd found you."

"For both of us, dear."

"I know. And in the end, he chose not to." I turned back to my salad. "He gave up being angry for us. I think I need to work on that, too. I mean, I'm hurt. I can't pretend I'm not." I looked up at her. "But I think we can hack together a relationship."

Mom smiled. "I think we can, too."

We went back to our salads and never mentioned Boston again.

Thank You for Reading

I do hope you enjoyed the book.

If you can do me one small favor, please. Can you go to one of the social media/retail profiles below and leave a short review? It doesn't need to be a lot, just honest.

BB bookbub.com/profile/anne-louise-bannon

g goodreads.com/author/show/513383.Anne_Louise _Bannon

f facebook.com/RobinGoodfellowEnt/

🐦 twitter.com/ALBannon

a amazon.com/stores/author/B00JCRXST2?ingress =0&visitId=bfadb491-d1ac-4575-84da-bb4f7d325a d9&store_ref=ap_rdr&ref_=ap_rdr

COMING SOON

Jannie and Rae Ann will be back for another adventure. I just don't know when or what's likely to happen. My next release will be from the Old Los Angeles series, *Death of the Drunkard*.

An inoffensive drunkard. A lot of reasons to kill him.

A bold shooting ends the life of Mr. Hewitt, the buggy manufacturer on a cold night in December, 1872. Physician and winemaker Maddie Wilcox is particularly puzzled, since it was clear that Mr. Hewitt was soon to die of his own dissipation. Nonetheless, she is drawn into searching out his killer by his grieving widow.

Maddie soon finds out that there were several people who might have been offended by Mr. Hewitt, including those hoping to bring the Union Pacific railroad to Los Angeles. As Maddie battles the usual winter colds and her own homesickness, the local men begin vying for her affections. Soon, Maddie realizes that she is searching for a killer determined to win the prize. no matter what the cost.

That Old Cloak and Dagger Routine

Stopleak

Deceptive Appearances

Fugue in a Minor Key

Sad Lisa

These Hallowed Halls

My Sweet Lisa

A Little Family Business

Just Because You're Paranoid

Freddie and Kathy Series:

Fascinating Rhythm

Bring Into Bondage

The Last Witnesses

Blood Red

Daria Barnes:

Rage Issues

Mrs. Sperling:

A Nose for a Niedeman

Brenda Finnegan:

Tyger, Tyger

Romantic Fiction:

White House Rhapsody, Book One and Two

Fantasy and Science Fiction:

A Ring for a Second Chance

But World Enough and Time

Time Enough

And I would be honored if you left a review for this and any of my books on the below sites. It really helps.

BB bookbub.com/profile/anne-louise-bannon

g goodreads.com/author/show/513383.Anne_Louise_Bannon

f facebook.com/RobinGoodfellowEnt/

twitter.com/ALBannon

amazon.com/stores/author/B00JCRXST2?ingress
=0&visitId=bfadb491-d1ac-4575-84da-bb4f7d325a
d9&store_ref=ap_rdr&ref_=ap_rdr

Connect with Anne Louise Bannon

Thank you for sticking it out this long! Please join my newsletter. It's the best way to stay up-to-date on my upcoming projects, blog posts and even the occasional game and giveaway.

You can sign up for the Robin Goodfellow Newsletter here: http://eepurl.com/zH0Ab or by visiting my website, annelouisebannon.com

And don't forget to connect with me on your favorite social media platforms:

BB bookbub.com/profile/anne-louise-bannon

f facebook.com/RobinGoodfellowEnt

a amazon.com/author/annelouisebannon

g goodreads.com/author/show/513383.Anne_Louise _Bannon

in linkedin.com/in/annelouisebannon.com

twitter.com/albannon

ABOUT ANNE LOUISE BANNON

Anne Louise Bannon is an author and journalist who wrote her first novel at age 15. Her journalistic work has appeared in Ladies' Home Journal, the Los Angeles Times, Wines and Vines, and in newspapers across the country. She was a TV critic for over 10 years, founded the YourFamilyViewer blog, and created the OddBallGrape.com wine education blog with her husband, Michael Holland. She is the co-author of Howdunit: Book of Poisons, with Serita Stevens, as well as author of the Freddie and Kathy mystery series, set in the 1920s, the Old Los Angeles series, set in 1870, and the Operation Quickline series, plus several stand alones. She and her husband live in Southern California with an assortment of critters.

www.ingramcontent.com/pod-product-compliance
Lightning Source LLC
Chambersburg PA
CBHW072027220726
48293CB00016B/500